PROMISE SEASON

Promise Series Book One

LEE EVIE

INTERSTICE
PRESS

INTERSTICE PRESS
First published by Interstice Press in 2019

Copyright Lee Evie 2019

Cover artwork by Rory Brockman-Tanham
Cover Design by Jenny Quinlan - historicalfictionbookcovers.com
Korean cultural edit and copyedit by Kim Stoker
Lee Evie asserts the moral right to be identified as author of this work

ISBN: 9780648732310

More Books by Lee Evie

Lee Evie has the following current and upcoming historical fiction titles set in old Korea.

Visit **www.leeevie.com** to find out more:

PROMISE SERIES:

Promise Season

Promise Thief

Promise Dream

JOSEON DETECTIVE SERIES:

A Song for Lonely Wolves

An Ode to Hungry Ghosts

A Hymn for Soldiers Lost

VERSE NOVELS:

Barley Fields: A Joseon Love story

To receive *Barley Fields: A Joseon Love Story* for free, sign up to Lee Evie's bookclub on her website at:

www.leeevie.com

for SOssy and Anna, forever ago,
you made me believe I could do this

Author's Note

This novel is set during the Joseon dynasty of ancient Korea.

At this time there was a highly-trained group of artist women called *gisaeng*, from outcast or slave families, who provided services to men of the upper class.

Gisaeng entertained men with music, dance, conversation and poetry, much in the same way as Japanese *geisha*.

PLEASE NOTE: This novel is written in British english, and some spellings may differ from those used in American english.

PROMISE SEASON

The Pavilion

The other girls press around me. Skirts rustle as they ready themselves for the long night ahead, pushing along a new girl who moves too slow. Laughter erupts as they touch and poke, working together to pull her inside a gauzy dress. This new girl, Wol-hyeong, was sold here only recently, kicking and screaming as she came.

Tonight will be her first night and my heart bleeds for her.

I try to be kind, to say gentle words as I help her into the dress we have prepared, but Wol-hyeong is blind to all around and I soon give up.

Another *gisaeng* whispers in my ear that the girl has been drinking, told the hazy effects of alcohol would make her night easier to bear. Now Wol-hyeong is unsteady on her feet, eyes glazed and unresponsive. She is drunk.

I sigh. Perhaps it is for the best.

It is late evening at the Pavilion and the summer heat is oppressive, air thick and humid in the way it always is before a storm. Cicadas hum in the lush gardens outside and dark clouds gather already beyond the windows. Before the new girl leaves I lean close to whisper against her ear.

"It will soon be over, Wol-hyeong. Just close your eyes and bear it and it will all be over."

She looks at me with unfocused eyes, her speech slurred and strange. "No. It won't. This is only the first night, *Unni*. I cannot bear to stay here for the rest of my life."

The name she uses for me means older sister, the first time she has referred to me so. I pretend it makes no difference.

"Yet that is just the way things are, Wol-hyeong," I say. "You have nowhere else to go, just like the rest of us. You must learn to accept your fate. It is not so bad, living here." I smile to offer encouragement as two of the other girls help Wol-hyeong to her feet and lead her away down the halls.

I watch them as long as I can, until the Pavilion swallows them up.

With Wol-hyeong gone I walk slowly toward the banquet hall. My head aches from the tautness of my hair, slicked back from my face and wound in high thick braids across my head. Entwined hair pieces are adorned with an elaborate jade pin. The pin moves back and forth as I walk, digging in beside my ear. By now I should be used to how heavy it is, after wearing my hair this same way for three long years. Yet I am not.

"Jang Seorin!"

The headmistress barks my name from where she waits beside the banquet hall doors, flanked by her bodyguard. She gestures impatiently toward the other girls already within the hall and I pick up my pace to join them, bowing low as I pass her by.

Inside it is crowded, colourful *gisaeng* mingle with noblemen of the high *yangban* class. Men lounge on cushions in front of tables spread thick with white dishes of bamboo shoots, ginseng and quince, grape preserves, and strong *soju*. Fine desserts and alcohol for fine rich men.

Most of the party are young today, resplendent in their finery and black *gat* headwear, presided over by only a few older nobles. All of them are dressed in the silk *hanbok* that signifies high status, shining robes awash in bright blues, greens, and red. It is clear they have been here a long time, eyes glazed and cheeks flushed red.

"It is a celebration to honour one of the young men," Jan-sil appears at my side dressed as I am, in whispering skirts and painted face. "He has passed the civil servant examination."

I nod as my friend hands me my *gayageum*. The instrument is heavy in my hands, yet a comfortable weight beneath my calloused fingertips. I have spent many hours working to master it, the single joy I discovered upon my arrival at the Pavilion. I run my hands across the *gayageum's* paulownia wood body, hollowed out and strung tight with twelve long strings, every nook familiar and loved. My mastery of it is my only pride and vanity, a skill which affords me opportunities the other *gisaeng* cannot have; a chance to step away from entertaining to perform or practise.

An escape.

"*Gisaeng*, play for us."

An older lord sits at the top of the hall, his voice booming above the room's chatter, arms spread wide as he addresses me. Heads turn and silence falls.

I smile and bow low, affecting a docile expression in my manner and speech. Letting it settle across my skin.

"*Nauri*," I address him in the respectful way. "You honour me."

I am more than perfect at masking my face and voice for them. No one in this room will ever know what lies beneath.

Perhaps even I no longer know.

Arranging myself carefully on the far side of the hall, I settle on the thin cushion Jan-sil has placed there for me, voluminous skirts spreading up to my elbows. I begin to play, practised fingers dancing across the strings of my *gayageum* as the room remains in rapt silence. Dark eyes drink me in.

It does not last.

Soon the laughter and slurred conversation rings out once more, a cacophony of men's deep voices and the higher chatter of attentive *gisaeng*. The women pour clear liquor from ceramic bottles each time a drinking bowl runs dry. These girls are everything they should be: shy and bashful, educated, intelligent, seductive, even silent. Always beautiful.

We are what we're wished to be.

I watch quietly from my cushion seat, for I do not mind being ignored. My music echoes through the hall as the crowd drowns itself in rice wine and liquor. The sky breaks and rain begins to fall. It hammers hard against the roof in a deafening thunder, heavier and heavier until my music is no longer discernible from the sounds of play within the hall. I continue regardless, head bowed now and eyes locked on the *gayageum*'s strings, the long instrument heavy across my legs.

With the rain comes servants. Women dressed in coarsely spun uniforms scurry inside to pull the shutters closed, picking their way through drunk patrons as they light candles and lanterns. Light spills red and gold across the floor, a soft warm glow to keep the gloom of night at bay. None of the men notice the presence of the servants. After fastening the latches against the howling wind, the women leave as silently as they arrived. Ghosts in the night.

Outside, the rain hammers on and on.

MUCH LATER THE temperature snaps to cool, humidity gone just as the lightning begins; great flashes flare across the wooden shutters as the storm rages on. My fingers grow stiff as they dance over the *gayageum*, until mid-song a string stretches and breaks, cutting flesh as it snaps. Blood stains my skin and I bite my lip at the sharp pain, glancing at the banquet patrons.

No one sees, the abrupt loss of music unnoticed.

After a few moments waiting to be sure, I finally stand and slip from the room, keeping one eye on the patrons as I haul my heavy instrument with me. I pad silently through the maze of halls toward our quarters at the back of the Pavilion. I am pleased to be away, even if only to retrieve a new string. My lips curl into a secret smile until a yawn breaks through. I will take my time re-stringing it, linger as long as I can.

Darkness swells inside the small storage room, shadows spilling from the corners across the cold floor. My lantern remains unlit and discarded beside the wall.

Still sucking my cut finger, I pause before the outer sliding doors, which are open to the night. The frame vibrates in time with the howling wind, gaping open onto the Pavilion's vast courtyards and wild wet gardens. The terrace beyond the small storage room is dark, water pooling into mud along pathways that wind through shadowed trees. The air tastes of rain.

The sliding doors are wide open.

Yet I am certain I shut them.

Carefully setting down my precious *gayageum* where it will remain safe and dry, I struggle with the doors, battling against the heavy rain. Water pools beneath my feet, soaking my indoor stockings. Cold against skin.

With the windows finally secured I think longingly of my bedroll as I drop to dry the floor. The room is dark and heavy, and I imagine forgoing the rest of the night's celebrations to sink into the soft depths of my blanket. Yet it is only a fleeting dream … for I am a *gisaeng* and a *gisaeng's* life is not her own.

Rainwater spreads far across the floor and, yawning, I follow it with my rag, drying impatiently. Water has spilled beneath the table, mixing with the long deep shadows and the darkness curling from the corners of the room.

Abruptly I stand still, listening.

I hear it again. Heavy laboured breathing, sharp and fast.

A man. Coiled like a spring in the darkness and hidden in the black.

Staggering backwards a scream erupts from my throat yet he is so quick, a hand hard across my face, fingers grasping my mouth to suppress yells before they have begun. I buck and kick, railing against him as his grip tightens. Warm breath against my cheek.

"I won't harm you," he hisses.

There is urgency in his voice. Desperation.

I do not believe him.

I throw my weight to unbalance him and kick again and again until we both tumble to the floor, a struggle of limbs and layered silk clouding around us. My heart beats jaggedly, blood roaring in my ears as I attempt to rip his hand from my mouth. Feet kicking hard at the low table, I twist and turn until the man exhales in a sharp gasp, my elbow finally connecting with flesh. Glimpses of a blood-streaked face emerge through the shadows, eyes wild and rolling as his body slumps, unfocused and dazed.

I rip myself away, staggering onto my feet to stumble for the door within seconds, holding my dishevelled hairpiece in place. He is almost unconscious, helpless and slumped on the floor, head pushed back and face angled to the ceiling, breath laboured. My chance to escape, to raise the alarm.

To be safe.

To fix my face and my hair and change my *gayageum* string. To return to the banquet hall where things remain unchanged. Stretching forward as far as I can see.

My feet do not carry me where I wish to go.

I remain locked in place staring down at the stranger. Blood soaks his chest, seeping between clutched fingers from some terrible wound on his stomach, hidden beneath ragged clothes. Half open eyes meet mine. Pleading.

Beneath the din of thundering rain, crunching footsteps splash along the gravel pathways beyond the sliding doors. I press shaking fingers against the doorframe, the thin structure all that obscures us from the lush wet gardens outside. Heavy footsteps draw closer. Men yell from the terrace, rough voices shouting back and forth through our complex. Searching for something ... for *someone*.

I look down.

For him.

The man grasps the hem of my *chima* skirt, clutching at the folded silk, material held taught and tight with startling strength. He does not let go as footsteps approach along the terrace.

Rattles and crashes erupt from within the room next door, as if it is being searched. The man stares at me, eyes wild.

"Help me."

2

The Stranger in the Room

Terrace doors slide wide open and flickering flame-light fills every hidden corner of the room. Over my shoulder the silhouettes of two men rise against the dark rain, both dressed in the guard uniform of the police bureau, their bodies imposing. One holds a lantern, peering inside with a thin pointed face. Sharp like a fox.

He barks like a fox too, voice just as piercing as his features. "You! What are you doing?"

One boot already hovers across the doorway, a threat that turns my skin cold.

The injured man lies pinned to the floor beneath me, and I am filled with terror of what must surely come next. Interrogation and torture. Death. The stranger remains motionless, watching me with burning eyes.

"I am doing nothing," I answer the guard finally.

The stranger releases a pent-up breath.

"I am only a lowly *gisaeng*, tell me why you have entered my private room at this late hour?" My voice is steady as I address the policeman over my shoulder, my body hiding the stranger's face from view.

But it is not enough.

The man beneath me is clearly an outsider, soaked through from the rain, his clothes and shoes covered in mud from the garden and his hands streaked with blood. He is no normal Pavilion patron. All the guards must do is look. My layered skirts won't hide his identity; our embarrassing position is not enough to distract these men, my idea will not work ... it will not.

Or it will.

The guard with the fox face squints through the darkness. "Have you seen any strangers in the hallways tonight, *gisaeng*?"

I release my breath and slowly shake my head.

He is not suspicious.

He is foolish.

I almost smile except the fox guard steps suddenly inside the room. Light from his lantern swings directly onto the stranger's face, illuminating sweat-covered skin and glittering eyes. I jerk to the side, using my body to block the light, plunging the stranger into shadow once more.

Too late, much too late and already I see my end coming straight at me, blood spilled across the road, screaming and tears. I already know what happens to traitors.

Except ... glancing back at the guard, his attention is not on the stranger at all.

All focus rests on me.

He scans my body with a lingering gaze, lips curling into a slow fox smile. "You are certain you've not seen anyone suspicious, *gisaeng*?"

"I have not." Anger clips my voice now, nerves strung much too tight. "How could I possibly have seen such a thing from here? Are you both fools?"

The fox guard's skin flushes and I think I have gone too

far, but already I am distracted. My hand still rests against the stranger's chest, covered in blood now, wet seeping between my fingers.

This cannot last.

Slowly I force myself to exhale, summoning whatever courage I have left to flash fury at the two guards, voice whip-sharp like the headmistress's, biting hard enough to draw blood. "Leave this room now! Or else I'll call the headmistress and tell her you've been disturbing our guests! She is greatly favoured by powerful men. Do you truly wish them to hear you have obstructed her business?"

The fox faced one seems almost amused at my outburst, yet already the other guard is flushed with embarrassment. He is very young. Perhaps even young enough for this to be his first time inside an establishment like the Pavilion.

"Forgive us, we will leave," he stammers, averting his gaze and attempting to draw back his partner. The fox man's eyes still roam my body.

"Perhaps I will visit you later *gisaeng*."

I do not bother answering the taunt; he could not afford the Pavilion anyway, yet I feel the stranger's fingers tighten against my skirt. I push harder on his chest and he groans. Stay down.

The younger policeman bows in apology and this time manages to pull the other guard from the room, sliding the doors closed behind him to shut out the wet night and lush dripping gardens. My vision adjusts in the shadows, my heart slows and roaring blood grows still. The sounds of the search party fade into the rain until the storm is all that's left.

In the sudden silence I am quick to climb off him. The stranger.

The man sits up slowly, his movements strained. He

presses a hand against his stomach, blood gleaming in the dark across his fingers.

"Your body is hurt," I say. Quietly climbing to my feet, I retrieve a layered skirt and offer it to hold against his stomach. "It will keep the blood at bay."

He waves me away. "I do not need it."

Grunting with effort he staggers to his feet, trying hard to hide his weakness. I imagine how easy it would be to press my hand against his chest and push; he would tip over like a sapling to the floor and I could scream for the guards, release myself from this hole I have dug. Leave that red road of traitor's blood behind.

I do not move.

Sweat shines on his forehead and the stranger spreads his hand against the wall to steady himself. Glittering eyes meet mine in the darkness, assessing and calculating.

"I need something from you," his voice is flat, without emotion. "Will you help me?"

I am taken aback. "I've already helped you."

"You have," he agrees. "You saved my life. And now you must face your choice and complete the task. Hide something here for me. Someone will return later to retrieve it."

When I don't reply he adds quietly, "It is important to many lives the guards who search do not find this thing. Please."

"I can't help you. I don't even know what you've done. Why do they search for you?"

His eyes burn with fever. And determination. "You *can*. You can help me."

"Why are they chasing you?"

"You already *have* helped me." He steps closer, ignoring my questions. "Hiding me is enough to implicate you

12

already. If I'm found here now you'll be marked as an accomplice, you'll be arrested alongside me. Help me with this last thing so I can leave here sooner. If I am gone you will be safe."

I wonder if he intends his words to sound as they do, so much like a threat. But already he is pulling a blood-stained silk pouch from underneath his clothes, reaching to wrap my fingers firmly around it as he pushes the bag into my hands.

"Keep this thing for me and I'll send someone to retrieve it soon. And that will be the end of it. I promise you."

Beneath the silk I feel parchment. I blink, heart racing as I close my fingers tighter and the paper crackles.

"This is so much more important than you can imagine." The stranger's grip closes over my wrist, painfully tight, willing me to believe in him. "Keep it safe."

I falter, another mistake, for already he is moving toward the shutters, expression alert and ready.

"There are still guards outside," I warn.

"I'll make it." He glances back over his shoulder. "Or I won't. Yet I cannot be found in possession of that thing. You must keep it safe, and if no one comes for it … burn it."

I peer at the silk pouch in my hands. "What is it? What's inside?"

He smiles and it changes his face. "I am putting my faith in you, *gisaeng*. I am trusting you." His hair hangs loose and wet across his brow and his jaw is unshaven. He's dressed in the attire of a common man, coarse and home-spun, yet beneath the dirt and sweat he is young and well made. A strong man.

He opens the shutters, hesitating. "Keep it safe. And

whatever happens, do not look inside. The less you know the better."

He smiles again and my chest twinges, blood singing through my body.

Then he disappears into the black storm.

3

Water Ghosts beneath the River

I sleep late as most of the *gisaeng* do, rising only when I can no longer bear the hunger in my belly. The kitchen is buzzing with rumours of a mystery man in the Pavilion, the servants bringing gossip alongside the breakfast dishes they carry. Jan-sil tells everyone who will listen how she was questioned by guards in the hallway. The other *gisaeng* lean close to whisper their own tales of encounters, embellished liberally in the morning sunshine.

I ignore the conversation yet cannot fault them for the gossip. Our lives within the Pavilion are small and boring. Week on week, year on year, nothing ever changes. Such an unexpected event will haunt our hallways for months to come, a relief from monotony to be grasped with both hands.

So I chastise no one for gossiping, sitting in silence.

In the afternoon I leave the Pavilion behind, restless in my mind and unable to keep the stranger from my thoughts. I make plans to wander by the river in the mountain woods, yet instead come across Wol-hyeong in the garden. She sits alone with head held high, the drunken glaze long lifted from her eyes. Her pale face is turned upwards toward the sun. What I see written there causes me to stop and keep her company awhile.

Lowering myself onto the wooden bench to join her, I hand over some of the fruit I intended to bring on my walk. Wol-hyeong takes it without a word, lifting slices to her painted lips. Sunshine shimmers across the high glossy rolls of her hair, dancing over the elaborate pins that adorn it. She truly looks the part now, a *gisaeng* in every way, even more beautiful than most.

"Are you well, Wol-hyeong?"

"No."

I hesitate. "You will be. I promise you that. If you do not continue to fight it." I hope it is true.

"I will never love a man, *Unni*." Wol-hyeong swipes the tears spilling across her cheeks.

I laugh. "You never know what will happen, Wol-hyeong. Though perhaps that is for the best. This isn't a place for real love after all."

Wol-hyeong is quiet and silence blooms, seeping into the spaces between our bodies. For a moment I imagine our shared experiences weaving us together and I am thinking of the past when she suddenly speaks.

"*Unni*... did Jan-sil tell you about the woman whose father came to save her?" She looks at me, earnest in her longing. "She said the girl was allowed to go home."

I frown and shake my head. "Did Jan-sil also tell you of the *mulgwisin*, the water ghost who lives deep beneath the river and pulls all the young men down to their watery deaths?"

I pause as Wol-hyeong slowly nods her head.

"Jan-sil tells tales," I say gently. "Some of them more beautiful than others, but all tales nonetheless."

Wol-hyeong sits still, drawing her fingers tight until they are white and bloodless. "I see … Jan-sil tells lies."

"Not lies," I correct carefully, for Jan-sil is my friend. "Simply distractions."

Wol-hyeong's face falls, and for a moment I regret what I've said, the truth. I should have left her as she was, filled with hoping.

Or perhaps I am kind to have done so.

I do not know.

"If you want to do well here you could ask the head-mistress for a skill," I venture, wanting to wash away the damage I have caused.

"A skill, *Unni*?"

"You will be trained in all the arts, of course, yet to become the very best at something. To learn to dance like Chungjo does, or to sing. Something to make you special, to make life easier."

She pauses. "Like playing the *gayageum*?"

I smile. "Yes, like the *gayageum*. Would you like to learn to play?"

She peers at me, her head tilted to the side. "If you teach me to play as you do then we will both be special, *Unni* … which only makes us less so."

I laugh, for clearly Wol-hyeong is intelligent too. Intelligent enough to do very well here, if she wants to.

"Yes, you are right." I lean closer to whisper, "Though I do not mind if you don't."

Her smile is small, yet it beats warmth into my heart and sets my memories stirring once more. Wol-hyeong watches me curiously, and I fancy she has read something of my thoughts upon my face.

"Seorin *Unni*," she asks tentatively, "how old are you?"

"Seventeen summers now." A woman grown.

"And were you sold here too?"

I look at my hands and hesitate before eventually shaking my head. "Not quite. Not sold."

"My father did. He sold me." Wol-hyeong surges on, barely seeming to register my words. "He couldn't afford to feed my younger brothers, yet I had hoped … I hoped…"

She does not finish but I know what she hoped.

I do not tell her that to buy back a state-owned *gisaeng* takes more money than her father received in selling her. Even if he changed his mind he could no longer afford her. We are women trained in art and poetry, in dance and music and intelligent conversation; we do not come cheap.

Yet because I do not tell her, Wol-hyeong begins to press me about my own history. I smile and do not answer, and cannot stop myself from standing and walking away. It is cruel of course, yet my own heart is something I cannot share so freely. Not anymore.

I go walking along the woods' path to the river and once there I paddle my bare feet in the cool waters awhile, thinking of the stranger. Does he live? Does he make plans to return here?

I cannot know for certain, yet there have been no whispers of a man arrested and I cling to this idea. He is safe. For now.

All around the cicadas hum, their song hanging thick in the tree boughs and across the water's surface. I close my eyes, reminded of my home and the times I spent sewing with my mother on our wooden *maru* when I was only a child. For all my words to Wol-hyeong of learning to live the life we have, I cannot help but think on it. And even after all this time I am still glad my father cannot see me now. I would be too ashamed to meet his gaze, embarrassed of my clothes and my hair and my painted face, things that mark me for what I now am, a lowly *gisaeng*.

A slave.

Yet it is his fault I became this way.

He did not sell me here, but it is my father's fault all the same.

For I was not always a *gisaeng*. Once I was naïve enough to trust my world would always be bright and warm as the summer.

I learned.

4

An Invitation

Three weeks pass and I grow certain the stranger is dead. I lie awake at night and imagine him collapsed beside a road somewhere, his body rotting in the summer heat, eyes glazed and locked onto the sky. Perhaps he died without telling anyone I have the small silk package locked away, hidden deep beneath folds of bright silk.

Perhaps no one will come for it at all.

You must learn to accept your fate. It is not so bad, living here.

My words to Wol-hyeong circle around my mind, over and over. Yet I am no longer ready to accept. Something has changed.

The stranger told me to burn the package and yet I do not. Instead I wait, until finally in the grey early morning one of the Pavilion child maids knocks on the door.

"Mistress Seorin, may I come in?" Her voice is thin and high, wafting through the latticed paper screen from the hallway.

I am still sprawled in a quilted blanket on the floor, buckwheat pillow thrown across the room. I sit and wipe my face, pinching my cheeks to wake up.

"Come in."

I do not know the name of the girl who enters. Was it Ok-hee? She is young, perhaps nine years old, with a sweet round face and quivering lips.

"Mistress, at the market this morning a boy talked to me. He gave me this letter. He said it is for you." She offers me a curled piece of parchment and I am relieved to see the seal is unbroken.

"Did this boy have my name?"

I turn the thin envelope in my hands. It is unmarked. Rough paper. Ridged beneath my fingertips.

"No, Mistress, only he told me it was for the one who plays the *gayageum*. I hope I wasn't wrong to disturb you so early, the messenger boy said it was so urgent."

I smile to reassure her. "You did the right thing. Thank you."

The girl is pleased. I give her a coin for her silence and then send her on her way. As soon as she is gone, I open the parchment with shaking hands to read the few short lines scrawled inside.

A time and a place. Nothing more.

Yet it is proof that he still lives.

The gladness that swells through my chest surprises me with its potency. In my mind's eye I begin to imagine the stranger whole and vibrant again, the images of his death slowly seeping away.

I study the letter.

I needn't have worried about the maid girl reading it after all. Even if she had wanted to, the note is not written in the common script, those easy letters created especially for the people to use, even for the slaves and lower-class peasants. Instead the words are painted delicately across the paper in classic *hanja* characters, a script only the *yangban* noblemen have the time or opportunity to study.

The stranger has been foolish in sending me such a letter. It reveals so very much about him. I bite my lips, assessing.

To have written it he surely must be well educated, not a dirt poor commoner as his coarse rags and untamed hair seemed to suggest. He must be *yangban* himself, a nobleman, to write a casual note this way. And even more interesting?

He presumed I could read it.

This presumption reveals he does not know much about the habits of the lower classes in Joseon, for no one who must work for a living has the opportunity for learning such as this. Although it is true a *gisaeng* might study the script as part of their education in the arts, not all of us would know. He could not have been certain.

He couldn't have known I spied on my older brother's lessons while growing up, hiding in the next room or crouched in the garden beneath the terrace. My father would not have approved of course, but he did not know. And when my brother, my *orabeoni*, found out, he did not tattle.

Instead he helped me, late evenings spent studying beside a flickering candle, watching the firelight warm his face. Memories more precious to me than life, dreams I relive while falling asleep each night, face pressed into my blankets and tears on my cheeks.

I sit and wonder who this stranger truly is, this man I have saved.

By helping him I have involved myself in something dangerous, for there is a need for disguise and hidden identities within this plot.

A clash of excitement beats suddenly within my heart.

Perhaps this is an opportunity. Perhaps it is leverage.

The first I have had in years.

"SEORIN...! JANG SEORIN!"

The headmistress calls me, her voice echoing loudly through the halls of the Pavilion. The sound reaches the wooden terrace where I sit practising a new song on the *gayageum*.

"I am here, Headmistress."

Halting my playing, I peer over the gardens as I wait for her approaching footsteps, dusk shrouding the plants and gateways in soft blue light. A group of labourers arrives through the main arched courtyard gate and for a single moment I think I see a familiar face. My heart stops beating.

My brother. My *orabeoni*.

Yet the familiar face changes into a stranger's and of course it is not.

I bow my head to clear it.

Old unwelcome memories often visit me these days, turning me tired and bitter. It will not do. And my *orabeoni*, my precious brother, he is dead.

I saw him die.

My features are schooled into a serene mask by the time the headmistress glides out to meet me, followed by her guard, a younger man with vicious eyes. The headmistress was once the most sought after *gisaeng* in all of Hanyang and it shows in the proud way she carries herself, in the graceful line of her neck as she bends low to speak with me.

"Seorin *ssi*, you are needed in the banquet hall again tonight. Are you ready?"

"Yes, Headmistress, I am ready."

"Good, go in now and pour drinks before you play, the

minister of defence is here and I know he takes particular interest in you."

"Yes, Headmistress." I bow my head as she leaves, taking another moment in the quiet to smooth my grimace before I venture inside for a final check over my hair and makeup. The minister of defence isn't the worst man to have shown an interest, but this news still fills me with distaste.

Sometimes I burn with hate for all of them, an emotion I cannot allow to run deep. I push the surge of anger away, remembering with shame how I had encouraged Wol-hyeong to adjust. As I collect my *gayageum* and walk toward the banquet hall I shake my head.

It is because of the stranger. Because he lives.

It has made me believe there could be something else out there other than this; this life, this stifling world. The idea seeps beneath my skin and slips inside my ribcage, planting itself like a small seed into my heart.

You must learn to accept your fate. It is not so bad, living here.

Inside the silk folds of my *jeogori* I clutch the stranger's note, tracing my fingers across the rough paper. Dreaming of something different.

5

Branches of a Camellia Tree

The market is hot and smells of fish and spice and sweating bodies. The summer heat beats on my back, the rough material of my *jeogori* scratchy and too warm against my skin.

Today I am not dressed as a *gisaeng*. There are no silk skirts or gauzy *jeogori*, instead I am a nondescript commoner girl, my hair pulled tightly into a long simple braid. It hangs unadorned down my back like an unmarried woman's plait should. No paint on my face, no bright colours, no calculated manners.

It is oddly freeing to walk through the marketplace as a commoner; no one notices me at all, no one cares who I am. It makes me wonder why I've never tried this before. What was I so afraid of? After all, there is nothing left for me to lose.

I scurry past food stalls, steam from simmering pots mixed with the yellow dust clouding the thin alleyways. The market is cramped and filled with the scent of frying *jeon*, a crisp pancake, and savoury grilled fish. I burst from a stifling alley into the wide-open space of the main street.

Leafy trees line the riverside and cracked stone walls radiate heat in the baking sun. By the time I reach my destination I am sweating, hair plastered to my forehead where it has escaped my thick braid, my *jeogori* damp against my back.

I pass through the elaborate wooden gates of the inn to find a sprawling complex inside: dining rooms and halls, public courtyards and sleeping quarters. A home away from home for travellers of every status. People swarm through the courtyards like ants inside an anthill, everyone focused on their own busy lives. No one has a spare glance for a servant girl like me. It makes me feel strange. Powerful.

Bold.

The letter has no further instructions. Just the name of this inn and a meeting time.

I stop just within the entrance, scanning the people wandering the garden. The laughing merchants taking tea on the balcony and the servants who scurry to serve them.

The stranger isn't here.

This is expected of course, to come here himself would be both foolish and risky, yet I feel an odd sense of disappointment nonetheless. My heart sinks as I scan the area for a messenger boy or anyone else who appears to be waiting to meet with someone.

There is nothing.

The thick scent of stew wafts through the gardens and I wonder if I'm meant to go inside. I take a last glance around the yard. Two little girls play by the courtyard wall, with a young police officer loitering nearby, wearing the blue uniform of a city district police bureau. And then finally a group of four commoner men huddled together near the balcony.

Nothing of interest.

Inside there is not much else; merchants, travelling noblemen and plenty of commoners. In the back-yards there are slaves.

No stranger.

No one stops me wandering around the complex. It's as if I have become invisible in my servant's garb, the feeling of it stealing warm and welcome across my skin. After so many years of being closely watched by the head-mistress, now it feels as if I could be anyone, *do* anything. Eventually my footsteps lead back to where I began, the entrance to the main courtyard, which has cleared now except for the police officer. He stands alone beneath the sprawling branches of a flowering camellia tree, looking hot and uncomfortable despite the shade. I stop to watch him for a moment as he throws yet another irritated glance toward the inn's main entrance gate.

Surely not.

The stranger would not have sent a police officer to meet me.

Would he?

I double back, focused on the officer as I move through the terrace and climb a set of creaking wooden stairs to stand on the inn balcony near the camellia tree. I peer down at him. He does not know I am here, his face hidden beneath the wide brim of his uniform hat, his focus still on the main gateway.

"Excuse me," I call out. "Excuse me."

The string of looped wooden beads hanging from his hat swing wildly as he twists, scanning me from head to toe. He is young, with sharp cheekbones and razor black eyes. Handsome, yet his disdainful expression ruins the picture. Scowling he waves his hand to dismiss me. "I have no money for you. I'm busy. Away with you."

I blink. Normally if a nobleman spoke to me thus I

would bow my head and obey without a moment's hesitation, yet today I am resistant. After all, today I am no *gisaeng*, yet I am no true servant girl either.

Today I am myself, a noble daughter in disguise, simply playing a part. I feel giddy and almost wild, for it has been three long years since I have been myself.

Sinking to a crouch on the balcony, I wave my hand until I've caught the police officer's attention again, lifting my chin boldly. It seems to me this unlikable young man must truly be the person I am meant to meet, if only because there is no one else here and it is well past the appointed time.

The man takes note of my dust covered skirt with disapproval. "Oh ho! Did you not hear me, brat? I said away with you." He turns, folding his arms neatly behind his back.

"I did hear you, yet perhaps you're here to meet with someone?"

He stops and squints, and I decide I rather like my vantage point. It forces him to crane his neck upwards, the sun directly in his vision. No one looks dignified when they are blinded.

The young man's squinted eyes fill with suspicion, travelling from my straw sandals over my faded clothes and back to my face. "You? You have a package to give me?"

He is not at all pleased, an expression I saw on many a man's face during that first year at the Pavilion, before I learned how to play the game of my new life. All those times I said something out of turn during a banquet or missed a note while playing the *gayageum*, all the mistakes I made before I learned the secret; *look and listen and never let them see beneath.*

It sends a savage streak of dislike humming through my bones. He is every inch a stiff nobleman, tall and disapproving with a proud straight back and a frowning line for a mouth. And it seems he was told nothing of me, of who to expect at this meeting today, for his expression is filled with surprise.

I find I rather enjoy his shock.

Taking my time climbing down from the balcony, I make him wait, ignoring his questions and taking pleasure in the impatience that rises in his voice. Finally, I leap the last distance to reach the ground at his feet.

Immediately I regret it.

He now towers over me, my head not quite reaching his shoulder. The sun blinds *my* eyes now and I blink again as every feature of his sharp face turns downwards.

"Did Kim Jae-gil send you?" he demands.

"Kim Jae-gil?"

Suspicion immediately blooms across his face so I quickly amend myself. "Yes! Kim Jae-gil. He sent me. He was the man who was wounded … the man dressed in disguise as a commoner." I smile, sidestepping the officer until the sun is no longer blinding me.

The injured man. The stranger.

Kim Jae-gil.

It suits him well.

"He told you?" The police officer's jaw is clenched tight. "He told you he was in disguise?"

"He did not. He said nothing."

The officer is still unconvinced, so finally I shrug and confess, "He wrote to me about this meeting using *hanja* script."

The young man's mouth turns down even further, immediately understanding my line of thought.

Not a fool then.

It doesn't make me dislike him any less. Especially when he begins studying me all over again, reassessing. His jaw tightens. "Yet you could read the note yourself? Or you've shown it to someone else."

"I showed it to no one." I am firm yet explain no further. I have no interest in revealing the truth to him. If he knew what I really am I know already how he would react. After all, a *gisaeng* is of the *cheonmin* class, reserved for slaves and tradesmen of the lowest rank imaginable; for men who slaughter animals and work with hides, for gravediggers and inn-keeps. For *gisaeng*.

If he does not already know who I am, then why should I be the one to tell him?

I take a deep breath, summoning my courage. "I want to meet him again. Kim Jae-gil. You arrange it for me."

"How dare you make demands? You cannot order a *yangban*!"

I square my shoulders. "I may not be *yangban* but I know what you and that man Kim Jae-gil are involved in. If you want my help, then you'll organise a meeting."

"We don't want your help! We don't need anything from a brat like you. Do you think I'll allow a commoner to threaten me?" He looms closer, blocking out the sun until I'm wholly lost within the shadow of his body. "Give me the package."

I should be afraid of his words and his size but I am not. I am not at all afraid.

Instead, I feel disconnected. Untouchable. After all, we're not here on official business. He's clearly involved in something unlawful. That much is obvious. I smile at him boldly. His hands are tied.

He simply doesn't know it yet.

"The package is not here," I explain calmly. "I have something you need and I do not care if you are a slave, a police officer, or the king ... I will not give it to you unless you bring me to meet that man."

Before the officer can react I lean up and grasp his elbow, tugging him further into the shadow of the building, away from a crowd of merchants arriving into the yard. He glances down at my hand with irritation and I know he wants to tell me a dirty commoner shouldn't touch his body, yet already he knows it will not make me stop. This causes me to smile too. He is a fast learner.

"Listen," I say. "I don't know what that man Kim Jae-gil told you about me..."

"He never said anything about meeting a brat like you." The muttered words already have less bite to them.

I ignore him. "It's clear you're both involved in something dangerous. And now I'm involved too. I didn't ask for this, so if I choose to help you further I want something in return."

He scoffs at me. "Money? Is that it? I can pay you right now and we will go our separate ways."

"No. There's something else I want. And I need to talk to that man about it."

"Just tell me and I'll send a message directly to him." The officer pauses. "If you give me the package first."

Now it is my turn to scoff. "Unlikely. Instead, why don't you organise for me to meet him and then I'll give *him* the package."

"Can you not listen to anything I say?" The man grimaces. "And why is your speech so casual? Do you know what rank I am?"

I ignore him. Two serving girls on the balcony are watching us. A common girl and a *yangban* officer speaking for so long in such a heated way is bound to draw unwanted gossip. I point this out to the officer and he glares down at me again, his expression darker only because he knows it's true.

"Fine. I'll arrange a meeting. But Kim Jae-gil won't

negotiate on this. And when I see you next you *will* hand over that package."

I shake my head. "I told you I won't bring it. I'll only bring it when I meet him."

Eventually he is forced to agree. He has no real choice.

I will not bend.

Reluctantly he names a market restaurant where we shall meet in two days' time, and then we pass together back through the ornate wooden archway into the bustling streets beyond the inn. A cart laden with large earthenware pots lumbers by, momentarily blocking our way as dust rises in clouds from the wheels. I feel dirt settle upon my skin, on my clothes, yet when I peer up at the officer his arms are folded behind his back, not a speck of dust daring to land on his blue uniform.

He says nothing, only gives me a poisonous glare, clearly about to leave without another word. I am unable to hold myself back. Abruptly I poke my tongue out at him, petty and childish, spinning on my heel to stalk away first in the opposite direction.

As I walk I reach to smooth the course material of my *chima*, spreading the skirt out and shaking to remove some of the heavy dust. I am certain it is the commoner dress that made me so childish, that intoxicating sense of anonymity and freedom. A dangerous kind of wildness.

Perhaps I shouldn't wear it anymore.

Yet I cannot quite wipe the smile from my lips.

6

To Watch and Listen, Silent

The marketplace on my way home is crowded and still stifling hot, thick with pressing bodies. A stall emerges from the dust, laden with shining slippers, deep pink and embroidered with thick blue blossoms. There is something about one pair that calls to me, dark blue at the tips and silver threads stitched in swirls around the heels. Running my fingers over the silk I think of Wol-hyeong, of the sadness that beats within her heart.

She isn't the same of course. Their faces are not truly similar. And Wol-hyeong is much older, even after all this time. Yet it does not stop me from picking up the slippers, holding them into the light to watch as they shimmer in the sun.

Would Wol-heyong smile if I gave them to her? Would the shadows lift from her eyes?

"Put them down."

A voice booms from behind the stall and a man's face appears, skin like leather dried in the sun.

"No *Ajeossi*, I was only looking…"

"Don't touch if you can't afford them. You make them

dirty!" The merchant reaches my side and pushes me away as a group of people squeeze by in the market throng. I stagger backwards, slippers dropped carelessly into the dirt. With a yelp I stumble into a warm soft form, robes fluttering around my face, soft silks and expensive embroidery.

"Forgive me..."

The words of apology forming on my lips are wiped clean away as the world abruptly turns upside down. Dust fills my mouth. Choking on the ground, hands lost in dirt and face pressed into the road. Stunned, I sit slowly, blood already seeping from a graze on my palm. People have stopped to watch, a circle of curious faces peering through the rising yellow dust.

"Dirty girl! You were trying to steal from me?"

My attention flicks toward the voice; the man I collided with. He is old and large, a beard of grizzle forming from a rounded chin. He still stands, unlike me, indignant and flushed red. I know immediately he is *yangban*, if not from his clothes and the way he stands then from the way he looks at me.

As if he is inspecting an insect.

The lord grimaces at his bodyguards. "Search her. She took something."

Men close in and I act without thought of consequence. I have not yet regressed back into a meek docile *gisaeng*, for better or worse.

For worse.

Springing to my feet I slide away before his men can reach me, slippery like an eel.

"It was an accident! I didn't mean to touch you."

No one listens.

Blood flushes the old man's skin, cheeks blotched beneath his straggly beard. It is a warning sign. An instruction to back down immediately, to grovel in the dust at his feet and beg his forgiveness; and even at that, I probably won't avoid a beating.

A shiver despite the heat.

Already I feel the threat of a rush mat wrapped tight around my body, the thick wooden clubs raining down across my back and shoulders. Skin painted black and blue.

I have felt that pain before, when I first arrived at the Pavilion and still believed myself to be a noble daughter. That pride was beat from me long ago, it did not take so much.

You must learn to accept your fate.

Despite it all my legs still won't bend.

Fire burns the fear away.

"How *dare* you." The old lord's face is simple to read. He cannot believe I have not yet kneeled, as even I cannot. He gestures wildly at his guards and they converge more quickly this time, ready for my dodging.

"Don't touch me," I hiss as one of the men takes hold of my arm. "I did nothing wrong!"

"If I say you did, then you did, market scum." The man shouts now, bystanders gathering closer to hear, to be entertained. "You question me? You must learn respect!"

My straw sandals scrape at the dirt as I am dragged toward the lord, unable to break free despite my wild struggles, kicking up clouds of dust that soon have me choking. The lord lifts his hand to strike me, swinging hard toward my head.

The blow does not connect. Someone else is there to grasp the man's wrist, halting all movement just a hair's breadth from my cheek.

The police officer from the inn.

I gape up at him as he pries the guards' hands from my body, unceremoniously yanking until I'm behind his looming shoulders. Slow with confusion, it takes a few moments before I realise the sneaky police officer could only have been following me, attempting to discover where I live. It fills me with ferocity despite the situation, knowing I was so close to losing my bargaining leverage before I'd even had a chance to begin.

"*Yeonggam*, please forgive this insolent girl." The sneaky police officer speaks in a steady voice, bowing deep to the old lord. "She does not deserve your attention. She has made a grave mistake."

The older man sniffs, smoothing his robe where it flaps weakly in the thick breeze. "This girl is yours, Lee Yoon? I'm disappointed. I never expected you to keep such a loose rein over your servants. What kind of household does your family run, Officer Lee?"

Officer Lee keeps his gaze lowered, except now he reaches with his free hand to force my head into a low bow too. His fingers push on the back of my neck until I bend.

"Please forgive her transgression this once, *Yeonggam*. If you allow me to take her home I will ensure she is rightfully punished."

I try to stand at that, but am shoved down again.

"Let me suggest a beating, Officer Lee. It will teach her manners."

"Yes, my lord, I will do as you say." Officer Lee straightens, shooting a dirty look in my direction, which I return immediately.

The lord peers down his nose at me. "What is your name, ungrateful girl?"

"It ... My name is Jang Seorin, my lord."

"If I see you causing trouble again I'll have you flogged."

I glare at the dust and say nothing as Officer Lee begins to speak to the lord in a pleasant way of the weather and their families, of politics and whispers. As if nothing has happened at all. Except his hand still holds me still beside him, wrapped like an iron bracelet around my forearm, the only sign he is not as calm as his exterior. I am impressed despite myself. He is a good actor.

They talk and talk while I stare at dirt until finally Officer Lee tugs sharply on my arm, the old lord distracted by a sweets seller. The officer shoots a furtive glance in my direction and mouths angry words I cannot understand, his black eyes communicating he wants me gone. I obey immediately, melting away into the market crowds, glad to be away from the *yangban* lord.

Glad to be rid of Officer Lee too.

I move quickly through the stalls, weaving between earthenware pots larger than I am, my body breathless and aching. There is a pain in my belly I cannot quite explain, something that runs far deeper than my brush with violence. The old lord in his resplendent silks has made me think of my father. Would *he* have been so cruel to a young girl covered in dust in the marketplace, a common girl he was sure had done him wrong?

I hope he was not that kind of man, yet cannot be certain. After all, I never walked the marketplace beside my father. I never knew how he conducted himself beyond the closed haven of our home.

It is suddenly difficult to push through the pressing bodies, the smell of sweat and dirt thick in the humid air, people too close as they crowd beside a troupe of entertainers beginning their dance. Drums pound and energetic performers jump between the commoners, faces hidden behind painted masks and feet kicking up great storms of yellow dust. Even the movements of the storytellers, the fervour of the watchers and their infectious joy, cannot distract me. I am dreaming again.

Of my home.

WHEN I WAS A CHILD, I dressed in gleaming soft *jeogori* and *chima*. Clothes made from the brightest colours imaginable. Each garment was covered in embroidery so fine and delicate along the voluminous hemlines, it was a marvel to me my mother had sewn them. Her hands were more deft and skilful than mine could ever be and I felt clumsy in contrast as we sat together practising embroidery in the open terrace of our house.

I remember her cool fingers against my skin, smoothing my hair back. Her smile.

Her words.

Remain silent like a mouse, Seorin. Obey your father and your brother, watch and listen yet never speak.

In those days I had not truly known my father. I was only a girl child after all. He was an enigma who lived in my house whom I was expected to revere and respect.

Yet I had loved him.

He was often absent as I grew older, as was my older brother, my beloved *orabeoni*, who was almost a man grown by then. He spent most of his time diligently preparing for his future as master of our house. He studied for the civil servant examination, and if he did well he would gain an official position at court just like my father. Both of them together, standing alongside the king. A secret inner world I could never be a part of, could never hope to understand.

My father loved my *orabeoni* and treasured him. I remember wishing with all my heart my father would one day look at me that same way.

He never did.

Instead it all turned to dust around us.

7

A Lesson and a Game

I am sitting on the terrace, practising the *gayageum* absently. A light summer breeze, cool and fresh, blows in from the garden and brings with it the scent of grass.

Wol-hyeong approaches along the courtyard path, stopping for a moment to listen to my music before she climbs onto the patio to sit on the polished wood floor at my side. I smile but continue playing, calloused fingers plucking and sliding across the strings.

Finally, she loses patience with my silence, leaning closer. "*Unni* ... Some of the other girls told me something..."

"Did they?"

"This morning, they told me the headmistress hates me." She pauses and peers at me uncertainly. "Is that true?"

I stop playing.

"Who told you that? Chungjo?"

She nods pitifully and I sigh.

"Don't listen to her. She's lying."

The girl wrings her fingers in her lap, moving

constantly as if afraid of being still. "I don't understand, *Unni*. Why would she do that?"

I raise my brows at her. "Because you are beautiful, Wol-hyeong. *Very* beautiful. And delicate like a flower. Chungjo is the most favoured *gisaeng* at the Pavilion. Can you not see what she might fear?"

Wol-hyeong considers my words carefully, hushed and quiet a long time. "Perhaps she feels threatened? That I may try to steal what she believes is hers."

I nod, satisfied.

Picking up my *gayageum* I resume playing. "Be careful with the other girls, Wol-hyeong. They're not all bad, but this place is like a *baduk* match, constant strategizing and plotting. All of us want to win."

Wol-hyeong pauses. "Win what, *Unni*?"

Her curiosity stirs at my memories again, that look on her face almost familiar. I smile yet it feels bittersweet.

"A bearable life beyond these walls," I answer. "How old are you Wol-hyeong?"

"I am fourteen."

"And Chungjo is nearing her twenty-first year, older than many of us still here at the Pavilion. She will not give up without a vicious fight."

Wol-hyeong is silent, thinking. "And do you also want to win, *Unni*?"

I laugh. "I already have." I motion toward the *gayageum* resting on my lap. "I was playing a different game, that's all."

Wol-hyeong nods as though I have imparted some deep wisdom, yet I know she still doesn't understand. She is screaming for someone to protect her, but that is not my place. She must learn for herself how to play the game or the others will never respect her. She needs to be strong, different to how I was at the beginning when I first came to the Pavilion.

It took me such a long time to learn not all the girls here could be my friends, that many saw me as a potential threat to their status and position within the house.

But I wanted none of it. Top *gisaeng*? A famed beauty across the capital city of Hanyang? I had only wanted to run away.

Yet the cruel tricks had gotten worse, especially from Chungjo who ruled over the other girls with an iron fist. Even now she is stunningly beautiful and ruthlessly smart, and as ambitious as a king's concubine. Her age means her years here are running out, and soon Chungjo must find a new way to keep herself.

Perhaps she will be chosen by a patron wealthy enough to buy her freedom from the state, who may even take her as his concubine. If she is lucky. If not, she will have to trade in sewing or medicine, or join an inn-keep. A hard life. And not what she is aiming for.

Chungjo wants the headmistress position, she wants it with every fibre of her being and she is not subtle in her methods.

Yet I had beaten her in my own way.

In only one single night of work I had targeted every one of those girls who harassed me and put an end to their vanity. It was only after her temporary fall from grace, when I did not attempt to claim her empty place, that Chungjo finally realised I was speaking the truth about not wanting her lofty position. Finally, she left me alone.

That was when I discovered the power of talent in this place, the art of music and what it can mean in regards to status. I chose another way to rise in the Pavilion and become important.

Chungjo is someone who must be watched, even

though I no longer fear her. In fact, I imagine I understand her. After all, there are no old *gisaeng*. All Chungjo wants is to secure a palatable future for herself. I find it difficult to begrudge her that.

Yet I still decide I will have a word with her about Wol-hyeong. I will tell her to back off the new girl and give us all some peace.

We sit together, Wol-hyeong and I, and I teach her about the songs I play, tell her what they mean. And then later I watch her walk slowly away, her head bowed low beneath the weight of her sad world.

It is hard to understand how lonely and difficult the first few months are unless you have lived them yourself.

They are excruciating.

Yet there is nothing anyone can do to help. That time simply must be endured. It is the only answer.

So, I say nothing and leave her be.

8

Dust in the Marketplace

Two days pass and I am dressed in my dangerous commoner clothes again, afraid of what they will make me do. Yet hoping too; longing for something thrilling to break the boredom of these last three years, even now when this meeting holds so much at stake.

The market restaurant where I am to meet Officer Lee is tucked within an alley, a tiny run-down establishment with low eating platforms spilling out onto the street. I sit primly on one to wait. But he doesn't come.

I am there such a long time I order tea and then ask if the auntie running the place has any private rooms I can sit in. The restaurant has only a few small wooden pallets inside an open pavilion, none of which are at all suitable for private conversation. The place is also buzzing with the loud conversations of slaves and commoners, a strange choice for a meeting with a *yangban* officer.

The *ajumma* auntie is a little taken aback at my request for a private room but still lets me use a tiny storeroom off the main building. Soon I am settled cross-legged inside, comfortably sipping steaming tea while I wait. I think again of Kim Jae-gil, of the letter he sent that now lies folded within my *jeogori*. Of the future.

I am bored by the time I hear him outside, asking the restaurant auntie if there are any commoner girls here waiting. I can sense her pointing to the little storeroom even if I can't see it and a moment later Officer Lee comes crashing inside, slamming the little doors with a loud clatter. He doesn't waste any time on greetings.

"Are you a fool? He wanted to flog you!"

I am taken aback that two full days has not cooled his anger, and my lips curl in distaste. I have already chosen to forget the marketplace incident. I scowl as Officer Lee hunches to fit into the tiny dim space, a hulking giant whose head scrapes against the ceiling.

"You were following me." I slide away to create room for him to sit, dragging my tea set across with me. "You were planning to double cross me and steal back the package!"

His mouth tightens, trying his best to be dignified despite the woven baskets and earthenware storage pots all around us. There is a long moment of thick silence where I know he is waiting for me to express my gratitude about what happened on the street, but I cannot do it. I tell myself it is the clothes that make me so rude, but truthfully, I think it is myself.

When it finally becomes clear I am not going to thank him, Officer Lee flings his robes out behind him and sinks onto the floor across from me. His knees are scrunched uncomfortably to his chest and his black, wide-brimmed horsehair *gat* is now squashed at the side, sitting crooked on his head. I almost smile but manage to stop myself. It will surely only exasperate the situation.

"So ridiculous," he mutters. "Where exactly did Kim

Jae-gil find you? A madhouse?" He clears his throat and then refuses to look at me any longer, glowering silently.

It interests me that my injured stranger, Kim Jae-gil, has still not disclosed my true identity to this man. Perhaps Officer Lee cannot be trusted?

I size him up thoughtfully. "When will I meet with Kim Jae-gil?"

The officer sighs. Loudly. "Kim Jae-gil says you should be waiting in the woods by the river tomorrow at dawn. Apparently, you'll know what that means?"

I nod. It can only be the section of wood near the Pavilion, we have no other shared history that I could know of.

Officer Lee continues. "He'll be there or he'll send someone else to collect you. That's all I know." He hesitates and then his voice lowers. "Brat, you're a fool to get involved in this. It's dangerous. Just take your money and go."

His words surprise me, sounding almost of concern, yet he ruins the effect when he adds his next ones.

"The sooner you leave this alone, the sooner I'm rid of you."

I pull a twisted face at him but he just keeps talking.

"And you should know the next time I see you digging your own grave in the marketplace I won't bother saving you from a beating."

I grit my teeth. "I never asked for your help. I didn't want it either." However untrue that may be. "It is me who will be happy to be rid of *you!*"

Officer Lee gapes but I'm finished with this conversation and his insults. Standing, I push past him roughly, climbing out through the little doors he is blocking and giving him a final shove for good measure.

"Why you … Don't touch me, brat!" I leave him spluttering inside as I slam the doors and run as fast as I can away from the restaurant. I don't stop running until I'm far enough away that he can't follow. Only then do I slow to a stroll, satisfied in the knowledge that the restaurant *ajumma* will force him to pay for my tea.

9

Hidden in the Mountains and Valleys

I often go walking in the summer, so no one is surprised to see me leave the Pavilion. I am dressed in my true clothes today, the extravagant garb of a *gisaeng*, hair bundled high on my head and rouge blushing my cheeks. There is no point pretending to be a servant when I meet Kim Jae-gil, he already knows what I am.

Yet he trusted me with his secret package anyway.

A slight warmth unfurls in my chest, traveling all the way into my fingers and toes, causing my heart to beat a little faster.

The river is rushing by, swirling against the banks and crashing over rocks lining its edges. There is no one in sight so I sit and wait, lowering myself onto a large flat stone and watching as water laps the grasses near my feet. My thoughts wander again to that night in the Pavilion when I first met Kim Jae-gil, the darkness of the room and his blood wet on my hands. The wavering tree tops bend and sway, warm wind rustling my clothes as a thick breeze rushes through the river valley.

Things are beginning to change. I can feel it.

Abruptly two men step from the woods and I launch to my feet, startled. I recognise neither. Kim Jae-gil must surely have sent them but both are dressed in dark clothes, like warriors, only their eyes showing behind cloth masks. Their hidden faces make me wary.

One of them peers at me closely, brow lowered. "Your name?"

"It is … I am Jang Seorin." I remind myself that I asked for this. "Are you taking me with you?"

The man nods and gestures for me to follow.

Officer Lee must have provided them with my name. Only a moment of hesitation passes before I do as he asks, setting off into the trees with the other masked man falling into step behind. We walk a short way through the underbrush and soon are met by a third man, his face also covered. This one holds the reins to three large horses who throw their heads restlessly at our approach. The man who spoke easily swings himself into a saddle and silently motions for me to get up behind him.

Taken aback, I blink at him. I am not very good with horses and the idea of riding one now with a man I don't know sets my skin prickling. Yet there is no going back. I take deep breaths.

The man is patient as I struggle to navigate my heavy skirts, and he pulls me gently until finally I am perched side saddle behind him. It seems so strange these silent masked men being sent here to collect me. Three, no less. It seems like a lot of trouble.

Why didn't Kim Jae-gil just come to the river and meet me himself? What is the purpose of all this mystery?

It is uncomfortable on the horse. I am jostled and bumped around, clutching onto the man's robes and balanced high on the horse's rump. Despite the discomfort, I try desperately not to shift my weight too much for fear of disturbing the man I ride with. He doesn't say a word as we travel, none of them do, even when I question them. I am left to my own thoughts and the further we move from the Pavilion, the more disconnected from reality I feel. I cannot remember the last time I was so far away from the *gisaeng* house.

It has been so long. It has been years.

We ride higher into the mountains. The twisted trees grow close together and the pathway closes in, forest thick enough to block the sunlight. Soon I worry about my planned alibi of taking a simple walk in the woods by the river. If I am away too long no one will believe it. And the Pavilion is a dangerous place. There are games being played behind those walls that outsiders could never hope to understand. Tigers and wolves ready to pounce on weaknesses, to twist and exploit until they emerge on top.

It is a dangerous place to be caught in a lie.

I am lost in thought when we abruptly jolt to a stop, high in the lush humming hills, lost somewhere far beyond the city. Before us lies a long winding valley, a simple village far below with maybe three houses and a tent dotted within a tiny clearing. It is nothing unusual, there are many nondescript mountain dwellings in these hills, homes for farmers and peasants and the sick.

Or places of sanctuary for those who do not wish to be found.

We begin the descent. To keep balance, I lean far into the saddle, the wide body of the man who rides before me taking up my entire view. Why does Kim Jae-gil expose me to this place? If it is a hidden village, then it is a secret. And if it is truly what I suspect it to be, then why has he let me see it? Why would he trust me?

He does not know me at all.

The village is all I expected of it, ramshackle and run

down, the houses in need of repair, and yet there are many people milling around among the buildings.

Too many.

Men holding weaponry beyond the simple agricultural tools expected of commoners, men who have been equipped with swords that glimmer deadly and bright in the sun. So many men they could not possibly all be housed here in this small place.

Glancing at the tree line I search for roadways through the forest, routes that must surely lead to a far larger camp hidden somewhere nearby. I see many well-trodden pathways disappearing into the trees. If I didn't know already, now it is clear that something terrible is happening within these hills, men amassing and training in secret, *yangban* noblemen wearing disguises and nursing injuries so deep they would rely on a mere *gisaeng* to harbour their secrets.

By the time we reach the valley floor the other two silent warriors have dispersed behind us, melting into the trees quietly. I am left alone with the man whose horse I share. We stop outside a vast canvas tent erected behind one of the dilapidated farm houses and he lowers me from horseback carefully, pointing toward the open doorway beside us without a word.

I hesitate a moment, fingers holding tight to the canvas doorway, clutching until my knuckles have turned white despite the heat. Taking a deep breath, I silently remind myself why I am here, promise myself I will not leave until Kim Jae-gil gives me what I want. Pushing past the heavy hanging canvas I step into the darkness within.

There isn't much inside the dimly lit interior, just the exposed wooden frame of the tent, like a visible skeleton holding up the roof. Roughly placed wooden floorboards spread underfoot, grass creeping between the slats. One long simple table sits in the middle, surrounded by heavy wooden chairs with a cabinet in the corner made of intricately carved wood. And Kim Jae-gil sitting alone beside piles of paperwork.

"Jang Seorin." Kim Jae-gil's smile reaches his eyes when he greets me, and I am left wondering how he learned my name.

I bow as he shuffles his paperwork, holding still with my head low as he carefully folds the maps and places them into the cabinet, locking it. My insides knot tight as I wait for him to finish. I do not know this man's position here but judging from his status as *yangban* and the manner of my arrival, he is someone who commands respect.

"Please, there is no need." Kim Jae-gil waves his hand until I rise from my bow. "Out here in the forest we are all equals."

I blink. Somehow, I cannot bring myself to believe it.

And yet, what could this man's story be, that he would say such a thing to one as lowly as me? Noblemen are not taught to think in such a way. Joseon's *yangban* class live a sheltered existence, only taught to care for their own kind, taught to walk all over everyone else. I am not certain even I would have learned the value of a slave's life if I had not fallen to become one myself.

Yet he tells me not to bow.

I realise I am still staring, gaze flicking downward as Kim Jae-gil gestures for me to sit. I quickly do as he suggests, arranging my skirts carefully in one of the heavy wooden chairs, using the motion to hide my confusion. His close attention causes heat to rise across my skin, a long drawn out moment of thick silence hanging between us. Until finally I can bear it no longer and speak.

"You are … recovered now? And well?"

Kim Jae-gil's smile grows wider, patting his stomach where he bled across my fingers the last time we met. As if pleased that I remembered. "I am well," is all he says, adding, "I believe you have something for me?"

I nod. Reaching inside my *jeogori* I hand over the silk bag without hesitation. Our hands touch briefly across the table, his skin calloused and warm, mine tingling.

Kim Jae-gil smiles as he opens the package and removes the parchment, inspecting the paper until he is satisfied nothing is missing. His eyes meet mine. "You didn't look inside?"

I hesitate a moment before slowly shaking my head. "No ... I did not."

His smile breaks wider. "Now it seems I owe you double. If this fell into the wrong hands it would mean death for many people, myself included. Today you have saved lives, Seorin *ssi*."

The confident smile remains as he places the parchment inside the locked cabinet, key slipped back within his folded warrior robes. "Lee Yoon told me you were unreasonable, he said it would be impossible to get this from you. Yet you hand it over as easy as that? No demands?"

I bristle at the mention of Officer Lee, a man who clearly enjoys telling tales, but calm myself as best I can. "I do have a ... request."

My heart thuds a drum beat against my chest.

"Go on."

"There is something you may be able to help me with, something I am unable to do myself."

Kim Jae-gil nods, rising to his feet to pour water from a jug on the table. The muscles in his forearms move beneath his skin as he places the ceramic cup before me. "You came a long way to ask me this I think. Drink."

"Yes ... *Nauri*." I add the honorary title to my address. Despite Kim Jae-gil's words of equality and his easy smiles, he is still *yangban*. They do not count our lives the same way they count their own. It is wise to be careful.

"Seorin *ssi*." Kim Jae-gil watches me. "Without you I would be captured or dead. That is the truth of it. I owe you my life."

I say nothing.

He sits again, drinking water slowly, taking his time. "I believe I can give you what you want."

I glance at him sharply, attempting to read his expression. "What is it you think I want?" I forget to be careful with my words and they come out snapping.

Kim Jae-gil only smiles. "Yet there are people here who will expect you to work for it. They believe you could be very useful to us."

"Useful … *Nauri?*"

He leans closer across the table. "I know who you are."

My breath stops.

"Jang Seorin. It is the name of the previous vice premier's daughter, a man who plotted treason against our current king and died for his sins. His family were executed alongside him."

He pauses.

"Except for you."

My hands tighten in my lap, forming fists until my nails dig deep into flesh. The world grows loud, roaring in my ears.

Kim Jae-gil watches me carefully, whispers, "Except for you … and your sister."

There is not enough air inside this stifling tent, I am suffocating now, drowning.

Kim Jae-gil stands and walks to my side. "Please. You are unwell. Shall we walk together outside?"

His hand presses gently down onto my shoulder and I want to push it off. No one has spoken to me of my sister in years. I have heard no news, no whispers, nothing. The warmth of his fingers seep deep beneath my skin and somehow, I let his hand stay.

"Come outside with me." Kim Jae-gil repeats the words more firmly this time and I stand, letting him guide me to the tent entrance.

The afternoon sun is blinding after the dimness inside. I must shield my face, Kim Jae-gil pushing me gently to walk ahead of him, hanging behind. He lets go of my shoulder. I miss the warmth of his hand after he has pulled away.

We walk from the village through a grove of low hanging trees, Kim Jae-gil taking the lead once more when we have drawn far enough from the village to be alone. He slows when my skirts become caught in the underbrush, patient and silent as he waits.

My thoughts are on my sister, her thin hands clutching my clothes, her wild hurt eyes. Eventually my questions cannot be contained. "How do you know who I am?"

Kim Jae-gil keeps walking and I watch his broad back until he turns and smiles at me. "You already refused Lee Yoon's offer of money. I wished to be prepared for whatever you asked, so I enquired into your background. It doesn't do to deal with unpredictable people."

I stop walking. "Is that why you let me see this place? Because you found out I am no threat? That I'm all alone?"

"You are an intelligent woman, but you are more involved already than I think you know."

We arrive at an open field, a vast expanse of yellow waving grass and sunlight, extending far below into a narrow rocky gorge. Stepping out of the trees, Kim Jae-gil beckons for me to follow. After the cloistered claustrophobia of the Pavilion's winding halls and the thick maze of alleyways that form the city of Hanyang, the open space makes my head spin.

Sky above, grass below. Nothing else.

Kim Jae-gil sits on the thick grass, motioning me down beside him. "Have you guessed what we are all doing out here? This camp, I mean, why all these warriors are gathering?"

I nod. Of course I have. I am no fool.

"You wish to kill the king."

Kim Jae-gil sucks in his breath at my blunt words. "You disapprove."

I shrug, gazing on the wide valley. "You will all die. Your families will die." I glance at him sidelong. "Or end up like me."

He is silent so long I am compelled to ask, "Tell me how that can be worth it?"

"What did your father tell you about the king? Did he explain why he joined the failed rebellion all those years ago?"

"My father didn't speak to me of important matters, *Nauri*. I was only a girl child." My words are laced with bitterness and I take a deep breath, reminding myself to stay in control.

Kim Jae-gil inclines his head. "No, I suppose he wouldn't have. Yet the king is mad. He drives our great country into the ground. He spends his time in paranoia of conspiracy, killing anyone he sees as a threat."

I raise an eyebrow. "It seems to me he is right to feel threatened. He is right to suspect conspiracy."

Kim Jae-gil laughs. "I suppose so. But he is also foolish, cruel, and bitter. He grinds the common people beneath his feet, giving them no chance to live good lives. Surely you have seen it? The taxes driven higher each year, the people who cannot afford to pay losing their livelihoods.

Families flood into the capital with nowhere left to go. Hunger and desperation are everywhere."

He speaks passionately, betraying true emotion, not too proud to display openly how he feels about these injustices. Unlike any nobleman I have ever seen before. Kim Jae-gil is a different kind of man and I cannot help but stare, his words raising Wol-hyeong's father to my mind; so poor he would sell his only daughter in order to feed his sons.

Kim Jae-gil runs a hand through loose hair, tied at the back of his head with a strip of cloth. "I knew your brother, Seorin *ssi*. Not well, but I knew him."

The breath leaves my body. "You … knew my *orabeoni*?"

"I did, yes. My family was involved in that first failed coup as well, yet your father and brother's bravery meant we did not fall. We lived to fight another day."

I blink, not knowing how I should feel.

I have never thought of my father as brave, only as foolish. He made a victim out of my *orabeoni* by sucking him into a vile inescapable abyss neither man could control. It was because of him my mother was arrested, that my sister and I…

I am not sure I can ever change my mind on this, no matter what Kim Jae-gil tells me. I will certainly never feel pride for what they did, whether their actions saved Kim Jae-gil's life or not. My mouth tightens. "So you are telling me you did not give up after their deaths. You have been plotting ever since."

Accusation creeps within my voice.

"Yes. Myself and many others." Kim Jae-gil takes no notice of my tone, eyes clear of guilt. "My father is gone now but I continue his work and will realise his dream."

I stand abruptly.

Unshed tears threaten to spill over and I will not let

him see me like that. Not giving up on the cause is surely Kim Jae-gil's way of honouring my brother's memory, yet I cannot help but think my *orabeoni* would have preferred Kim Jae-gil rescue his younger sisters from slavery instead.

At least I hope he would have.

"I pray it is worth it, *Nauri*," I say finally, my back still turned to him.

"It will be." Kim Jae-gil sounds so utterly certain. "We will not fail again."

I walk away at that, nothing left to say, stepping quickly through the long grass back the way we have come. By the time Kim Jae-gil catches up I am composed again, controlled.

What's done is done.

All that is left is the future.

"Then, you will help me find my sister?" Words I have practised so many times before, waiting and hoping for the chance to say them aloud. My hands shake. "By now she would be..." I have to think. "She would be eight years old."

I stop to face him.

"She cannot end up like me. I will do whatever I must to change her fate. You said your people here would have use for me in return for aid in finding her? I can do it. I can do anything."

Kim Jae-gil watches me. "Are you certain?"

I nod immediately. I don't need time to think it over.

"If you can find her and free her, if you can ... send her somewhere safe, somewhere she can have a good life, then yes. I will do whatever you ask."

"And what of you?"

I smile, almost amused at his naivety. "I am not asking for myself. Help my sister, and that will be enough."

There is something dark in his face at that, a flash of pity I suspect. Whatever it is I lower my gaze to avoid it.

"I'll talk to the leaders here," Kim Jae-gil says finally. "I promise I'll do my best for you, Seorin *ssi*."

"Thank you, *Nauri*." I offer a true smile to show how much I mean it. Kim Jae-gil smiles back, quick like lightning, and then we are silent, walking again toward the village.

When we reach the tent, Kim Jae-gil immediately waves to one of the men in black and within moments he has brought a horse. The man stops a respectful distance away to wait as Kim Jae-gil draws me aside.

"You saved many lives by keeping that package safe. I promise people will be sent out immediately to search for your sister."

My head buzzes and I smile back shyly, ideas already unfurling inside my chest, threads of hope I thought burned out long ago. Kim Jae-gil has reignited them, set them moving again. An image of my sister, somewhere green and hidden, an image of her safe, it seeps inside my heart until I do not believe I will settle for anything less ever again.

"Do not tell anyone about this place." Kim Jae-gil's eyes blaze. "What we are doing here is a continuation of your father's work, if you help us it means he did not die in vain. We will make better lives for the people of this country. I know it is possible."

I say nothing for I do not care about his cause or what my father died for, only those sweet images of my little sister, free under a great blue sky, grass beneath her feet. Except then Kim Jae-gil leans so close his breath touches my cheek, his skin smudged with dust and eyes flecked with light, and he places his hands against my waist and lifts me high onto the horse. I grasp at the saddle and find my balance as Kim Jae-gil steps from the restless animal.

"I will send a message to you when I have news of your sister," he says. "And you will be contacted about a task soon enough."

And then he smiles, an open disarming expression I have no reaction for.

One kick to the horse's belly from my escort and we are gone, struggling up the mountain pathway back into the trees toward the valley ridge. I glance over my shoulder toward the little hidden village.

Kim Jae-gil has not moved. He stands alone in the clearing watching us until we are too far away to see. The forest comes between us and he disappears.

THE WAY down the mountain is steep and unsteady but we make good time, the late afternoon sun sliding between tree branches and the summer wind blowing strong. Over and over again Kim Jae-gil's words run through my mind. And no matter how many times I hear them I know in my heart that he is wrong.

My father did die in vain, I know he did.

Yet in this strange twist of fate, the only way to save my sister from the hell my father left us in, is to help Kim Jae-gil complete the work my father began.

Suddenly I laugh out loud, startling the man who escorts me. He says nothing, only glancing back at me strangely. Even I can hear the sound is tinged with bitterness.

10

The Task

I glide softly through the halls of the Pavilion, listening to the girls talk within their rooms. Chatter fills the building with light and laughter. I hesitate outside Wol-hyeong's door, my hand hovering over the latticed wood panelling.

I have spoken to Chungjo and she will no longer bother Wol-hyeong, I have made sure of that, yet I do not want to put the girl's heart too much at ease. Chungjo is not the only danger within these walls after all, and it pays to remain on edge; it pays to remain careful.

My name is mentioned within the room, Jan-sil's voice rising with excitement as she speaks with Wol-hyeong. I press my ear closer to the door.

"In one night, Seorin snuck into those girl's rooms and ... she cut off all their hair! Right to their scalps in parts!"

I hear giggling inside and a shocked gasp as Jan-sil continues. "Chungjo couldn't see anyone for weeks and weeks until her hair was long enough to cover with a hair-piece again! And the headmistress didn't even do anything about it! She said it served Chungjo right, and that maybe she'd think twice before bullying a new girl again!"

A tinkle of laughter rings from behind the door, clear like a bell.

Wol-hyeong? I have not heard her laugh before.

The sound is sweet and light. I am unable to hide my smile as I enter the room to ask if they wish to visit the marketplace with me.

OUTSIDE, the summer heat is not as heavy as it was only yesterday. Already the seasons turn and, soon, the lush green will fade and autumn will come. I wonder how many years it's been since I saw the trees shed their leaves in my hometown. The mountains there are so beautiful in the fall.

I shake my head to clear it, concentrating on the confections that Jan-sil offers, soft rice cakes dusted in sweetness. They taste sugary and tart on my tongue and I smile at the way Wol-hyeong closes her eyes in pleasure as she bites down.

Like my previous visits the marketplace is crowded, throngs of people winding through the alleyways and lanes. This time, though, we are not jostled or pushed; instead merchants and sellers gesture to us with wide beckoning smiles, certain of the money we have for spending.

I ignore them as we walk, passing a young woman whose pink skin is pocked with old sickness scars. She stands in a servant uniform behind a fish seller's stall, her arms filled with dried pollack and salted roe, some rich family's dinner. She watches me as I pass, a hint of envy, lingering on my fine silk skirts and on the coins that jingle in my purse, mine for the spending on whatever beautiful trinket that takes my fancy. I peer back at her until she is lost among the crowd. It is a strange feeling to be envied.

A Pavilion maidservant trails behind us, our chaperone, on account of my inexplicably getting lost in the woods some weeks before. She walks with her head lowered and doesn't speak with us; a ghost needed only to accompany but not to interact. She is slightly older than I and more awkward, with broad shoulders and too many teeth.

A slave like me, yet different.

Wol-hyeong walks just ahead of me now, her fingers running absently over the jade trinkets of a market stall. She smiles shyly when she realises I'm watching and quickly replaces the dark jade hairpin she has been admiring, fingers lingering on the perfectly carved shape of a rose.

She is older than my sister of course, for my own sister would still be but a child. Yet there is something about this wisp of a girl that conjures memories anyway; the wide eyes, the simple sweetness and shy smiles. I cannot look at Wol-hyeong without imagining how my sister might be today, how she might be when one day she reaches Wol-hyeong's age.

Will she grow to be as beautiful as Wol-hyeong? Has her life been as hard? Or has it been worse? I hope more than anything she has found some happiness since we were separated, if only snatched moments. I hope she has been strong and found a reason to live through her experiences during our family's fall. I hope she is waiting for me.

I hope she knows I will come.

The others walk ahead and I motion for them to go on as I hang back to buy the dark jade hairpin for Wol-hyeong. I smile as I tuck it inside my *jeogori*, planning to present it to her later at the Pavilion. I have noticed Jan-sil and Wol-hyeong spending more time together of late, a development that eases my heart. Sometimes though, like now when Wol-hyeong believes no one is watching, I catch her gazing into the distance with darkness in her eyes. Her inner demons have not yet been fully vanquished. Though perhaps it is wrong of me to hope they ever will.

After all, these days my own have returned in full force.

At that moment I feel a sharp tug on the voluminous folds of my blue *chima*. Glancing down I find a pudgy little boy peering at me hopefully.

"Miss, a letter..."

I take the paper from his sticky grasp as he grins proudly, his mission complete. He raises one hand up to me, palm open and waiting.

Although I tsk at his boldness, I drop more coins than I should into his plump little hand. Immediately the boy scampers off into the dusty crowd as I glance over at Jan-sil and Wol-hyeong, still walking ahead with our maid.

Heart beating hard I unfold the fragile paper. The letter contains the name of a nearby inn. Nothing else. Yet I recognise his hand in the writing and already I feel his name on my lips.

The man who will help me, who will save my sister.

It has been weeks, an agony of waiting, chewing my mind into pieces while I sat quietly practising my *gayageum* on the terrace, my thoughts no longer within the Pavilion's walls.

I cannot wait any longer.

I decide I will risk disappearing and deal with the consequences later. Perhaps a mistake after my lengthy absence last time, which did not go unnoticed, yet still a decision I do not care to examine any further.

It is done.

Before the other *gisaeng* or our chaperone turn back I am already lost in the market crowds, melting between the food stalls and winding around merchants who shout their wares into dusty streets. Walking quickly down a shady pathway, I slip between two restaurants, the air filled with the thick savoury scent of cooking meat. Doubling back through winding alleyways and crowded roads I find the inn from the letter easily; a place girls from the Pavilion have visited many times before to entertain passing merchants, men raised up in a world that values money over ancient family clans. Even so, such men will never be respected, never allowed to fill official government positions. *Gisaeng* though, they can certainly afford.

Reaching the inn, I duck inside, hovering uncertainly within the first hall only to be met by an old man with a hard leathery face and no words to say. He takes my sleeve and leads me up a flight of creaking stairs to usher me into a gloomy room at the very back of the inn, a private hidden place. The doors are closed firmly behind.

A man sits cross legged on the floor behind a low table, the only person in the room. A tea set with two cups sits before him. His mouth breaks wide, and a tingle spills across my spine.

"Seorin *ssi*, it has been a long time."

"Yes *Nauri*, it has."

Three weeks in fact.

I know this because I have been counting.

Now he is before me I feel strangely nervous and I wait in heavy silence, still hesitating beside the door. Kim Jae-gil carefully pours tea from the steaming pot, spice and floral scent filling the room. He should not be serving someone like me. My skin flushes hot and uncomfortable as I watch his smooth movements, until finally he gestures to the seat across from him. A flat deep blue cushion has been placed on the floor on the opposite side of the low table. I obey, settling myself slowly upon the polished wooden floor, one knee up against my chest and my skirts spread about my body in the elegant way I have been taught.

"I sent someone to watch the Pavilion," Kim Jae-gil says. "But you have not left for days." He glances at me with dark eyes and motions for me to take the tea.

"I have. I walk by the river often." I leave the rest unsaid; that I was hoping to see him there; that I was waiting for him.

"I see." Kim Jae-gil breaks into that easy smile again. "My man only watched the main entrance. How foolish of me."

I shake my head. "You could not have known."

Keeping my gaze lowered I peer intently at the calm surface of my tea, unable to look at his smiling face directly. Hope burns inside my chest, wrapped inextricably around easy smiles and promises of freedom. "You have news of my sister?"

"I do. I have sent men out to investigate where she was sent after being made a slave. They travelled to your home-town one week ago, though I have not yet heard how their investigation fares. It is possible we will not hear a report for many weeks yet. But I trust them to do this job."

I continue to stare into my tea. "Thank you, *Nauri*." The words are not enough to convey my feelings.

"Wait until we find her," Kim Jae-gil answers lightly. "And then you can thank me."

I nod, a weight lifted from my shoulders.

"There is other news, Seorin *ssi*." Kim Jae-gil waits a moment as if I might have forgotten. "You said you would help us."

"Yes. I did and I will."

He pauses to drink his tea, a slight frown playing across his face. "I do not want to ask you this but think I must.

The leaders at the camp believe you can help us in a way our trained soldiers cannot."

I blink. What could I possibly do that they cannot?

A flicker of resignation crosses Kim Jae-gil's features before he speaks, as if he finds the words distasteful.

"We believe there is a spy among our higher ranks."

The magnitude of this statement fills the room, fills my mind with a road awash with blood and my father's body lying motionless on the stony earth.

"Betrayal will end with death," I whisper.

Kim Jae-gil nods. "That first night we met in the Pavilion something went badly wrong. There were government soldiers waiting for me. They knew where I would be, a secret only known by our inner circle. The night I met you I was ..."

He stops speaking abruptly. That night hangs between us, the darkness and heavy rain, the feeling of my body pressed against his. Quickly I lower my gaze.

Outside I hear the sounds of the bustling market, people shouting and laughing, merchants calling out their wares.

Inside the room silence hangs thick and heavy.

Kim Jae-gil finally clears his throat.

"It happened that way because someone betrayed us. I think someone has been planted within our organisation by the government, or perhaps someone is being paid to leak information."

Immediately I think of Officer Lee. My skin prickles at the opportunity I may have lost if he'd managed to tail me all the way back to the Pavilion. He would have forcibly taken the little package from me and I would have spent the rest of my life rotting away inside the Pavilion walls, my sister lost forever.

I'm furious simply thinking on it.

Perhaps he wished to steal the little package for himself.
A spy? Or simply an insufferable fool, I do not know.

Kim Jae-gil is oblivious to my thoughts. "Whatever the case, it is a person high within our ranks, proven by the specific nature of the information they have leaked, yet we have been unable to learn their identity."

I shake my head slowly. "Then how do you still stand? Your mountain stronghold, why has it not been raided by the military?"

"Indeed, why not? I can only believe the spy is feeding select information through to the government, piece by piece. Perhaps he fears he will no longer be useful if he reveals all he knows at once."

I nod. Always a game, every step careful and deliberate. Just as we play within the Pavilion. "I still do not understand though. How could I help find this betrayer if your own men cannot?"

Kim Jae-gil shifts on his cushion. "No one knows about you. We believe if you were dressed as a maidservant you could move freely around a household, you could listen to servant's gossip. Watch people unnoticed. What do you think?"

Sneaking and spying. My hands grow clammy as I grip my fingers tightly into fists. Yet it is not only fear that invades my body, but a sense of excitement too, sudden and unwise. The same feeling as when I wear my commoner garb.

Perhaps this is something I can do.

I glance at Kim Jae-gil with renewed determination.

For my sister's sake it will have to be. There is no backing out of this deal now.

"Whose house would this be, *Nauri*?"

"There will be a government meeting at an estate outside Hanyang soon. Minister Choi's household. He is one of ours but this will still need to be done carefully. Quietly. Many officials will be present, men loyal to us and those who remain on the side of the king. All the men we suspect could be the spy will be there. We think it will be the best opportunity we have to find the truth."

I nod. It sounds dangerous. Yet ... *outside* Hanyang. Beyond the city. Somewhere far from the Pavilion. A thrill runs up my spine. I take a slow sip of tea to calm myself.

"How will it … work? What must I do?"

"Minister Choi will have his own men searching within his house, but we are also sending someone else to attend who will investigate the officials during the meetings. You will keep an eye on the things he can't. Simply keep your head down and report back to Lee Yoon if you come across anything out of the ordinary, no matter how inconsequential it may seem."

"Report back *to whom?*"

"Officer Lee Yoon. You have met him before."

I nod in stiff agreement. "I have." Kim Jae-gil raises an eyebrow as I ask sceptically, "You trust this Officer Lee enough to send him?"

"Why would you ask?"

I hesitate before telling him how Officer Lee followed me, yet I do not get the reaction I hoped for. Kim Jae-gil seems more amused than anything.

"Officer Lee may have followed you, yet he was at that time …," Kim Jae-gil pauses and I realise he is teasing me, "…under the strong impression you were blackmailing him for an audience with me. Believe me, he thought he was doing the right thing. I trust him with my life."

I wrinkle my nose. "So, you are certain he is no spy."

Kim Jae-gil grins. "Officer Lee is too righteous for underhanded dealings."

"Yet not too righteous to become involved in treason."

Immediately I regret my blunt words, though Kim Jae-gil only laughs loudly, filling me with relief that I have not irreversibly offended him. He is standing now, walking around the table to crouch beside me, abruptly serious again. This close, I notice the bruises beneath his eyes, the worry that tightens his mouth.

"Seorin *ssi*, do you truly think you can do this?"

"I am certain, *Nauri*. Yet how will I leave the Pavilion? I cannot come and go as I please."

He smiles. "Leave that to me. I have already set plans into motion. Just be ready to follow along. It will be soon."

"Yes, *Nauri*."

"It will be dangerous," Kim Jae-gil warns. "Please understand, if you are identified as part of our movement by one of the king's loyal men, it will mean your life. And the spy himself, the man you seek … he does not want to be found. I am sure he will do anything to avoid it. Do you understand what I'm trying to say?"

Wolves on all sides.

I sit thinking, letting his words sink in. There is no going back. "If that were the case, if I am caught, if I … die, what of my sister? She is only a child."

Kim Jae-gil holds my gaze. "Our agreement still stands. She will be found and given a new life. She will be protected."

"Do you promise me?" I whisper the words.

"Yes. I promise you, Seorin *ssi*."

He reaches forward and for a moment I think he is about to take my hand into his. He doesn't. Instead he lightly rests his fingers on my shoulder. He is not smiling anymore.

"It is time to go."

JAN-SIL WATCHES me suspiciously when I meet the other girls again. I find them waiting in the exact spot where I left them. When I say I got distracted and lost I am sure she knows I'm lying. She doesn't say it, but I feel her curious gaze burning into me the entire walk back to the Pavilion.

Wol-hyeong on the other hand barely seems to have registered my absence. More than once, as we walk, I catch her lost in the distance with a wistful look on her face.

I make it my mission to cheer her, and later that night I present Wol-hyeong with the jade hairpin I bought for her from the marketplace. I am rewarded with a glowing smile of gratitude unlike any I have seen before. It almost makes me believe I have family again, that smile, it makes me wish I could offer Wol-hyeong her freedom alongside my sister.

Yet the moment is broken by Chungjo, who bursts into the room to say a messenger has arrived from the country-side with a proposal for the Headmistress. The whole Pavilion buzzes with the news and not long afterwards I am summoned to meet with the headmistress in her quarters.

She sits before a low table on a pile of shimmering cushions, flanked as always by her guard, the tall young man with broad shoulders and vicious eyes. She informs me an influential noble lord from a distant province has heard of my skill on the *gayageum* and requested my presence within his home. He has offered the headmistress so much money for only a few months of my time that she cannot possibly refuse him, and so I am sent to pack immediately. The headmistress tells me it is an honour to be sought after in such a way and that the minister of defence will just have to wait, no matter how annoyed he may be with the arrangement.

Like Kim Jae-gil instructed, I am ready.

By the next morning, in the early grey light of dawn, I am accompanied from the Pavilion by the countryside lord's messenger and four of his servants. The servants all stand tall and strong, holding themselves like soldiers, with shiny new swords glimmering from the lacquered scabbards they hold tightly in their hands. They take me away in a beautifully painted *gama*, a palanquin they carry strapped upon their shoulders, only stopping when we reach a sprawling inn on the outskirts of Hanyang. There I meet a young peasant girl who swaps her clothes and wooden identification tag with mine.

Dressed as a *gisaeng* with her hair high and her face painted with powder, the young girl departs the city inside the *gama*, and I am left alone on the busy streets of Hanyang disguised as a maidservant, an address clutched on crumpled paper in my hand.

And I am free.

11

A Simple Servant Girl

We meet as instructed outside the gates of his house, a large sprawling complex hidden behind high stone walls. Officer Lee is not pleased to see me. He is even less pleased than I am that we must work together this way, and immediately voices his displeasure. He asks how it is that someone like me was selected to accompany him to Minister Choi's household in Damjang, the tiny rural village lost deep within the mountains where the meetings will take place.

I raise an eyebrow at his lack of welcome and at his question, for it seems Kim Jae-gil has still not chosen to share my full history with this man.

And yet he assures me there is trust between them.

I wrinkle my nose and, unable to help myself, I bite back. "You're so rude, Officer Lee. Is this how you welcome your guests?"

Huffing, he simply strides through the open wooden gates, boots crunching heavily across the gravel courtyard of his home. I scurry to keep up.

"Don't get any ideas, brat. You're no guest here. Stay

out of my way and blend in with the servants until we leave for Damjang. And *try* not to do anything foolish." He halts and turns so abruptly I almost slam right into him. He bristles. "If that is *at all* possible."

"I am not a fool." I glower as he walks away, calling loudly after him, "I know how to behave!"

"Good. Now go find Housekeeper Kim and tell her you'll be starting here today. She'll put you to work and show you where you'll be sleeping."

As simple as that. I am dismissed.

I gape after him as Officer Lee climbs the stone steps to the house, clearly finished with me. His home rises imposingly before us, black tiled roof shining in the morning sun, polished boards gleaming on the terrace and inner chambers clung with shadow. The manicured gardens are deserted and lush with late summer.

Beneath my breath I remind myself the Pavilion is far grander than this place, as are many of the houses in Hanyang I have visited as a *gisaeng*.

Yet suddenly I feel very small.

"You're just leaving me here? I don't know where your Housekeeper Kim is!"

Officer Lee ignores me completely. Until I follow after him, feet quick like lightning dancing up stone steps. Taking hold of his sleeve, I tug sharply. "Officer Lee!"

"I told you not to touch me!"

Forcefully trying to shake me off only makes me more determined, until…

"*Lee Yoon?*"

We both freeze at the sound of the voice.

Emerging from the house's inner shadows is an older woman dressed in an absurdly bright *hanbok*, her plump mouth open at the sight of us, lips quivering.

"Mother!"

Officer Lee throws me off and clears his throat awkwardly. "Mother, this girl is ... this is our new maidservant, newly arrived today. She is ... she comes under Minister Choi's recommendation, she is..."

Officer Lee's voice trails off.

"She touched you." The woman looks at me with unfiltered distaste. "She does not know her place."

My body tenses. What is this? A punishment already. A beating? This woman clearly does not know why I am here. I glance at Officer Lee, pleading.

"Mother, please. Father is aware of this arrangement. Come, I will explain." Already he is by his mother's side, firmly guiding her inside the house and far away from me. Not once does Officer Lee turn back, though Lady Lee does, throwing a warning look over her shoulder that I have seen many times before.

One step out of place and you will pay for it.

I sigh. Walking lightly back down the stone stairs I am soon alone in the courtyard, drenched in warm sun but cold inside. I must be careful, for a mistake now at Officer Lee's residence could mean the entire purpose of my window of freedom put at risk. I swallow my pride, spreading a hand across the rough material of my maidservant's clothes, worn and frayed. Now is not the time for bravery, nor for boldness. This is a place for a *gisaeng*'s mask, head down, eyes down, silent and obedient.

Disappointment settles across my skin.

This will not be a pleasurable stay.

A FEMALE BELONGS to her father when she is a child and then after marriage, to her husband. If she is widowed she belongs to her eldest son. A life passed back and forth between men, no power and no influence.

Except within her own home, where she is mistress of all, responsible for everything that occurs within her walls.

Perhaps that is why Officer Lee's mother watches me so hard. I am like a stone in her slipper, a cog out of place. A disruption.

Housekeeper Kim, the inner household's head servant, does indeed put me to work. Backbreaking heavy work until my hands are raw and chapped, and my skin bleeds from cracks near the nails. I hold my fingers up to the sun, move them in the light. They are no longer a *gisaeng*'s hands, no longer slender and pale. These hands are for working. Each day the calluses on my fingertips fade away a little more, my heart aching for my *gayageum*, my hands changing from a musician's into a servant's, cracked and raw.

I hardly see Officer Lee during the time I spend in his household. Instead I am scrubbing and cleaning and washing everything in sight, all under the watchful eye of Housekeeper Kim and sometimes even Lady Lee herself. Apparently Young Master Lee never spends much time at home, and with a mother like the lady I begin to understand why. Clearly, she has not yet forgotten the sight of my dirty hands on her precious son's body. And each day it seems I must pay again for this past transgression.

The servants in the household all accept me easily enough, and I am assigned a room in the women's quarters with a girl named Chaewon who has a plain wide face and strong hands. She is very patient with me, showing me the tasks I must do, explaining how the household works, the inner servants like myself and the men who work the outer yards. Chaewon helps me when I fall behind in my duties, and sometimes we giggle together like children, whispering of the lady and our work, of Housekeeper Kim or some little bit of city gossip. Soon I count her as a friend in this strange busy place.

I learn that Officer Lee has two younger sisters, both similar to my own age, Da-in a little older and So-hye a little younger. Quiet pretty girls who sit in the garden practising embroidery and whispering to each other softly. Both are kinder to me than their mother and often ask me questions about where I lived and what I did before I arrived at their household. They are persistent enough that I invent a very simple backstory, yet I sense their boredom and isolation, their thirst for news of life beyond their walls. Soon I spin strange exciting tales about my past to entertain them, silly adventures or even just rumours I have heard at the Pavilion. Nothing too scandalous of course, but I certainly amuse them. Soon I am invited back every evening as dusk falls, an arrangement I am positive their mother knows nothing about.

It is on one of these evenings in the dim garden that Officer Lee's two sisters huddle together on a bench, with me sitting cross-legged at their feet. I am deep in the middle of a ghost story I once heard at the Pavilion, a story set during a terrible famine that raged across the countryside in the aftermath of war. My voice is low as I describe the married couple, explain how they were driven to desperation through utter poverty, helpless as their precious children slowly starved.

"Finally, unable to bear this pain any longer, the couple unearthed corpse-flesh from a gravesite, removing one single leg from a man recently dead." I smile at their gaping faces. "Yes, it was a terrible thing to do, yet it was only with the intention to feed their starving children. Except…"

I pause, letting the tension rise, until So-hye, the

youngest sister, cannot contain herself.

"Except what?!"

"Well, it seems that the dead man's ghost … he trailed behind his missing flesh and followed the married couple all the way to their home! And there he—"

I lapse into immediate silence as Officer Lee emerges from the overhanging trees behind the girls, a frown so black across his face that I bite my lip. I do not know how long he was standing there in the dusk. Or how much of my story he has heard.

Enough, I suspect.

"What are you doing out here in the dark?"

He addresses the question to his sisters only, yet when they jump in fright he scowls pointedly at me. His look says I am a constant source of irritation, despite the fact I have not seen him for days.

Unable to stop myself I glare back. I am not pleased by his interruption either. Nor the lecture on young women's decorum that will surely follow.

I huff and turn away, only to be drawn back immediately at the sound of Da-in's soft voice.

"*Orabeoni.*"

I stare at her, at the word that still hangs in her bow-shaped mouth. She is smiling, unabashed and wide, the expression reaching deep into her eyes. Her younger sibling So-hye smiles too, for it seems they are both very pleased to see their brother. Somehow I had not expected it. I am thrown askew, ungrounded, a deep ache driving through my stomach. For I once had an older brother, an *orabeoni* too.

And now I do not.

The affection between them is evident, bared for the world to see. Flashes of open terraces and lush summer gardens engulf me; my older brother's warm hands enveloping mine as we practised calligraphy on thin curling paper. I watch Officer Lee carefully, and for a moment there is something about my brother in his face, in the way he looks at his sisters as if they were precious, to be cared for and loved.

I turn away, blinking.

So-hye is alive with excitement. "*Orabeoni*, our new maid has been telling us stories! This one is so frightening!" She giggles. "Tell him the story, Seorin. Go on."

I shift uncomfortably on the grass. "Oh no *Agassi*, young lady, I am sure your brother is very busy. He does not wish to listen…"

So-hye waves her hand to cut me off, all fire and impatience at fourteen years old. The same age as beautiful fragile Wol-hyeong from the Pavilion, yet so very different. She grins at me widely, her excitement infectious. "*Orabeoni*, the story Seorin tells is a ghost story! They go to a graveyard and dig up a body to…"

"Don't tell them stories like that." Finally Officer Lee bothers to face me directly. "What are you filling their heads with, do you want them to be as wild and insolent as you, brat?"

"*Orabeoni*!" Da-in's pretty brows draw close. "How can you speak to Seorin like that? We asked her to tell us, so if anyone deserves your anger, it is me, for I am the eldest between us."

I gape at her, unused to being defended. My lips twitch at how easily she admonishes her brother, in a way I never would have dared with mine.

"Da-in is right, *Orabeoni*. Seorin did nothing wrong." So-hye pouts, holding the expression until finally Officer Lee's broad shoulders droop, utterly defeated by his two diminutive sisters.

The storytelling sessions will continue.

If I were alone I would have laughed out loud. Instead I smile at him sweetly, relishing in his defeat more than I should, receiving only a dark scowl in return, until I notice Da-in watching. I wipe my face clean, focusing on the grass. I feel her thoughtful gaze on me until So-hye asks their brother about his day, distracting her.

Officer Lee sighs at the question. For the first time I notice how tired he looks, dark circles smudging the skin beneath his eyes, hands holding tight and bloodless to the lacquered casing of his sword.

"It was fine." He is not convincing. "We are investigating a few cases at the office, nothing important."

"What cases?" Da-in asks, and I am pleased for I also wish to know.

Officer Lee though is apparently not in the mood to speak of it, excusing himself to change from his uniform before the evening meal. As he leaves he gives me one last pointed look. "You be careful what you tell my sisters, hear me? They're not bold commoners like you, brat."

His words have no real bite so I only smile politely as he strides toward the house, leaving us alone once more in the dusky lush garden.

"Don't mind our *Orabeoni*," says So-hye. "He is sharp with his words but is a good man beneath it all."

Da-in nods. "Yes. He has had worries pressing him down of late, I fear." She peers at me, as if deciding whether I can be trusted.

It seems I can.

"...I think there is something going on with Yoon," she whispers. "Though I cannot be certain what it is. My father too, lately he has been ... different."

Her forehead creases and I lower my gaze, not wanting Da-in to know I am well aware of exactly what scheme her foolish brother is involved in. In that moment I want very badly to go and slap some sense into that fool Lee Yoon. To put his family at risk like this, these beautiful innocent girls, how could he do that? Does he not understand what will happen to his sisters if he makes even the smallest mistake?

It seems he truly is just like my own *orabeoni*.

For if he is not careful, he will sacrifice it all just as my brother did. His family and his home. His sisters.

His life.

I AM MORE sombre in my dealings with Da-in and So-hye after that evening in the garden, the pressure of the task at hand beginning to weigh me down. It is hard to be close to them with what I know, unaware as they are that their future hangs so precariously within their brother's hands.

I am relieved when we finally begin preparing to depart for the meeting in Damjang. It is announced that myself and my new friend Chaewon, as well as four other manservants I do not know well, have all been chosen to accompany Officer Lee on his journey. I am not sure what Lee Yoon said to his mother to be allowed to bring me, or what purpose he could possibly have told her I would serve, but the lady of the household didn't object. I suppose even a woman as formidable as she still understands her duty, first to her husband and second to her son. I watch her as we depart from the Lee family's courtyards, out onto the busy streets beyond their household. She stands next to her two daughters on the stony earth, peering after her son as he leaves. Lee Yoon never once looks back.

It is furiously busy in the city and takes a long time to reach the outskirts of Hanyang. All around us are dancers and masked acrobats, with commoners and nobles alike lining the streets to get a good view.

Officer Lee is above it all, tall and untouchable at the head of our procession. Chaewon and I ride far behind in a small wagon stacked high with carefully wrapped boxes. Their bright coverings shimmer in the warm sun, grass green and blood red with patterned silk tied in perfect knots. Chaewon and I take the opportunity to enjoy the bustling city atmosphere, a reprieve from my weeks of hard work, and for Chaewon, from a lifetime of it. Leaning back against the trunks we drink the city in, whispering and giggling.

When I ask, Chaewon tells me the wrapped trunks and boxes are gifts for the household we will visit and I peek beneath a sun-yellow cloth to find a beautiful lacquered box, inlaid with mother of pearl. I don't check inside but it is clear the gifts are expensive, hence the presence of the four manservants that accompany us on foot. I think they must be guards, considering how heavily they are armed. I notice now that Officer Lee too is carrying a weapon, a long sword slung onto his saddle near his knee.

Once beyond the capital walls we are free to press on more quickly, and soon the journey turns from thrilling escape to exhaustive tedium, the stony road jostling Chaewon and I until our bodies ache. Alongside the pathway the scenery remains the same. Trees pressing closer, rising higher, thick with scraggly bushes and reaching branches. The air in the mountains grows chill, breath clouding at my mouth by the time night falls, leaves blushing red and gold with impending autumn.

The first night is spent at a roadside inn, Officer Lee locked away inside a private room and the rest of us banished to shared quarters. Chaewon and I toss and turn on the floor among a mess of commoner women and screaming children. The air inside the cramped space is thick and humid despite the change in season and my sleep is filled with fitful half-dreams of my sister. Now though her face is Wol-heyong's, creased with despair and so much older than she should be. I wake with tears dusting my cheeks, throat parched and lips cracked.

By the second night of hard travelling we have moved deep within the mountains, nothing for miles in any direction beyond the isolated stretch of road we follow. Exhausted we all sleep where we fall, except for Officer Lee who has a tent set among the trees. He doesn't once turn my way, his face expressionless and controlled at all times. The dark circles beneath his eyes are the only sign he is just as exhausted as the rest of us.

I try to get comfortable under my shared blanket. The dark forest seems to hum with strange noises, each one causing me to flinch and wake anew. Ghosts? Or wild animals? Chaewon does not stir at my tossing and turning, much too tired to reprimand me. Soon she is snoring lightly, and it is not long until I follow, descending into a deep sleep, too exhausted even for dreaming.

12

The Winding Mountain Path

"You cannot remember him?"

Chaewon blushes as she speaks, touching the palms of her hands to her warm cheeks. "He is one of the master's servants. Perhaps you haven't met him yet?" She smiles in embarrassment as I try to recall her man's face. I am sure I came across him during my time in the Lee family household, yet his features are a blur.

We rock back and forth on the cart, moving, always moving, our legs dangling over the end and our feet swinging above the disappearing road, knees touching. Chaewon's whispered confession is a welcome distraction from the ache of endless travel, our group trudging through yet another thick mountain pass of forest and winding road. The trees here are heavy with yellow and gold and already the air is growing cooler, despite it being only early afternoon.

Chaewon's blush remains as she tells me of her future, of a small home outside the Lee household they might one day have if they are lucky, of a wedding and a baby. I nod and smile and steadfastly ignore the tinge of jealousy that clutches my heart, ashamed to be so petty.

I console myself that my sister may yet enjoy that kind of life, if I succeed.

And that will be enough.

I wonder if my sister could write to me in the Pavilion once she is settled, if she remembers the skill at all. I wonder what reading those letters would feel like. Will she eventually write to me of a husband and baby when she becomes a woman grown, no longer the little girl she is now?

I am lost in the images, barely listening to Chaewon's low voice until abruptly she breaks off into an odd strangled gasp. Sudden movement erupts from the woods to our left, the wagon lurches violently and Chaewon is no longer at my side.

Glimpses of black blur against the red and gold of the trees, the forest alive where it shouldn't be. Men? Officer Lee is shouting, his household guards drawing weapons, scrapes of steel against wooden sword casings. Where is Chaewon? A horse screams as the wagon tips and I scream too, no time to move, to think. A blow smashes hard across my face. The cart upends beneath my rolling body, slamming me heavily into the dirt. I am winded and momentarily stunned, black clouding the corners of the sky above. Treetops. Reaching branches. The black recedes and high inhuman shrieks replace the buzz in my head, the world sharpening, refocusing. The clatter of hooves draws near across the stony earth. Rolling over in the dirt I shrink in terror, arms wrapped over my pounding skull for protection, cowering from lashing hooves.

A man shouts somewhere down the road, the sound faded. I think it must be Officer Lee but cannot know for certain. The razor clank of metal on metal moves much louder and closer, two men stagger toward me, locked together in vicious battle. I scramble to crawl aside, skirts catching beneath my feet, underneath my knees, face to the dirt once more and blood on my lips. One of the men is a stranger, dressed all in black. With a grunt he plunges his weapon deep inside our guard's belly and the man opens up right in front of me, raining blood and guts. Screams rip from my throat as gore splashes my face, the sounds of his life leaving him in a soft gurgle as his body thumps to the ground heavily. My hands are wet and slick with his life-blood as I scramble backwards and away, moving desperately toward the overturned cart. I fall beneath its shelter toward Chaewon's huddled form inside.

"Chaewon!" I scream her name.

When I grasp her body she pitches forward, wide eyes open and a half smashed skull. I cannot help it, I have no reverence for the dead, filled only with horror I shove her hard away, scrambling backwards from the cart. I can't see any horses now. They are gone, their terrible shrieking fading on the mountain wind.

Whimpering, I swing wildly toward a sudden burst of screaming, a man slashed down where the forest grows thick and twisted alongside the road. Our last manservant. Gone. Dead. Beside him Office Lee still stands in fighting stance, ragged and dirty, his chest heaving. He has dropped his sword but scrambles to grasp another where it lies embedded in a dead man's chest, swinging blood-covered steel toward his opponent's face, a masked man like all the others. The attacker throws himself against the ground to avoid the blow, squirming onto his back yet already raising his blade to strike.

I take a staggered step toward them, shout to Officer Lee in warning but already his blade swings down with a terrible heaviness. A finality that is rewarded when the fallen man's eyes widen above his mask and he grows stiff and still.

I scream Officer Lee's name again, and he whips around to meet my gaze, panting heavily, only to follow my desperate gesturing toward the steep slope above the roadside, the mountain peaks towering high above. More men in black descend toward us, slipping quietly and steadily between the trees with weapons ready and gleaming.

Officer Lee is by my side, shouting and grasping my arm hard with dirt-smeared fingers, dragging me away over the side of the road and down, down, down, scrambling past strangled trees into the steep valley ravine below. I clutch him for balance, hands grasping at his robes, anything to stop myself falling. My skull rattles with every step, chest heaving and vision blurry.

My eyes roll back past Lee Yoon's blood-streaked face to the steep slopes above. There are fewer masked men than I thought, only two or three still standing. I was certain there were fifty, no *hundreds*. But then one man draws his bow. Three is as dangerous as fifty, for the other two follow suit, bow strings taut as they take aim. I scream a ragged warning and Officer Lee shoves me faster as arrows rain above. Feet sliding among loose crackling leaves, my fingers grasp creased bark and stunted trees, breaking the skin, snagging my fingernails.

I fall.

And Officer Lee is hit.

The bolt drives deep within his shoulder, with enough force for him to scream. His body pitches forward, slamming into mine and both of us slide wildly down the slope, leaving only my screams and a wake of ruined vegetation and exposed red earth. Twisted bushes whip by, fingers scrabbling at roots, stones, breath knocked from my lungs until I'm flung to the valley floor among tall sharp grass, head twisted and still spinning. Staggering to my elbows, to my feet, I crawl across razor grass toward Lee Yoon where he lies gasping nearby, stunned.

"Officer Lee." I slap lightly at bloody cheeks until his black eyes clear, until he is trying to sit. I help him, heaving his massive body upright, his topknot twisted and coming loose. Glancing back up the slope I see nothing. "Are they gone?"

Lee Yoon's focus follows mine, taking in the quiet trees above. "No ... Help me."

I nod, biting down my panic, for Officer Lee is calm. He knows what to do. Except blood seeps thickly from the back of his robes onto my hand, sticky and hot. The bolt shaft has broken off during the fall, leaving only the arrow-head still sunk deep within his shoulder flesh. A short-splintered nub of wood protrudes from his shoulder blade.

Staggering to his feet, Officer Lee's attention is elsewhere, still watching the mountainside far above where the road lies. I am certain I see the undergrowth move. I am certain we have only moments before we are attacked again. Officer Lee manages to stand with my shoulder wedged beneath his arm, though I am taking much of his weight. My legs shake from the effort, one of my straw sandals lost in the wild descent. Officer Lee gasps, face turning grey.

"You are hurt, Officer Lee." I reach to carefully touch his shoulder, bloodstained and covered in a carpet of dirt and grit. I am not familiar with wounds, yet I have witnessed childbirth in the Pavilion. Too much blood escaping the body is no good. This I know for certain. My breath catches when my hand comes away from his shoulder wet and red.

He doesn't look at me, still peering at the steep slope above, scanning for movement. "Run."

I stare at him. "What?"

"I said run, brat. Go."

"No."

"Run!" He shoves me away and I fall hard into the long grass, shocked. Officer Lee staggers to retrieve his sword where it lies half hidden in the sharp undergrowth. The blade is caked with dirt, debris stuck to metal slicked with blood. He turns to face the rising ravine, his back to me. I see the man coming down the hill now. Officer Lee wades toward him through the long grass, silent and deadly, wide heavy sword raised and ready for striking.

"Go!" Officer Lee screams.

This time I do, scrambling away across the dirt with tears streaming down my face. I throw one last wild glance behind, glimpse him standing there waiting, straight and steady despite the blood running down his back, hand tight on the hilt of his sword.

And then I don't watch anymore, I just run. Run and run. I don't stop until I can't breathe, until I'm unable to take another step because my chest pounds and my legs are heavy like rock. I trip over a tree root then, falling hard to the stony ground where I stay with my head spinning and face touching dirt. How far have I gone? How far?

I cannot go further.

I lie still, chest heaving, gasping. And sobbing.

It feels as if an age passes before I am able to force my body to roll over and then I lie peering at the yellow swaying tree tops. The sky is bright overhead and I see scraps of blue shining between reaching branches.

There was no warning, no indication. Chaewon and all those men. Dead.

Lee Yoon.

Dying.

I sit slowly, unsteadily crawl across to a gap between

two rocks, two huge boulders among many that rise into a cliff on the mountain side. I don't know where I am. I don't know how to get back to the road. I don't know if I should go back to the road.

I crawl into the small hollow and lie still, eyes closing. It is still so bright, only mid-afternoon, sunlight creeping between the rock walls to dust my skin in warm yellow sunshine. Yet my body is beaten, and sleep comes tearing into my mind, for if I cannot shut it all out even for a moment I might scream.

Yet my dreams are much worse.

WHEN I WAKE, I am alone. The sunlight slants through the trees, turning the long grasses yellow and illuminating the trunks so they all burn orange.

I smell blood.

It's on my hands, on my face, in my hair. The front of my ruined *jeogori* is rust brown and dried stiff with it. The thick stench in my nostrils lurches me back to my hometown, back inside my nightmares. I scream as my father's head rolls across the dirty country road, as I watch my beloved *orabeoni* weep before he too is executed, his blood spilling in pools beneath my feet, mixing with my father's.

My mother's face. No longer soft and calm. Her skin sallow and smeared with grime, fingers reaching for mine between thick wooden bars.

The promise I made her.

The promise I have failed to keep.

"Seorin!"

The thick scent of blood and my little sister calling my name over and over.

"Seorin, answer me! Seorin."

I am lightheaded, lost in the stench of blood, choking it down. I cannot bear it. I pound my head but it sticks there like a haze, thick and strong and overwhelming. Clutching my hair, I bend until my face touches the stony earth, trying to banish the searing images, gasping.

They will not let me go.

My father's hea—

"Seorin?"

The voice is low. Officer Lee crouches in the entrance of the hollow, his body filling every space; his face streaked with dirt and blood. He says my name again.

My father is gone, banished. Only Officer Lee and the waning sunshine remains.

I am unable to stop the great heaving sob that wracks my body. Covering my face I sink toward him and after a stunned moment he uncertainly touches my shoulders with his hands, whispering, "Everything's fine now, brat ... You're safe ... You're all right." He is close and I smell his skin, the scent of his clothes beneath the dirt and sweat. And there is blood too, yet it is not all there is, not anymore. The rest stays in my nightmares where it belongs.

I cry until my tears dry up, until there's nothing left to release. Immediately Officer Lee's hands pull away from my neck, from my hair, untangling himself and clearing his throat awkwardly. He does not meet my eyes. "Were you hurt?"

I shake my head, slapping tears away. "No."

"Good." He pauses. "Can you walk?"

"Yes. I can walk."

"Good. You're going to have to help me." He motions toward his leg. "I hurt it, and they'll be searching for us." He watches me curiously. "You were ... making a lot of noise. We need to be elsewhere when they come."

I flinch, unable to look at him as I crawl from my

hiding place into the open forest. Thinking of the arrow lodged deep within Officer Lee's shoulder fills me with shame. It was not I who stayed behind to battle men. I screamed from nightmares while Lee Yoon lived one. I take a deep breath.

"My apologies for … what you saw. I was dreaming."

"Dreaming?" Lee Yoon's mouth tightens as I move to his side, hauling his arm over my shoulders. "What did you dream of then? The attack?"

I do not answer, only grunting beneath his sudden weight, ready to help, ready to prove my worth. I *will* find my sister, not die forgotten in the forest beside an unnamed stretch of mountain roadside.

"You were hurt?" I ask him.

"As you see." Officer Lee gestures to his left leg, blood-streaked, face grim.

There is indeed something very wrong with his left knee. He can barely walk, unable to press much weight on it at all, the limp severe and the limb twisted.

"Can you feel your toes?"

"Yes. I feel them."

"That is good then."

When he doesn't answer I glance up. His bloody face betrays nothing, though I am certain Officer Lee knows what this means as well as I do. If he had aspirations of being a great warrior, they are wiped clean now, for a wound like his rarely heals straight. It is something everyone knows. Though because he says nothing, I say nothing too.

Officer Lee looks down at me, leaning heavily on my body for support.

"Ready to go?"

I nod and together we shuffle slowly further down the slope.

13

Like Stones beside the River

B y the time we have followed the mountain ravine to the riverbank, night is already falling, the last of the sun's rays hitting the rocks. We collapse beside the water, both of us exhausted, though soon I slide closer to get a better view of Officer Lee's shoulder.

Some of the girls at the Pavilion know much about medical care, studying for their own interest or for extra money. Some I am sure, like Jan-sil, might even pursue it as a career when their time at the *gisaeng* house runs out. I sigh. "I do not know anything of wounds."

Lee Yoon scoffs but the sound turns strained. "How does it look then, brat?"

"It looks bad, I think. I do not know. The bleeding has stopped though." I try to pull his robes further over his shoulder for a clearer view but he prevents me.

"Leave it. It's fine."

"What about your leg?"

"That's fine too."

I glare at him. "You are a liar, Officer Lee."

Normally my boldness would draw a rise from him yet

Lee Yoon doesn't even bother to answer, reaching instead with dirty fingers to touch the gash above his left eye. His eyebrows draw close and his mouth tightens. One side of his face is slicked red with blood, blinding him.

"Don't touch it," I say. "It will only get worse."

I heave my aching body to the riverside, tearing off a strip of my rough woven *chima* hemline. Wetting the cloth in the streaming water, I carry it back to him. "Let me clean your face at least. That much I do know how to do."

When I crouch before him, Officer Lee turns his head away impatiently. "I said I'm fine!"

Irritation gnaws sharply at me. I am trying to help, trying to make amends for what happened earlier and he still looks down on me.

"I do not care what you say," I snap. "And stop moving!"

I grasp his chin firmly in my hand and force his head still. He is shocked enough to stay motionless as I carefully wipe the blood and dirt from his eye, the shadow of bristle along his jaw rough beneath my fingers. I work in silence as darkness gathers around us, clinging in long shadows to the trees and river rocks.

Officer Lee's eyes are closed now, his face a drawn mask of calm, yet underneath flickers of pain attempt to escape, twitching at his jaw. I pretend not to notice and keep wiping at the dirt and grime.

I do not know what makes me ask it, the growing darkness perhaps. Or the utter isolation of the mountains. Manners seem wasted out here.

"Officer Lee … why have you involved yourself in all this?"

Black eyes flick open. "What do you mean?"

I continue to clean his face, moving carefully onto the deep cut itself, pressing clean cloth to the open wound.

"This plot, this conspiracy against the king, why are you involved?"

He lets out a snort. "What do you think you know, brat? You don't even fully understand what you're involved in yourself." He looks at me sharply, holding my gaze. "Don't ask questions like that."

I lower the wet cloth. "Of course, I know. I'm not a fool. Is that what Kim Jae-gil told you? That I didn't know?"

Officer Lee hesitates then curtly nods his head.

I laugh, the sound echoing above the rushing water. "True, you are correct, when I met you the first time I did not know. Or at least Kim Jae-gil hadn't told me himself yet, but of course by then I'd already guessed."

"You guessed? How could you possibly have guessed?"

"Stay still!"

I'm silent for a long moment, weighing my options. Finally, I admit the truth. "The silk package that Kim Jae-gil left with me … I opened it. I wished to know what I was carrying, so I … read the letter."

"What? You did what?" Officer Lee jerks away from me.

Rocking back onto my heels I shrug, rattling off some of the names on the list, names of ministers, of politicians, of powerful men I have never met and will never have cause to meet. The names of heads of noble families whose signatures were scrawled on the parchment Kim Jae-gil left behind in the Pavilion, a list of nobles and officials who have sworn allegiance to Kim Jae-gil's cause. Allegiance to a plot to kill the king.

Officer Lee's eyes burn bright, reflecting the last of the light. "Do you have any idea what those names are? How *dangerous* it is for you to have that information?"

"Of course, I do! I know exactly what they are. The

names of your collaborators, Officer Lee, the names of other traitors just like you."

Officer Lee physically flinches, almost as if I've slapped him. "How can you say that? You're involved too. You're helping us..."

"I have different reasons from you."

His mouth tightens. "And exactly what are those?"

I cannot answer. To tell Officer Lee my reasons would be to tell him who I am. And I find I am not yet ready to do that. I know how he would treat me if he knew the truth.

I say nothing and we lapse into thick silence until he finally speaks, surprising me by offering his secrets first. "It's because of my father." He presses his lips together. "He believes in this cause, believes this is right. I won't go against him."

I sit forward, peering at his half clean face. "Why?"

"Because he's my *father.*"

"Sometimes our fathers aren't right, Lee Yoon." I am suddenly angry. I reach for his chin again, wiping vigorously at his cheek.

He eyes me curiously. "My father tells me the king is a madman, a true madman. He says the whole of Joseon would be better if he were gone."

"Better for whom?"

"Better for the common people."

A ragged laugh escapes my throat. "What do nobles know of the common people? You want to save them? Make their lives better? Have you even spared a single thought for Chaewon? She died because of you! Or what about those other manservants? Did you know their names? You want to save the entire country yet you cannot even protect your own people."

My words are cruel and they fall like stones into the

silence, heavy and harsh. I don't know why I say them, except there is a fire brewing in my belly, a spark of fury long suppressed. And Officer Lee is so very naïve, despite the years he has on me. All at once I want very badly to explain it to him. It is important he understands.

"Fathers don't know everything," I say, still holding his face tightly, still wiping at his skin. "Sometimes they are just as foolish as the rest of us. Tell me, have you thought about what will happen to your family if something goes wrong?"

He looks at me now, black eyes shining through the darkness. I can tell he doesn't want to hear it but I tell him anyway, I can't stop myself.

I don't even try.

"If you are caught and your rebellion quashed, your father will die in front of you and then afterwards you'll die too. Both of you in the street for your friends and neighbours to see, heads lopped off on the road. And your mother? She will die too. Except *her* death will not be so quick. She will rot away in jail, dying alone of starvation and disease."

I wipe at his face harder, my fingers gripping tightly at his chin. "And your sisters? If they're lucky they'll live out the rest of their days as slaves to some wealthy family, humiliated and forced to serve some young noble girl just like Chaewon used to serve them. Or even worse, they'll be sold to a *gisaeng* house and men from the palace your father used to know will visit and..."

"Shut your mouth!" He grasps my wrist tight and we sit locked still, tension heavy between us. His breathing is thick, hand shaking.

"Wipe your own face," I spit out at him, jerking from his grip and throwing the cloth hard at his chest. I find my feet and stride toward the water. I am filled with so much anger it burns behind my eyes, inside my chest, deep within my belly. All of it, aimed directly at him and I do not even know why. It's none of my business why he chooses to involve himself in this plotting, it's none of my business if he dies.

Only my sister matters. That is all. And I will give her the chance to grow up free. Give her what I could not have myself.

A noise draws my attention back to Officer Lee. He has struggled to his feet in the blackness of night, limping away into the wood that lines the riverbank.

I almost call out to stop him. I almost do, but then I hold my tongue.

I let him go.

14

A Forest and the Valley Below

I wake to the sound of voices.

It is dark, pitch black. I lie stiff with fear, listening as the murmuring gets nearer, louder. Two men, maybe three, I can't be sure. I roll over on the crackling leaves and place my hand firmly across Officer Lee's mouth. His eyes snap open and at first, he tries to weakly struggle, all his strength long gone, but I clutch harder until his attention turns to me, placing a finger to my lips in warning.

We are exposed, camped beside the river with only a few low bushes for shelter, lying on a bed of pine needles and fallen leaves. He is not doing well. I saw it when we settled for the night, awkward silence thick between us after our altercation beside the water. I saw how he tried to hide his pain. But now he is a ghost in the darkness, the colour blanched from his cheeks, dark shadows clinging to his skin. Hiding his condition is no longer possible and I wonder if he has slept at all, for now he has lost his chance.

Officer Lee slowly pulls my hand from his mouth and breathes, "How many?"

I feel him shift awkwardly on the crackling needles,

reaching for his sword. I shake my head, silent and scowling, hands gripping tighter to his shoulder. Too many. He is wounded and has lost too much blood. It is certain he would lose.

The noises grow louder, heavy steps over dry crackling leaves as they search. We lie huddled together in the darkness barely breathing, every muscle in my body wound tight with fear. The crunching grows closer, whispers in the darkness, a flash of metal catching moonlight between dark trees. I suck in my breath, fingers clutching tighter to Officer Lee. Until they pass us by.

The men disappear back into the night.

We do not dare move, afraid any noise might bring them back. It is cold in the autumn forest, the sharp air becomes clouds of frost at our lips. Yet Officer Lee has sweat beading his forehead, fever in his eyes. I reach out silently to touch his face and he startles, eyes to mine, blurry, as if lost in a half dream. His skin burns.

Stopping was a mistake.

I should have forced him to keep moving after we left the river, forced us further away from the men who search. I glance at him again, whispering, "Can you walk, Lee Yoon?"

He nods and pushes himself off the ground with determination, yet it is me who must haul him to his feet when his strength runs out. I can barely hold his weight. He is too big, too tall. Too heavy.

Wedging my shoulder beneath his arm I attempt to keep him up, already panting from the effort, sweating despite the cold. We do not talk as we struggle through the forest, aimless as we stumble slowly in the opposite direction to the men who search. Officer Lee's breath becomes louder and more ragged with every step. His body grows heavier, his feet clumsy.

"I must stop," he gasps finally, and when I try to lower him to the ground I realise his back is slick with blood. Halfway down he collapses and I cannot hold him, his head rolling back hard against the dirt.

On my knees I try to hold his heavy head straight, black hair slicked to his sweaty forehead. "Lee Yoon *ssi*," I hiss. "What are you doing? Stay awake." I shake his head softly to rouse him, hand on either cheek. Slowly his eyes open but they are unfocused, disorientated.

"Brat..."

I see the whites of his eyes and then he is gone.

"Stay awake. Please." My desperate whispers echo through the night forest, throat raw and cracking. "Please stay awake!"

He lies so still beneath my hands that I am reminded again of my brother sprawled lifeless on the roadside. But no, this time there is a heartbeat, soft and steady beneath my desperate fingers. He needs a doctor. I can't do anything for him out here. I can't do anything at all except watch him die. I feel the rise of panic, the cold awareness of my utter incompetence. If only I had learnt the art of herbs and medicine instead of the *gayageum*, if only I was skilled at survival instead of at pouring a man's drink and smiling prettily, if only...

I blink back salty tears, swiping them away as they slide down my cheeks to mix with the dirt smeared across my skin. I don't want to be alone out here.

"Please wake up," I whisper into the darkness. "I don't know what to do, Lee Yoon. I don't know how to save you."

Officer Lee doesn't stir, quiet and still as the dead. I lower my head onto his chest. It rises and falls softly. He still lives, he is still here. "Please wake up."

But he doesn't.

AT DAWN he is still unconscious.

Blue morning light gives the woods an eerie look. Mist and dew cling to the trees and rocks, the leaves of early autumn shining yellow and gold. I am huddled against him to combat the biting wind, to try my best to keep his bulky body warm. His skin is clammy and cold on his arms and neck, yet his face burns like fire.

I shift him carefully, turning his body just enough to see the mess of his shoulder in the dawning light. The head of the arrow is still there, embedded deep within his flesh. I war with myself on whether I should try and remove it, but it seems too terrifying a task. My tampering could make it worse. I can't be sure of the outcome so decide I cannot take the risk. The arrowhead stays where it is, the surrounding flesh inflamed and red.

In the distance the rumbling river rushes down the mountain pass. It will flow out into the open valleys below, crashing and swirling against rocks and fallen tree trunks as it goes. Deep water, cold and deadly.

My choices are limited. Officer Lee is dying.

I make my decision. If we both die in the process so be it. I try not to think about my sister, I try not to think that if I die now I have truly failed her. I can only hope that Kim Jae-gil will honour our bargain. By now, she would be eight years old, still so very young. Yet I must trust him on his word.

It is excruciating dragging Officer Lee's limp body back toward the river. At first, I try to lift him but he is so much bigger than me, at least a head and shoulders taller, and heavy beyond my capabilities. Desperation tightens my chest, and furious frustrated tears build at the back of my throat as my struggles get me nowhere.

"Wake up." I whisper it over and over again as I pull at him, inching our way down the slope as I slide and drag at his heavy unresponsive body. "Wake up. *Wake up!*"

But Officer Lee is gone and there is only me.

We die, we live, it is only up to me.

Forcing myself to keep dragging him, I grip his arms and try my best to cushion his head as I haul his enormous limp body over rocks and roots and around trees. The bed of fallen leaves helps a little, and I hope it cushions his flesh against the hard ground as I tug him down the hill, gasping with an exhaustion that is bone deep and raw.

I do not give up.

It is an awful journey but I reach the riverbank, collapsing into a shaking sweating heap, lying on my back to peer up at the wavering tree tops. The wind is heavy here, swirling through the branches and rushing across the river rocks. I lie still, resting with my eyes closed, the sun flickering on my face as the trees move, visible behind my eyelids. Orange fire and then blackness, light then dark.

The water is icy, gushing and frightening.

My brother once taught me how to swim, my *orabeoni*. I remember the stolen summer afternoons spent paddling in the languid river behind our home, the feeling of joy and freedom it brought to be able to do something none of the other noble girls could do, no matter how improper.

It has been a long time but I do not think I could have forgotten.

I rip off much of my *chima*, knowing the billowing skirt will only drag me down, heavy and constricting when soaked with water. I take off my *jeogori* too until I'm wearing only my underclothes. I don't care about modesty, I care about life.

I undress Officer Lee too, pulling off his voluminous robes so there is less to weigh him down. Again, I inspect the wound on his shoulder. The naked flesh around the arrowhead is dark.

I slide my body into the water alongside the bank, planting my feet wide apart to combat the current and ignoring the ice of it, how it sucks away my breath. Then I drag Officer Lee in as well, so very careful to keep his head above the surface. I lose my footing but grasp the bank with one hand, desperately gripping his body with the other. I won't let him go. I won't let go. And then I let the bank slide away, I let the rushing waters carry us.

The hours that pass are agonising, shattering. Officer Lee never once wakes and at one point beneath the water I feel his entire body shudder and then grow still. I am so frightened he is dead yet when I drag him half onto the bank I find a faint heartbeat when I press my ear against his chest. I cry when I hear it, exhausted tears of relief, I cry until my head hurts and I collapse into the river mud.

I rest for a short while and then I pull him back into the river and keep on, determined to find someone, find anyone who can help us.

By the time the valley widens out it's almost evening, the whole day passed in a blur of exhaustion and pain and terror. My legs are bruised all over, my hands bleeding and raw. But I can live with bruises.

As the river widens the current and depth almost disappear. Soon there are sand banks spreading through the middle and the sluggish water is much too shallow for me to float Officer Lee's body any longer. But I can also see the distant outline of a settlement on the high banks ahead, just a few ramshackle houses and trails of smoke rising into the dusky sky.

I drag him onto the sandbank beneath a rising cliff of jagged yellow rock, fields of green waving grass between us and the village. I haul his body as far as my remaining strength can manage and then fall to my knees beside him. Touching his blanched face I lean down and whisper his name, close against his ear. He does not move. I am too afraid to check his heartbeat. He looks dead. Lee Yoon might be dead. "I'll bring someone back, Yoon," I breathe. "Wait here for me. I'll come back. I promise you."

And then I get up and limp across the fields for what seems like an eternity, climbing a gentle hill that feels like a mountain until finally I reach the first house in the village. A woman comes out holding a fat baby. She screams when she sees me.

"Help me," my voice rasps and I keel over in exhaustion.

There is bustling movement as others emerge from their homes, I am aware of it, though the world is changing around me, swirling at the edges. I am covered by a blanket and someone helps me to my feet.

"You need to rest, child, come inside," beckons an old man. He is stooped and grey.

"No, please. Yoon ... Officer Lee. I left him by the river, by the cliffs. We must go back." Weakly I struggle against a young villager, one of the men who helped me up.

"We'll send men, *Agassi*," he says. "You must stay here and rest." I am led toward a house, spent, my legs shaking.

"By the cliffs," I breathe. "I don't know if he..."

I break off, unable to finish.

"Take her inside." The older man's voice rings with authority. He seems to be the leader here. "The rest of you, get ready to search by the cliffs."

I am guided into a small *hanok* dwelling even before the search party have gone, the sounds of preparation clattering outside, shouts and calling. The woman with the fat baby spreads out a bedroll for me on the floor.

"You must take those off," she indicates my wet ripped

clothes. I nod but my fingers are so cold and stiff I can't seem to undo the knots and the woman must help me herself, setting her baby down onto the blankets. She gives me new clothes made from rough homespun cloth and I gratefully pull them on. They are warm and soft against my bruised skin.

"Lie down," she says. "Sleep."

But I shake my head. I need to know they find him. The woman sighs but doesn't stop me from heading back outside to wait.

It takes the villagers so long to return I wish I had insisted I go with them. Fear eats me alive as I move in staggered circles, limping and kneading my fingers against my new skirt until the woman orders me to come sit beside her.

Finally, I hear the shouts of the returning village men, see them lowering a limp sandy body from the back of a spindly horse. He could be dead; it looks as if he's dead, but the men are urgent as they haul him, as if there is still time left.

Officer Lee is brought inside a house on the edge of the village and the woman tells me quietly it is the home of the valley's physician. I follow them inside even though she tells me not to.

The dim room is already stuffy with so many people crowding around Lee Yoon's body, stripping his torso of his remaining robes. I hang back against the wall, watching with wide eyes as the physician rolls him onto his belly to examine the arrow entry wound in his shoulder. He glances at me from the floor. "You didn't take out the arrowhead."

I feel panicked. "Was that wrong? Should I have?"

"No, it is better. It may have helped a little with the bleeding."

He turns back to Officer Lee's body, snapping out orders to the other men for cloth and hot water and herbs. I slide down the wall and huddle there as everyone buzzes around. No one asks me to leave so I don't. I watch as the doctor removes the arrowhead and cleans the wound. He covers it in dark green crushed herbs and then turns his attention to the cut above Officer Lee's eyebrow, to his twisted knee. The doctor's jaw tightens after running his fingers lightly over Lee Yoon's leg, head shaking. Lee Yoon does not stir.

I close my eyes as the doctor works, feeling rather than seeing the forms enter and leave the room over and over again. I must have fallen asleep for when I next open my eyes the doctor is gone and the room is empty except for Lee Yoon. A candle flickers and burns low.

I slide across the floor to touch his face. He is sweating but his skin is cooler to the touch now, his breath coming strong and steady when I place my hand near his mouth. I reach to push loose strands of hair away from his sweat covered forehead. His eyes flicker beneath closed eyelids but he stays asleep.

I smile and lie down exhausted beside him.

He will live.

15

Reprieve

The village is small, just a few scattered houses on a hilltop, stony yards overlooking the wide slow river far below. Agricultural fields spread across the hills in waves of green and yellow crops, reaching to the very edges of the mountains. It is quiet, a thousand worlds away from the bustling streets of Hanyang.

When I ask about Damjang, the other village where the meeting is taking place, the old man who is head of the community tells me we are still very far away. I am glad of it, glad to be lost in this isolated place, glad to be surrounded by people who are kind and warm. People who make me feel safe.

Officer Lee sleeps for two whole days and the doctor tells me quietly that he was very close to death. If we had been out in the forest any longer Lee Yoon would certainly have died. He *nearly* died.

Yet he didn't.

I sit in the dusty courtyard outside the doctor's house, settled cross-legged on the raised wooden *maru* platform the villagers use to cook and eat upon. I am helping the woman who lives across the way weave straw sandals, enjoying the quiet calm of the river views and the silence. Her young daughter, a pudgy-cheeked toddler named Jemi, stumbles about clumsily nearby. It is peaceful and I concentrate on my work as Jemi's mother teaches me how to twist and knot the pieces of straw between my fingers. Just as my own mother once did with a needle and thread. Slowly and with patience.

Jemi calls our attention to a small squishy thing she finds in the grass, a slimy insect held up for our inspection. I cannot help but laugh, and unbidden I think for a moment of having my own daughter one day, of teaching her to sew on a polished wooden terrace. Of smoothing her wild hair back with cool careful fingers as she shows me the little precious things she has found in the garden.

I shake my head and the images fall from my mind, waning with the rushing river wind. No, I hope I never have a daughter, for the daughter of a *gisaeng* can only become a *gisaeng*, a cycle to be repeated, over and over again.

From within the doctor's house I suddenly hear murmuring, coughing, and immediately I bolt upright, dropping my work as I scramble to the household entrance. The screen is thin and Officer Lee's raw voice sounds inside, rasping but steady. I cautiously push open the shutter.

The doctor is crouched over him, wrapping his patient's shoulder securely with a cloth bandage. Lee Yoon looks terrible, ravaged, but I hardly notice, climbing inside so quickly I barely find time to kick off my shoes. Leaning back, I straighten them where they have fallen, smiling widely at Officer Lee, a simple kind of happiness flooding my body.

"Lee Yoon, you are awake."

The doctor grunts. "Yes, yes, the sleeping lord has finally woken. Come here, *Agassi*. You can finish this for me. I need to speak to someone about cooking broth. Your officer must eat."

Lee Yoon says nothing. He is watching me; has been watching me with dark eyes since I first came in, face carefully blank. I bow to the doctor as he shuffles from the room. He closes the shutters behind him, leaving only dim light and shadows in his wake.

I drop to my knees beside Officer Lee, reaching to touch his forehead with the back of my hand, ignoring his flinch. "Your fever is gone." I am pleased. "How do you feel?"

"I don't feel good."

"You nearly died, Officer Lee, I don't feel good either." I smile widely again, unable to hold it back. The truth is I feel very good *now*, seeing him awake is a small kind of miracle. I lean forward to thread the bandage across his chest and his gaze follows my hands as I work. There is tension in his body, muscles beneath his skin pulled taut.

"That old man tells me I should thank you for my life, brat."

I tsk. "He isn't just some old man, Lee Yoon, he's the physician, and it seems to me we both saved each other's lives." I stop winding the bandage and rock back on my heels so I can meet his gaze. My smile fades. He is staring again, a strange expression on his face.

"Yet he said you carried me."

"In a way, I suppose," I answer uncertainly. "Well, not carried. I dragged you. And then I just let the river ... bring us here."

He says no more, looks as if he couldn't even if he wanted to, exhausted as if he might drop where he sits. Yet the mood in the tiny room is heavy, his focus still locked on me. I don't understand what is wrong so turn back to his shoulder, yet it suddenly feels uncomfortable now to be leaning so close, to feel his breath against the side of my throat. I finish tying his bandages quickly.

"Lie back down, Officer Lee. Rest. I'll go and get the broth for you." I smile, trying to reassure him. "You'll feel better after you've eaten."

"Your face is hurt."

I reach to touch my bruised cheek self-consciously. "Mmmh. But the physician says it will heal soon enough."

He says nothing, the air thick between us until I open the tiny shutters and light pours inside. Jemi and her mother are still busy in the courtyard. I shake my head to clear it, sliding back into my shoes and shutting the doors slowly.

Lee Yoon watches until his face is hidden from view.

DAYS PASS SLOWLY in the village once Lee Yoon wakes. The repetitive routine sucks me in until I almost forget I have somewhere else to be, almost forget I have ever lived a different kind of life. Every day is the same, yet unlike the boredom of my life at the Pavilion, here I find simple pleasure in the monotony. A part of me thinks life could be better, easier, if I stayed here forever.

I rise early with the sun to help the woman I stay with cook breakfast for her family. Before we eat, I take her fat little daughter with me to feed the chickens, the small girl more of a hindrance than a help as she chases the birds on thick clumsy legs. She always forces me to carry her home afterwards but I don't mind. I enjoy the feeling of Jemi's heavy solid body in my arms, it reminds me of carrying my own precious sister when she was just as small.

I take breakfast to the doctor's house after that, and often the little girl tags along too if her mother is busy and needs me to keep an eye on her. Together we feed Officer Lee his breakfast and everyday he is stronger, the colour returning to his skin.

I spend my afternoons sitting outside the doctor's house on the low wooden platform in the courtyard, weaving shoes from straw or crushing herbs or preparing food. Whatever the villagers need from me I can do. As I work Officer Lee rests inside his room, the shutters flung wide open to let in the light and rushing river wind.

And he sits there watching me.

In the evenings I help cook dinner, and, after Lee Yoon and the doctor have eaten, I tell a story. At first it is for Jemi's sake, just a silly story to send her off to sleep, but soon I notice the doctor is often around whenever I am beginning my tale, working quietly on something or other nearby. Sometimes even the old stooped village elder arrives as well, either visiting the doctor or checking on the patient. And Lee Yoon is always listening, always watching. His expression remains blank and unreadable as I weave tales of head-strong princesses and brave warriors, stead-fastly ignoring the black eyes that follow my gesturing hands.

The close touch of death is a strange thing and change is to be expected, with Lee Yoon no different from other men who have experienced it. His old ways will return soon, I am certain of it. And sure enough on the sixth morning when the little girl and I arrive with breakfast we find Officer Lee already waiting for us. He is outside, sitting expectantly in the doctor's courtyard beneath the autumn sun, his left leg stretched out straight and awkward on the wooden *maru*.

"Officer Lee! Did you come out by yourself?" I am

pleased, the last few days have seen him growing healthier, the deep strain beginning to vanish from his face.

"I did. I'm doing much better now, brat. It must be your extraordinary stories; they've cured me."

He is his old self and I roll my eyes as Jemi climbs onto the platform beside him to shout, "Saying *brat* is rude!"

Lee Yoon just laughs and nods down at her. "I know, sometimes I am very rude, little one. Don't copy me or your mother will beat me." He smiles even wider now, the first I've ever seen him with such an expression, eyes scrunching and a dimple digging into his left cheek. He turns back to me, his smile fading. "What?"

I quickly turn away, focusing on my hands as I serve our breakfast. "Nothing. Are you hungry?"

"I am. What have you got for me today?"

"You know exactly what I've got for you today." I hand over a bowl of rice porridge, filled with local vegetables and forest greens, careful not to touch his skin.

Officer Lee sighs, taking the bowl without noticing my strangeness. "I know, but I thought perhaps today there would be meat."

I tsk at him. "Don't be a fool, Lee Yoon."

"Oh ho! How can you call a nobleman that, brat? Don't you know anything?"

He is already shovelling food into his mouth so I don't take any notice of his ridiculous words, acting as if he were on the streets of Hanyang and not lost in the mountains. Besides, Jemi is always ready to protect me, complaining immediately about Lee Yoon's bad words to the doctor when he steps outside to join us.

Yet Officer Lee *is* a nobleman. It surprises me how well he fits into village life, how respectful he is of the doctor and the village elders, how kind he is to the little girl and her mother, all common people who should be far beneath his notice. I wonder if I had it wrong, if I misunderstood him back in Hanyang? Or perhaps it is nearly dying and being saved by a village of lowborn people that made him change his attitude.

I cannot know for certain and I do not ask, yet I see the way he is with the villagers, I watch him and I notice. And every day he gets stronger, until he is limping back and forth in the courtyard testing his strength. His knee does not heal as well as the rest of him and I overhear the doctor one night explaining to Officer Lee that his left leg will never be exactly right, from now on he will always walk with a heavy limp.

I do not know if this news bothers Lee Yoon, for I cannot read his expression. When he looks at me he simply smiles, scrunched up eyes and dimple, but there is more hidden beneath the surface, things he will not let me see.

Sometimes too I think of Kim Jae-gil as I work. I think of the promise he made me so sincerely, and I wonder what he is doing and whether he is safe. I wonder if he ever thinks of me at all.

And other times I forget him for days.

I SIT in Officer Lee's room, candlelight flickering across the bare walls. I've just finished the long tale of a clever thief who courageously stole from the rich and corrupt, told for the sake of small Jemi who now sleeps soundly sprawled across the floor. I smile at her peaceful expression, touching her hair softly and thinking again of my sister, trying my best not to let hope dawn for this reunion between us that is not yet a certainty.

Trying and failing.

Officer Lee sits silently watching us, lost in his thoughts

as I am lost in mine, and I catch myself wondering what it is he dreams of in moments like these. A better future for the people, like Kim Jae-gil? A new, kinder king with no madness in his veins, lower taxes and less corruption? Or perhaps something else entirely. I cannot know for certain. Our eyes meet but I am used to his stares now, no longer feeling the need to fill the spaces between us with words.

It is Officer Lee who breaks the quiet first. With a sigh he leans over, his voice low and tired. "It is time to leave. Everyone will be out looking for us, we cannot lead them here."

I peer down at the sleeping child, strangely torn. "Already? Are you well enough?"

"I am. I could have travelled already, but I wanted to wait until I was stronger. The meetings will still be running in Damjang, there is still time. But that place won't be like this. We will need to be ready." His gaze flicks to my face. "Someone tried to kill us."

This is the first time he has spoken of the attack and I'm not ready yet to think on it. "I've really liked it here," I say softly.

"I know. I have too, brat."

There's something in his voice that makes me look up.

"I nearly died, but it was..." he pauses, and then just sighs again.

We are silent for a few moments, watching Jemi's chest rise as she sleeps, her breathing soft and rhythmic. I sigh. "When will we go then?"

"Tomorrow. I've already spoken to the village elder. He's agreed to give us a horse."

"A horse? You mean their *one* horse? Really?"

"I don't want to walk out of here looking like we need to be saved," Officer Lee explains. "We need to arrive healthy and strong to show we're not so easily beaten."

Seeing my lingering worry he suddenly smirks. "It's fine. We'll send the horse back to the village when we reach Damjang and I've already agreed an amount in payment. That will be sent back too. If that's what you're worried about."

"Oh..."

He grins now, slow and wide. "You think I demanded their horse for free?"

I tsk as if he is foolish for suggesting it, and do not admit that he is right. I wave him away.

"You worry too much, brat," Lee Yoon says, but then his smile fades and he grows serious once more. "When we get to Damjang we'll need to be careful, it's likely whoever tried to have us killed will be there as part of the meeting."

I look at him sharply. "Why would you think that?"

He shrugs. "It seems to me someone wanted to prevent me from attending, so my not being there must benefit someone somehow."

"You mean someone else found out about your conspiracy? The government then, the king himself? You think they found out who you are, what you're involved in?" I pause, breathless, thinking suddenly of his sisters left unprotected at home, helpless and not at all prepared for what might happen. My fingers clench to stop them shaking. "Then ... does the king know about your family? Will he be going after them next?"

Lee Yoon lowers his eyes, takes a deep breath. "I hope that's not the case. It depends on who tried to kill us." His mouth is pulled tight. "I do not believe the government organised the attack."

"But who else would want you dead?" I pause, turning the possibilities over in my mind. Indeed, why *would* the king organise such a quiet death for a traitor like Officer Lee? I watch his face in the candlelight, the warm glow playing across his skin. There would be no quiet death. The king would have an example made of him.

I shiver.

"So, it is not the king then," I finally relent. "Who else does that leave?"

Officer Lee sighs. "By now rumours must surely have spread through our organisation that I'm investigating the one who betrayed us. They'll know I've been sent to find out who it is. It would be in that person's best interest if I never arrived to the meetings."

"And that person could be anyone who is attending."

Officer Lee nods wearily.

I shake my head, daunted by the task ahead, my thoughts whirring. "Is the king aware? Does he know there are ministers within the palace who wish to depose him?"

"I believe he does. I am told he does."

"Then why does he not act?"

"Without evidence and facts, without knowing for sure who is involved, what can he do? No one is able to act. It is why we must identify the spy. One small mistake and everything that has been built will crumble."

"It is like walking on a cliff edge," I breathe. "One wrong step..."

Candlelight dances across Officer Lee's skin. "One wrong step."

I am thinking of my words beside the river, the terrible future I painted for his family. I wish now I had never been so harsh.

"We will find the spy," I tell him firmly, hoping it is true. It is late and our heavy conversation has tired me out, making me think again of the last conspiracy raised to dethrone the king. Of how much it cost me.

"I'll take her home," I say, leaning down to collect Jemi into my arms. She murmurs and sighs but does not wake.

The child is heavy so Lee Yoon helps me lift her, steadying her head against my shoulder and leaning across to open the doors to the courtyard outside. Cool air rushes against my skin.

"Goodnight, brat," he says quietly.

I feel his eyes on my back as I cross the courtyard outside.

16

The Promise

I wake too early, restless and filled with bad dreams.

Down at the riverside in the dawn light I pull straw sandals from my feet, tugging the *beoseon*, my white socks, off and dropping them onto the rocks. The water is ice cold against my bare feet and I shiver as I step in, one foot and then the other, reaching down to splash more onto my face.

I think of my mother again, of the last time I saw her. She was clutching my hands and stiff with fear, for already my sister was taken from us, my brother and father killed. I was the last to leave her, and for a long while it was just the two of us alone, cells side by side, hands clasped through thick wooden bars.

I remember the look on her face when she told me to be strong, a fierceness I had never before seen within her, my mother who was only ever small and quiet and obedient. My mother who was already sick, deep coughs wracking her delicate body, eyes yellow and skin sallow.

And yet she had made me swear it.

Find your sister.
Find her and live well.
Together.
And then she stared me in the eye.
Daughter, promise me.

She demanded it, and I repeated the words after her, until they were set in stone between us, until they became real. I remember my promise to my mother more clearly now than the moment I made it. Now it is only the shadow of a memory and it swirls and fades in my mind like wood smoke by the fire. Her face too, fades. And my sister's as well.

Yet my promise does not.

I plunge my hands deep into the freezing water, tired of ghosts, and then carefully dry myself on the riverbank amongst the long grasses, taking my time before climbing the hills back toward the village.

Officer Lee sits outside the doctor's home, alone in the courtyard. He watches me approach and then together we sit silently in the sunlight, awaiting the beginning of the day and the changes it will bring. Officer Lee massages his knee and I ask him if it hurts.

"No."

I pull a face. "You are a liar, Lee Yoon."

It makes him smile, eyes crinkling, dimple appearing. "It's fine. It will be."

I nod, choosing to believe him before biting my lips. "I admit I feel rather afraid of what it will be like when we reach Damjang."

"It will be easy, brat. Do nothing. Just listen and learn, that is all."

"And you?"

"I will do the same."

There is silence between us, until curiosity gets the better of me and I pry where I should not. "Why were you chosen for this task? Why did Kim Jae-gil not come himself?"

He looks at me sharply, then carefully relaxes his expression. "My father holds great sway in the inner circles of our group. He put my name forward for this position."

My heart sinks. His father is just like mine, drowning his own son willingly for more power, more money, for a better position. Out loud I say none of it. "He must place great faith in you."

"Unlike some."

I pause. "What do you mean?"

Officer Lee turns away, as if not to answer. Yet the words seem to drag from his mouth. "Kim Jae-gil believes I have doubts. I am sure he no longer trusts me, though we grew up together as brothers."

My mind falls back to Hanyang and I answer without thinking. "Kim Jae-gil said he trusts you with his life. He told me himself."

Though as soon as I've said it, I remember the details Kim Jae-gil never chose to share with Lee Yoon. My true identity, the location of my home in the Pavilion. His promise to help my sister.

Kim Jae-gil keeps secrets from Lee Yoon, this is true.

I remember doubting Lee Yoon myself, what feels a thousand years ago, that afternoon in the market inn beside Kim Jae-gil. Back then I had believed Lee Yoon could be the spy they sought so desperately.

No longer.

My trust in Officer Lee has laid roots, growing down and outwards, a foundation to stand on.

I turn back to Officer Lee for I wish to know if Kim Jae-gil is right, if Lee Yoon really does have doubts about the movement. Yet he is watching me strangely and I cannot understand the bitterness I see in his expression. When I try to question him, the easy honesty we have shared is gone and it seems our conversation is now over.

He limps inside with no more words, leaving me alone to ponder my mistakes as the morning wears on and the time to leave draws closer.

I AM sad to be going. Sadder than I can quite explain. When it is time I say goodbye to the woman who let me stay in her home, who clothed and fed me; kissing her fat daughter Jemi on top of her head.

Another life, another world.

Officer Lee comes outside dressed in commoner clothes, his hair pulled high and neat into a topknot with his own black *manggeon* band in place across his forehead. I watch him smile as he thanks the villagers for bringing him back to health. He limps toward the horse and swings himself awkwardly onto its spindly back. One of the villagers uses his hands as a step for me and I climb up as well, clutching at the material stretched across Lee Yoon's back to keep steady. I'm barely settled when he swings the beast around and urges her to a canter, no time for last goodbyes. We pound along the dirt road leaving the village, passing by the river and the fields. I am holding on too tightly to wave to the villagers and by the time I am brave enough to turn back, the houses have already disappeared into the trees.

Officer Lee taps my hand, wound tightly around his waist. "All right?"

"Yes," I answer breathlessly, the awkwardness between us faded and long gone. Things how they should be once more. "But slow down. It's ... *too fast!*"

But I'm laughing too.

I feel the horse slow slightly but still we fly through the trees like the wind, early morning sunlight flashing through the canopy and dry autumn leaves crackling beneath hooves. The mountain air is crisp and cool, filled with the scent of the river and trees. I grip tighter and laugh again.

It feels like flying.

IT IS MUCH LATER in the day when we come across the searchers.

We've reached one of the main mountain roads and we hear them before we see them, the thunder of hooves, shouts of men calling to each other. Officer Lee tells me the mountains must be crawling with guards from Damjang sent to find us. Soon we are surrounded by men on horses, some dressed in the local magistrate's guard uniform, and one young man plainly a *yangban* noble. He is clearly used to being obeyed, barking out orders and shouting at us.

"Identify yourselves."

Lee Yoon inclines his head and answers calmly. "I am Officer Lee Yoon. This maidservant and I are the only survivors of an attack on our travelling party. May I ask who you are?"

The new group is restless, their horses shuffling back and forth as the men all eye us closely. The young lord peers hard at Officer Lee.

"We've been searching for you since news of the bandit attack reached us in Damjang. I am Choi Chan Young, I believe you know my father, Minister Choi. It is our estate in Damjang that is holding the meeting."

Young Master Choi bows his head low to Officer Lee. "Our family takes full responsibility for the bandit attack that occurred on your journey to our estate. I promise we will hunt down the individuals involved and bring them to justice in your name!"

"Bandits?" Officer Lee shifts slightly in the saddle. "You believe they were bandits?"

Choi Chan Young frowns. "What else could they be? We've investigated the scene, they took everything you were carrying, left only the bodies behind." He pauses. "In truth we suspected you must be dead, Officer Lee."

"I see," answers Lee Yoon, still noncommittal.

Choi Chan Young frowns again, irritated. "Officer Lee. Please. Allow us to escort you to my father's house. I know he will be very pleased you have survived. He has many great things to say about your record and integrity."

The young lord pulls his horse around on the trail without waiting for a response, ready to victoriously lead the search party home. He throws a glance over his shoulder at me and then barks an order to the guard at his right. "You! Take that servant off Officer Lee's horse. She will ride with you."

The guard nods and urges his horse toward us but Officer Lee does not move.

"She is fine with me."

Choi Chan Young's expression sours, though he tries to hide it, smoothing his features quickly. His voice when he speaks is calm and controlled. "Please. You aren't thinking straight, Officer Lee. You've been through an ordeal, I understand that. But you do not want to arrive into my father's estate like ... *that*." He looks me up and down. "People will talk."

I feel Officer Lee's body stiffen and quickly I lay a hand lightly against the small of his back to calm him, careful that the others cannot see. Sliding off the horse, I move toward the assigned guard without a word. Choi Chan Young nods in approval.

"Smart girl."

17

Damjang

I am discarded from the horse the moment we arrive at Choi Chan Young's grand sprawling estate. The home has a variety of separate structures and courtyards, each encircled by high stone walls backing onto the autumn yellow forest.

I scurry to get out of the way as the search party mill dangerously around the yard, their horses stamping and tossing heads restlessly. One of the guards is shouting at approaching servants, and a few ladies dressed in beautiful bright *hanbok* step from the house to witness the spectacle.

My arm is grasped and I am pulled aside, a man in light blue robes wearing a wide-brimmed black *gat* is gaping at me. It takes a long moment to recognise him dressed so differently, his hair in a neat top knot underneath a *manggeon* headcap instead of loose around his face, clothes richly coloured and made from the finest of materials.

Yet it is Kim Jae-gil who stands before me, warm hands pressing upon my shoulders, eyes alert and dancing across my face.

"*Nauri*," I exclaim. "Why are you here?"

"I came to speak with Officer Lee." Kim Jae-gil urgently searches the crowd of men and horses in the courtyard, lingering on faces. "Is he with you? Is he alive?"

I turn to point across the crowded courtyard. Just as Kim Jae-gil is dressed so unexpectedly as a true *yangban* today, Officer Lee is barely recognisable in commoner clothes; a strange reversal. The two men nod at each other in greeting, Kim Jae-gil visibly relieved to see his friend, yet Lee Yoon's expression is hard. He stands watching us from across the bustling yard.

I turn back to Kim Jae-gil, allowing him to draw me further away, almost to the corner of the terraced house. There is a moment of silence between us, almost awkward, and words flow from my lips just to fill it. "What is it you wish to speak of with Officer Lee? You have come such a long way."

"Seorin *ssi*, something has happened in Hanyang he must know. I could not entrust a messenger. Yet when I got here they told me you never arrived." He is breathless. "I've been waiting for days. I thought..." He leans close, expression questioning. "I thought you both must surely be dead."

I nod, moving out from under Kim Jae-gil's warm hands, taking a step back so we are no longer quite so close. "*Nauri*, is there any word of my sister?"

Kim Jae-gil seems taken aback. "No … I'm sorry. There is nothing yet." He moves forward again. "Can you tell me what happened on the road? Were you attacked? Do you know by whom?"

I shake my head as Officer Lee reaches us, his eyes hard and flat like stone. Kim Jae-gil grasps his friend's shoulder in welcome and calls Lee Yoon his older brother in greeting, reminding me again that these two men have shared a childhood. I take some steps back to give them privacy, the relationship they share layered with too many complexities and suddenly I feel like an outsider even after all Lee Yoon and I have shared.

Together they speak urgently in low voices. I cannot hear what is said but Officer Lee's expression grows more strained by the moment, head bowed low to hear Kim Jae-gil's news.

When the master of the house, Minister Choi, comes outside, Kim Jae-gil moves to stand at his side as the older man pays his respects to Officer Lee, offering the same reassurances of justice and punishment as did his son, Choi Chan Young.

Finally Minister Choi leads the men inside, leaving me to follow at a respectful distance for lack of anything else to do. Choi Chan Young notices and speaks in a low voice with Officer Lee before sending a servant back to take me away. I throw a glance at Lee Yoon and he nods, mouth pulled into a taut line.

CONSIDERING I am Officer Lee's only surviving servant I am surprised by how little I see of him. There is no opportunity to speak privately and he doesn't set me work to do either, so at first I am listless and idle, though soon enough the girls in the kitchen notice and put me to good use. I then spend my time cleaning platters and chopping vegetables, cutting herbs, and cooking rice.

Although it is strange that Officer Lee and I share the same house yet never meet, I suppose it is not unlike my experience staying with his family in Hanyang. In that place I was only a lowly servant, and here again in

Damjang I am reminded of my place within this world, of my status and worth.

And if I were ever able to forget for a moment, young master Choi Chan Young's sour expression every time he passes me would be reminder enough.

I imagine how Choi Chan Young might look if he was told the full truth, that I am a runaway *gisaeng*, travelling outside Hanyang illegally, with no permission except a lie and the identity tag of somebody else.

I imagine how Officer Lee might look at me too, and the thought makes me feel sick.

Kim Jae-gil though, is different.

He knows exactly what I am and yet he treats me well all the same. He smiles when he passes me in the hallways, always making pains to seek me out within this bustling house, somewhere quiet and private where we will not be seen together. For he too is aware of appearances.

It is on one such night that I receive the message. A whisper from a child through my shuttered sleeping quarter doors, a mouth to the gap between the wood and then the pitter-patter of small feet running swiftly away across the courtyard. I stir and sit, half-believing the whispers were from a dream, for the maid I share with still sleeps soundly.

Outside it is too early for the household to wake and too late for the nightly revellers to remain. Soon the darkness will lift and the courtyards will overflow with sunshine, yet for now the air is chill and the ground hard with frost. I walk silently to the terrace within the outer gardens, stepping carefully up stone steps into the open pavilion.

Tree branches hang loose in the wind beside the terrace, cushions and empty bowls and saucers strewn across the floor. It seems a party was held here earlier, ending not so very long ago judging from the leftover fermented vegetables spilling from white porcelain platters. I step, grimacing, over a discarded *jeogori*, gauzy and sheer as only a *gisaeng* would wear, and settle down to wait for Kim Jae-gil.

If he has asked to meet me here, in this quiet place so late at night, surely he must have news. My heart beats in time with the mountain winds. Perhaps he wishes to meet because of my sister. Perhaps he calls me here in the dark of night because he has good tidings. My veins sing and my lips curve into a smile until...

I notice a low familiar shape sitting motionless in the terrace corner, half lifted on a flat cushion. A *gayageum*.

I sit watching the instrument, drawn to the gleaming paulownia wood body, the hollowed spaces and the strings that catch the darkness. I resist.

Yet no one comes.

Out here in the garden it is quiet. I remain alone in the space between midnight and dawn and there is no one left to listen. My fingers find the smooth hard wood, taut strings cold in the frost, uncared for and unloved. Tightening and loosening I work the strings until they ring out clear in the night, until my fingers dance and sing, eyes closed and head bowed low.

It is a slow song, music mournful to suit the night, rushing wind carrying the sound away into the mountains. Soon my unpractised fingers hurt too much, callouses gone, and I must stop with one last note ringing out into the darkness.

Inspecting the damaged skin across my fingertips I startle at the creak of wood from the entranceway. A figure stands frozen at the edges of the terrace, motionless.

Lee Yoon.

I stare back, blinking in the darkness.

In a scramble I push the *gayageum* aside to stand quickly

and ungracefully, bowing low as a maidservant should to a *yangban* lord, heart beating too fast. It has been days since I've seen him properly, longer still since we've been alone together. Smoothing my skirts I steal a glance but it is too dark to see his face. Was it him who sent the message to meet? Not Kim Jae-gil at all. Yet still he does not move, hovering at the edges of the terrace with the dark trees wavering at his back.

"My apologies, Officer Lee," I say into the thick quiet. "I was waiting … and I saw …"

"You play?"

His voice sounds strange in the darkness, but he steps forward now. Close.

"Yes…"

"How?"

This makes me smile, straightening my back to face him. "Just as anyone does. I practise hard and then—"

"No. How did you receive such as opportunity?" He pauses, the silence heavy. "As a maidservant."

I inhale sharply but say nothing.

There is suspicion glittering in his black eyes, close enough now, and the truth tugs at my chest ready to escape. I take a deep breath.

And I tell him what I am.

"I … work at a *gisaeng* house. I found the … opportunity there."

I cannot look him in the face, except suddenly he laughs, the sound tinged with … relief? My gaze finds his and he is smiling, eyes crinkling, dimple returned to wherever Damjang has banished it.

"I'm sure the *gisaeng* of your household order you around something fierce, brat. I don't envy anyone being at their beck and call." He reaches one boot to touch the edges of the discarded *jeogori* still lying on the floor, expression changing and voice turning hesitant. "It seems to me you could have done something better with your life than just be a servant, and I'm ... sorry you were born into a world where you could not."

My mind runs blank. He does not understand me, does not see the truth I've tried to tell him and now he says ... something no one has ever said to me before.

I stare at him.

Something has changed in Lee Yoon.

Slowly I sink to the polished wooden floor, no words left for him. He follows, settling on a flat embroidered cushion, fussing with the beaded strings that hang from his wide-brimmed *gat*. He smiles shyly, eyes crinkling again and in that moment I know I will say nothing about the mistake he has made, the easy silence that has returned between us too welcome to ruin with words.

Or with truth.

I bite my lips. "Officer Lee, was it you who summoned me here, so late at night?"

"Not me, no. Kim Jae-gil is late it seems. I do not know why he calls us, he didn't tell you?"

I shake my head. "No."

We lapse into silence again, a long stretch, only the hum of insects in the forest and the rushing wind for company.

Lee Yoon clears his throat. "You were ... Your music was ..." A self-mocking smile flashes across his face and then just as suddenly it is gone. "You play beautifully ... Seorin *ssi*."

I blink and do not know what to say.

Many men have complimented my playing over the years, many times over, yet this is different. There is a simple sincerity behind his words that turns my skin warm. I cannot meet his eyes.

Footsteps crunch through the dark garden frost and Kim Jae-gil slowly emerges from the night. By the time he reaches the terrace I am standing, body already bent into a low bow for the approaching nobleman. Officer Lee remains on the ground, watching. "You're late," he says.

"My apologies. Minister Choi kept me far longer than expected." Kim Jae-gil displays one of his easy smiles, as if his life and Officer Lee's did not hang precariously in the balance. "I must leave you both now."

I am surprised. "You will return to Hanyang?"

"Indeed, I have been away too long already. This was only meant to be a short visit." Kim Jae-gil waits while Lee Yoon stands. "I wished to say goodbye to you both in private, so we could speak freely. I am well aware of the danger I must leave you in." Kim Jae-gil places a firm hand on his friend's shoulder. "You must be careful, *Hyeong*," he says, calling him older brother.

Officer Lee nods, mouth tight. "We will be safe."

"Keep faith in our cause, and do not forget why you must succeed in this."

Lee Yoon bristles. "I do not forget, Kim Jae-gil."

The two men speak together in a rush of hushed whispers, of names and places I do not recognise, speaking cryptically of an event looming in the horizon that both seem to be afraid of. I watch as they talk, and listen, for they do not attempt to hide their words from me, though I do not understand their meaning.

The two men are like morning and night, Kim Jae-gil filled with energy and brightness, while Officer Lee grows grimmer with each word that falls from his lips. Soon his brow is furrowed and his jaw tight.

Kim Jae-gil does not seem to notice the tension in the air, and finally it seems their words are spent, for he steps to my side instead, reaching to lightly touch my chin. Just a brush of his fingers and then it is done, yet I find my hand reaching for that same place on my skin, uncomfortable. Officer Lee stiffens beside me.

"Seorin *ssi*, remember how proud your brother would be of your bravery." Kim Jae-gil's eyes glitter in the growing morning light, face flushed with blue.

I say nothing, for it seems wrong to speak of my brother here, now that my past could so easily become Lee Yoon and Kim Jae-gil's future. Besides, Officer Lee knows nothing of my brother, and it is not Kim Jae-gil's place to tell him.

I glance up at Lee Yoon but his face is carefully blank.

Kim Jae-gil clears his throat. "Please, will you walk with me? My horse waits at the front gates."

I am startled, yet allow him to draw me from the open garden terrace as he exchanges final words with Lee Yoon, who is left standing stiff with tension on the polished wooden balcony. I glance back at him through the dawning light, dew catching the morning sun as Kim Jae-gil walks me further into the garden.

Soon Lee Yoon has disappeared amongst the trees.

WE STAND at the gates beside a restless horse and my whole body is tense, my belly knotted. Kim Jae-gil does not feel the same discomfort it seems, for he lingers with me far longer than he should, as if we have nothing to lose. "It is places like this that make men wish for a better world, do you not think?"

I glance across at where he has gestured, the mountains and the little village of Damjang nestled among the over-hanging trees. "*Nauri?*"

"People here are satisfied, they do not go hungry." Kim

Jae-gil glances toward the grand house behind us. "Minister Choi is a good man, and provides for his community well. If the capital could be ruled so carefully, none of us would have any reason for dissent. Have you heard that women in Hanyang have taken to selling their hair to keep poverty at bay?"

I nod slowly. "I have." After a pause I cannot help but add, "And selling their daughters, as well."

Kim Jae-gil watches me with blazing eyes, as if my statement is proof I am now wholly converted to his cause, as if we are comrades who together will change the world.

He nods. "Yes. I am sick of patiently waiting and hoping for things to get better. The time to act is now, and if more brave men and women like yourself were willing to risk all for change, our organisation would not need to hide in the hills and quake in fear of old men and corrupt politicians."

"Like myself, *Nauri*?" I am alarmed by his fervour.

He smiles. "Of course. How is it *gisaeng* are often described? Is it not said that you have the body of a low born, yet the mind of an aristocrat? Why should a woman as intelligent and educated as yourself live life as a mere slave? Do you not also wish for change? Do you not also want the chance for a better life?"

I do not know what to say, thinking of Officer Lee's tight expression, the doubt that crept into his eyes when Kim Jae-gil spoke of the future. My brother died for this cause, and yet nothing has truly changed.

I stare at Kim Jae-gil and all of my doubts remain, though his words do spin tales, building something bright and gold within my mind, a place where things could be different from the way I have always known them to be.

Kim Jae-gil smiles at me, different now though, almost self-consciously. "My apologies, Seorin *ssi*. My mind runs away with me and I voice too much of what I think. Or so I am told."

It is my turn to offer a cautious smile. "Your dreams are strong, *Nauri*."

"They will not be dreams forever." His voice is filled with certainty. "Soon we shall make dreams into reality, no matter how cautious our leaders are determined to remain. Change is coming, this I promise you. You should begin to dream too. Soon you may have the opportunity to live in a different world."

He turns then to calm his horse, slotting his sword into the strapping on the saddle. I am left unsettled by his words, of possibilities I am sure could not be real.

Did my brother also dream of changing the world?

Did my father?

Down below at the edge of the village a small group of waiting guards have amassed on their own horses. Kim Jae-gil's men, ready to escort him back to Hanyang.

"Jang Seorin," he says, placing a warm hand on my forearm, fingers strong and firm as if to impart strength. "You must be careful here. If you come across anything unusual take it immediately to Officer Lee. He knows what to do and he'll protect you if anything goes wrong. Be careful. Be safe."

He smiles his easy smile as I nod, morning sunshine playing across his skin, and then he swings into the saddle. Before I can say anything, he is gone, down into the village streets, lost from sight in the maze of houses below.

I stand outside by myself for a long time after he has gone. What he said, what he believes the world can be, I cannot understand it.

I know my place.

I stare at my hands in silence before finally heading back inside the complex.

18

To Tell a Lie

I slice greens in the kitchen of Minister Choi's house until the head cook calls for me. "Outside, quickly! Go. Someone wants to talk with you."

I scurry into the yard, for when the head cook asks something of you, obedience is wise. Wiping my hands on my apron and trying to tame my wild hair, I find only a young girl standing under a shady tree.

At first, I am disappointed, certain Officer Lee had called for me after so many days without contact, yet soon my curiosity is piqued. What business could a girl like this have with me? She is one of the noble daughters visiting the estate judging by her richly embroidered dress, and she is flanked by two personal maids, both of them dressed far better than I.

I bow low, respectfully. "*Agassi*. You wished to see me?"

The girl's eyes run me up and down. "I heard you are the servant who was attacked on the road with Police Officer Lee Yoon."

I nod, confused. "Yes, *Agassi*."

"I want to hear your story then. Tell me."

I blink at her before remembering my manners and bowing my head once more. "*Agassi*, surely Officer Lee himself would be a better person to tell you this story."

"He won't tell me," she says in a petulant voice. "My brother won't tell me. I just want to hear what happened!" She almost stamps her foot in frustration. "*You* tell me! You were there!"

I glance at her maidservants for guidance and one quickly steps forward, a warning look flashing across her thin face. "This young mistress is the daughter of Minister Choi and the younger sister to young master Choi Chan Young."

I take her statement to mean I should do as the lady commands and hurry myself about it, so quickly I launch into a very short and rather censored version of what happened on our way from Hanyang. Even so, the young lady is clearly enthralled by my sparse tale, as are her maid-servants, all of them listening with bated breath.

When I am finished the young girl strides off without a word of thanks and I am left to hurry back to the kitchens before I get in trouble.

Yet it does not take long before word spreads in whispers through the estate that I have a thrilling story to tell, and all the maids and stable boys want to hear it for themselves.

And I find that most are able to offer their own tale in return.

Some bring me useless bits of market gossip but others are genuine tales of comings and goings at the estate houses where they live back in Hanyang, or rumours of their lord's newest friends. None of it is at all incriminating, any servant knows better than that, but much is interesting and I store it away until I get a chance to impart the knowledge I have collected to Officer Lee, who perhaps will know what to do with it.

Except I do not find a moment alone with him to tell him anything. Not that day, nor the next. Officer Lee is busy with meetings, always I see him disappearing down a hallway or into a room with one of the ministers, only ever in glimpses.

On the third day I have had enough.

It is late at night and my work in the kitchen is finally done. The other maidservants trail across the courtyards to the shared women's quarters, but I linger in the kitchen until the space is empty, slipping quietly toward the big house. I know which room is his, for often I have been asked to deliver tea to the main house by the head cook, and on one occasion I saw Lee Yoon slip inside a small room in the guest hall.

A tea tray rattles in my hands. Winding through dark corridors I stop in front of the door I am certain belongs to Lee Yoon. Deep breaths and hesitation, yet footsteps approach from the far end of the hallway so I balance the tray in one hand as I push the iron ring handle and slip inside.

A candle burns and Lee Yoon sits on his open bedroll with his ruined knee stretched awkwardly to the side. He gapes at me as I press a finger to my lips, waiting in silence beside the door until the footsteps have passed by and moved down the corridor.

Silence falls and Lee Yoon says nothing, his face blank like a mask. His expression causes me to frown as I pad quietly to place the tea set on a low table against his wall, flickering candlelight barely piercing the gloom. I settle close before him on the floor, my voice in hushed whispers. "Can we speak, Officer Lee? I have news I must tell you."

He looks at me coldly. "Do you really."

"Yes, really." I frown. "What is the matter with you?"

He doesn't answer, black eyes dancing across the floor, the ceiling, the walls. Anywhere but on me. Abruptly a terrible thought occurs to me. "Have you been avoiding me?"

"Don't be a fool. What reason could I possibly have to avoid you?" He waves me away and I think he will actually tell me to leave, except instead he leans close, voice a hissed rush in the thick darkness. "Why did Kim Jae-gil choose *you* to send on this venture?"

I am taken aback. "I don't ..."

He leans closer, speaking low so no one can overhear through the paper-thin walls. We are almost face to face. "Why is it he so badly wanted to send *you*, even when I told him no? What else did he ask you to do for him on this journey?"

"He didn't ... I'm not ..."

His expression flashes cold and hard. *"I know nothing about you.* Jang Seorin is not your real name. How much of what you've told me is real?"

"Y ... you are wrong, Lee Yoon. Seorin is my real name. It is ... only I ..."

I flinch when he reaches for my wrist, his fingers clenched and bleached of colour. My breath comes sharper and faster, a hum in my ears.

"Do not lie to me. In the village on the last day, I saw your identification tag. The name on it was not Jang Seorin."

It takes too long for me to understand and by the time I do he is struggling to his feet, limp evident in his strained movements, pulling me after him as he grips my wrist. I clutch at his sleeve with my free hand and dig my heels into the floor.

"Please ... *Stop*! It *is* my real name. The tag you saw ... it is false. Borrowed."

He stops, skin awash with candlelight. "False?" He still holds my arm but his grasp is different now, loose.

"Yes. I swapped mine with another girl before I left Hanyang. It was the only way I could get out of the city. Kim Jae-gil organised it for me when he asked me to come here with you. I'm only..."

I break off, breathless, uncertain.

I am a gisaeng. *A lowly slave.*

The truth. The truth. The truth.

I stumble over my words, hearing myself speak them from far away, as if it were someone else. "I am what I look like. A commoner. I'm a servant. Kim Jae-gil recruited me after I helped him, after I gave him the letter back. He thought I might be useful and I agreed because he said he would pay me. I am what I seem."

I look up at him, my stomach dropping like a stone to the floor. "I am no one."

Lee Yoon does not move, and slowly I let go of his robes. His black eyes cannot be read, his expression carefully controlled once more, empty like the surface of a lake. The longest moment passes before finally he lowers his gaze. "You have something to tell me, then?"

I nod, blood pounding in my ears.

I lied to him. I lied to Lee Yoon.

Not a lie by omission. He asked me and I chose not to tell him what I am.

A true lie.

"Yes, I have news for you," I say. Pushing back the sickness that creeps inside my belly I launch into the tirade of small gossip I have gathered from the other servants. Officer Lee listens intently, frowning occasionally and asking questions in a low voice. After a time he guides me back to the floor and we sit across from each other once more in the candlelight, heads bowed close to ensure our whispers remain secret.

I speak for a long time, telling him everything I have learned, no matter how trivial, talking and talking until I have almost forgotten the lie. "I heard the Park family's eldest son was in marriage talks with the prime minister's daughter, and they have been engaged for over six months." I shrug, for I do not know if my gossip could be useful. "I was told neither family are here in Damjang though, both live in Hanyang."

"Yes, their marriage is not surprising." Officer Lee frowns thoughtfully. He avoids meeting my gaze. "An alliance between those two houses would be a formidable opponent to us. Both the Park family and the prime minister's family are fiercely loyal to the king." He pauses. "Or at least they're invested in the positions they've gained from his favour. It is strange though that neither family has officially announced the engagement after such a long time. Why keep it a secret they are making a marriage alliance? Such a match is to be expected."

I shrug, tired now. "Is that strange?"

When I yawn Officer Lee grimaces at me. "Time to go I think," he tells me, black eyes soft again. "It's late. Go to bed, brat." He hesitates and then attempts a smile. An apology. "You've been helpful tonight. I am grateful."

I turn away for I do not deserve it. I am beside the door before he has managed to struggle to his feet.

"Good night, Lee Yoon," I say quietly as I slip from his room. I do not wait for his reply, padding silently through the dimly lit hallway toward the outer yards and the women's quarters. I am outside in the crisp chill air before I remember the tea tray left inside Lee Yoon's room.

I do not return for it.

It was the right thing. A lie to save myself humiliation. To avoid the look that will come creeping onto his face.

Officer Lee is a means to an end, I owe him nothing. Why should I endure his disdain if he were to know the truth?

A slave girl and a *gisaeng*. He would be disgusted.

I lift my chin and square my shoulders.

Despite Kim Jae-gil's shining words of a changed world, I know better. Soon I'll be back in Hanyang, shut away inside the Pavilion where I will stay for the rest of my life. Or until I am no longer beautiful and young enough to be wanted.

The rest of it will fade with time. It must.

My sister will be safe because of me. It will be enough.

19

Creeping Doubts

Outside in the yard I bend over a pot of fermenting vegetables, dishing the sticky red mass into a smaller wooden bowl. Far from the main house, this garden of heavy pots lies at the very edges of the enclosure near the forest, only a wall separating us from the mountains. I glance to where he leans against it. "If Minister Choi is on the same side of the rebellion as you, why is his son like that?"

"Choi Chan Young? Like what?"

I shrug. "Horrible."

Officer Lee displays the barest ghost of a smile. "He is not always horrible. Not in front of his father at least." He shifts against the wall, readjusting his position. I have noticed his leg pains him much these days. "Besides, just because he's on the same side doesn't mean he's necessarily a good man. There are plenty of dishonourable people in our organisation."

I stand biting my lip, the bowls forgotten. "Then how can you know you picked the right side? How do you know what you're doing is right if the people standing beside you aren't good people?"

Officer Lee grows still and doesn't answer. Immediately I regret my words. I sigh, wiping my hands against my rough *chima*. There is nothing to be gained by questioning him over something that can no longer be changed.

"Why did you come out here, anyway?" I am trying to change the subject. I glance over as I continue with my work. "Don't you have some meeting you should go to or something?"

"I do."

"Is it boring then?" He frowns at my guess but doesn't deny it either, which makes me laugh. "Well, hand me that before you go." I point.

"This?"

"No, the other one." I take the ladle from him. "How much longer must we stay here? How long will your meetings last?"

"They're not *my* meetings, brat ... but, a few more days at least, I would say."

"What do you all talk about in there anyway?"

I am distracted by my work so it takes a few moments to realise Lee Yoon hasn't answered. When I look up he simply shrugs.

"Politics. Money. It's not really important."

"It's not?"

I frown at him. Something is wrong.

"…What is it?"

"We're running out of time." Officer Lee presses both hands over his brow. "If we don't finish this before we go back to Hanyang then … I don't know what will happen. We must resolve this. Now."

I am uneasy, certain I know exactly what will happen.

Officer Lee's whole world hangs in the balance now; his family's lives and the burden of it is beginning to show.

"We'll find out who it is," I tell him, trying to sound confident. My sister's life hangs in the balance too. If Kim Jae-gil and his organisation fail, there will be no one left standing to retrieve her for me.

Officer Lee says nothing, only lowers himself with effort to sit on the dry grass, resting his back against the stone wall. He rips at the yellow blades with his fingers, twisting and twirling until the grasses fray apart. He makes no move to return to the meetings inside the main house.

I stop my work to watch him.

There is no one else around, only the rising mountains beyond the wall, the treetops turning gold and yellow. I put aside my bowl of fermented leaves and move to crouch before him. The wide brim of his *gat* hides his face and instead I focus on his ever-moving hands. His fingers are long and the palms wide, veins visible beneath his skin.

"Officer Lee. Tell me what is on your mind."

Lee Yoon glances at me sharply, something uncertain in his black eyes, though it fades quickly when he shakes his head. "It seems I am worried about a great many things these days." He pauses and then laughs, the sound bitter. "Kim Jae-gil told me the prime minister suspects my father of illegal activities. He is suspicious, but has no way to prove my father's involvement. Yet. It is the message Kim Jae-gil carried, all the way from Hanyang, at my father's request."

Slowly I shake my head. "That is…" I have no words, worry swelling inside my chest.

"Seorin, we must be even more careful now the prime minister knows the truth. He may have sent messages here as well, to other officials loyal to the king, asking them to watch me. We cannot know for certain. That man is famous for his determination, he will find evidence … or he will *create* evidence. Nothing will stop him now he has a target." Lee Yoon stops speaking and drops the twisted grass from his hands. "It seems this is a battle we are losing."

I have nothing I can say. Instead I reach out to touch his ruined knee lightly. Lee Yoon glances up and a smile creeps across his face. Small and strained. But it is something.

"I must go," he tells me, hauling himself up from the dry grass until he towers above me once more. "Please tell me anything new you learn, as soon as you can. We are running out of time."

I watch as he walks away across the yard, his limp heavy and awkward. He pretends it does not hurt but I know better.

20

A truth Embedded Deep Within

Serving in the grand hall is not my favourite task. Minister Choi's guests are seated across from each other, deep in discussion and barely aware of the servant girls as we work around them.

These men are like peacocks, preening in the candle-light, showing off their richly coloured feathers. I remember Kim Jae-gil's words before he left for Hanyang; how Minister Choi was a good man who served his people well. I glance to where he sits now in his bright silks at the head of the table, his wealth and power on display in all the extravagant dishes and decorations spread before his guests.

When I lay down a bowl for young Master Choi Chan Young I pull a secret face at Officer Lee who sits beside him. It is foolish of course, but I cannot help myself. Lee Yoon is horrified and glares at me fiercely over his own bowl. Yet nothing today can dampen my mood.

For today I have finally heard something that may help us.

The guests eat and drink, and when they have finished

their meals I am sent to collect all the dishes again, piling them on trays and enduring countless trips back and forth to the kitchens until it is done. On my next journey back to the grand hall I see more people arrive at the estate. Women stand in the dark yard outside, their heads covered with high winding braids; bright flowing silks draped across their bodies.

Gisaeng.

I watch them from the balcony until they are gone from sight, drawn into the bright warm lights of the main house like insects to a flame. One of the girls is followed by a manservant who carries a *gayageum* and my eyes are drawn to the smooth carved shape of it, my too-soft finger-tips aching.

Inside the grand hall I quickly lay out the bottles of liquor, hoping to disappear again before the *gisaeng* arrive and the space becomes too crowded to navigate. As I pass Officer Lee I raise my eyebrows at him, tilting my head toward the door. Outside I wait impatiently until he appears.

"What is it?"

"I must speak with you. I heard something important." I glance along the walkway and see the shadows of women arriving. Before he can reply I have ducked away down the hall to avoid the *gisaeng*, their appearance marked by a mass of swishing silk skirts and wide smiles at the grand hall door.

AN HOUR PASSES and still Officer Lee doesn't arrive.

I am in the kitchen, hard at work by the light of a single candle, scrubbing and washing until all the dishes are clean again. Another girl is sent to help but I tell her she can leave if she wants, that I will pretend she stayed if the head cook asks. Despite her curiosity about why I would offer such a precious gift, the girl's night of freedom lures too bright for hesitation. She hugs me tight and disappears into the deep night.

I work alone and wait for Lee Yoon. I know he will check for me here because it is where I always am, where I am every day from dawn until late. But I wait and still he does not come. And soon his lengthening absence begins to fill my belly with tension.

The information I have heard does not make sense to me, not fully, yet I am sure he will know what it means. This place is dangerous, Damjang.

I think we need to leave.

I dry my hands on a cloth, careful of my tender skin, careful not to scrape my fingers worse than they already are from so many hours scrubbing in the cold water. I think of my precious *gayageum* and wonder if the state of my hands will soon mean it is impossible to play. Already the calluses on my fingertips are gone, replaced by new blisters and hard skin in all the wrong places.

Someone approaches outside, heavy panting and feet pounding unevenly across the gravel toward the kitchen. I whirl around as Officer Lee throws himself into the room, clattering through the doors with panic seeping from every movement. He does not stop until he is close, grasping my shoulders. "Seorin. Are you hurt? What has happened?"

Breathless he pushes me stumbling back from the door, away toward the far wall.

"Lee Yoon, what is wrong?"

Throwing a wild glance around the kitchen, Officer Lee searches the deep shadows where the flickering candle cannot reach. "Was someone here? Did someone come looking for you?"

"No." I reach out my hands to calm him, fingers against his chest. "No. I was only waiting for you. I've been here alone waiting for you."

My words seem to break through and finally he meets my gaze. I raise my eyebrows, waiting as his breathing calms. I can almost hear his heartbeat slow, his pulse become steady again beneath my fingertips.

"Good," he breathes. "Good." As if unaware he does it, his fingers reach to softly touch my hair where it has escaped my long plait.

I blink, startled. "Tell me why you're like this, Lee Yoon."

"Someone searched my room." He is calmer now, his body still. Stepping away he sits on one of the benches lining the walls, careful of his damaged knee which doesn't bend so well. "They left a letter and I am certain..."

"A letter? What was written on it?"

"It was a warning. It said I should leave Damjang now if I want to live. It said they would prove to me they were serious, they would *prove* why I should go." He hesitates. "I thought, I was certain it must mean you..."

He does not finish, words trailing away into nothing, yet I understand what he believed.

There is no one else to harm here that belongs to him.

I may only be a lowly servant, but I would be enough to send a message. My body grows cold yet I hold my expression carefully blank, for Officer Lee still watches.

Quietly he says, "Either the prime minister is trying to put pressure on me, hoping I make a mistake, or the spy is trying to scare us away before we find the truth of their identity."

I nod in agreement. Stepping close against his side, I lower my voice. With him sitting, our eyes are closer to level. "Yet I learned something today. It is why I wished to speak with you. Earlier I was with one of the Choi daughter's personal maids..."

"Choi Se-ryeong's maidservant?"

I shrug. No one told me the name of Minister Choi's bratty daughter.

"I suppose so. The point is the maidservant told me her mistress has become engaged to marry the eldest son of the Park household in Hanyang."

Lee Yoon's brows draw together. "Yet ... you have also told me the son of the Park family already holds an understanding with the prime minister's daughter."

"Exactly. It is what I have heard, yet both cannot be true."

He shakes his head. "Minister Choi is on our side, he can't possibly be planning to marry his daughter into the Park family. They're our enemy. They are loyal to the king. Was the maidservant mistaken?"

I pause. "I do not think so. The maidservant said it's meant to be a secret. The young mistress told her by mistake."

Officer Lee frowns, candlelight flickering across his skin. "Then the true question is, if Minister Choi *did* agree to marry his daughter to his enemies, what could he hope to gain from it?"

He bites his lip, lost in thought. "Minister Choi has sworn to us he will oppose the king, yet really I believe he had no choice." He looks up at me. "The king was angry with him. There was no chance for the Choi family to rise under the king's rule. They are rich, yet will gain no further political power under the current king. This is why Minister Choi and his family sided with us. A different king will mean better opportunities for advancement."

Lee Yoon's eyes are blazing now. "If Minister Choi believes he has a chance to redeem his family before the king he may choose to betray us. The promise of an alliance through marriage to one of the most powerful families in the country, the Parks, could tempt him. Minister Choi would have to believe betraying us could really benefit him, otherwise the risk would be too great."

I nod slowly. "Connections mean everything." This I already know.

Officer Lee reaches to adjust the wide brim of his *gat*, pushing it back from his face. There is nervous energy in the way his hands move, betraying his unhappiness at this new possible truth.

I say the words aloud for him. "If Minister Choi's daughter were to marry into the Park family, a family beloved by the king, then Minister Choi would have assurance his own family by extension would be protected once the rebellion is destroyed. Even though he had sided with you at the beginning."

I think again of Kim Jae-gil's words, how he assured me Minister Choi was a good man, a man who cared for the people above all else. I should have known better.

I clear my throat. "You believe Minister Choi is the spy. You believe he is feeding information to the king." I pause as another thought occurs to me. "Then it must have been Minister Choi's men who attacked us on our way here. He attempted to murder you to halt your investigation."

"Yes." Officer Lee rubs a hand over his jaw. "Minister Choi thinks all will be forgiven and forgotten by the current king. He is a fool to believe it."

I crouch in front of him, slow understanding edging into my mind. "Then you don't believe the Park family will really marry their son to Choi Se-ryeong? You think they are lying to trap Minister Choi ... and bring down the rebellion. Hence the second engagement. The true engagement."

Officer Lee doesn't answer for the longest time, until finally he nods. "Yes. Otherwise the Park family would never agree to such a match. Marrying their son to Choi Se-ryeong is not as advantageous politically as joining with the prime minister. There will be no marriage between Choi Se-ryeong and the Park son." His mouth grows tight and he clenches his hands against his knees. "This is why the other match, the true match between the Parks and the prime minister's daughter, was never announced. They will use this deception to destroy our organisation, and then the king will surely destroy Minister Choi as well."

I swallow. "What will you do?"

"I … I do not know. First, I must bring this knowledge back to my father. Immediately. He will decide with the others how to proceed."

I pause, still crouched before him in the darkness. "And what of Choi Se-ryeong, Minister Choi's daughter? What becomes of her?"

I do not much care for the girl. She is rude and spoiled and selfish.

Yet she is also an innocent in this, used like an expendable piece in a game she does not even realise she has joined.

Lee Yoon shakes his head. His words are careful and measured. "I do not know what will happen."

He lies. We both know.

Choi Se-ryeong will suffer along with her family, no matter which side of this struggle for the throne succeeds.

Just another powerless, foolish girl.

Outside a door slams in the distance and both of us jerk at the sudden noise. I listen for a tense moment until the quiet descends again. We are still alone.

"Officer Lee, do you suspect Minister Choi is the one who sent you this warning letter?"

Lee Yoon nods. "I do. He is clearly attempting to scare me away before the truth emerges. In the hall tonight he spoke at length with me, he said he has suspicions about who the traitor may be." He hesitates and then laughs bitterly. "He was trying to implicate someone else. And if you had not learned about this promised marriage alliance, I may even have believed him."

I bite my lip. "This means all that Minister Choi knows of the rebellion, the king must surely know as well, does it not?"

"No, if Minister Choi had already informed them, there would be no need to continue the deception of a false engagement. We would be dead already." Lee Yoon presses his hands over his face and takes a deep breath. "We must return to Hanyang and inform my father and the other leaders. They will decide our next move..."

Voices echo from the darkness beyond the kitchen. We both tense as urgent footsteps approach, boots crunching on gravel outside. Lee Yoon is on his feet, tugging my arm but I pull back.

"It could just be the head cook coming back to check on me."

Yet Lee Yoon has already blown out the flickering candle.

Abruptly we are plunged into thick blackness. Blinded and disorientated, Lee Yoon's hands clutch at my shoulders, pushing, then half-lifting me over a slim door frame, shoving me forward into a narrow storage space, tall shelves rising on either side.

Pressing forward into the black I stumble over rolled mats and large cool earthenware pots, Lee Yoon's body pushing me against the wooden shelves, rocking them precariously. The jars clink together.

Deafening. Horrifyingly loud in the thick silence.

Lunging for the shelves, Officer Lee clutches the rack behind my head to hold it still, steadying it just as the sounds of people entering the kitchen ring out beyond our hidden space. Slivers of light from dim lanterns spill between the shelves and we both draw utterly still, hardly daring to breathe at all.

I listen carefully to the muted voices, wanting to recognise the head cook's low tones or perhaps a maidservant's light laughter. Yet it is a man who speaks and I hear only the sound of Choi Chan Young's voice, the son of Minister Choi, a man who must surely want us dead.

Slowly my vision adjusts to the black, Officer Lee emerging from the darkness above, shadows clinging tight to the sharp lines of his face. His breath ruffles my hair and I mouth silently up at him, *What are they doing?*

Lee Yoon does not answer. I can almost hear his heartbeat, can see the sweat beading on his skin, the veins in his tensed arms holding tightly onto the shelves behind me. Like I do, he surely believes that Choi Chan Young has come here to find me just as the letter warned he would. Wild fear grows like a living thing in my belly. If we are found here by Choi Chan Young we could fight, yet Lee Yoon has no weapon, only a ruined knee. Still, we might survive it. Though even if we did, out here in Damjang, in this isolated mountain range so far from the capital … we would not last long. Not if the most powerful man in the region has decided he wants us dead.

My breathing is too loud, my heartbeat surely echoes through the kitchen outside. Choi Chan Young can hear me, he must know we are hidden here. And yet…

"No one's here, Master Choi."

The voices drift into our hiding place and my eyes jerk back to Officer Lee's. Dim light creeps through the cracks in the wall, a warm glow that illuminates Lee Yoon's face. I think they are searching the kitchen. How can they not find us? How could they not look here?

I hear Choi Chan Young say, "It will not matter. If he has not gone tomorrow then that will be the end of it."

"Master?"

"You know what to do. If he's still here by dark tomorrow. And the servant too. We cannot wait any longer."

Officer Lee shifts abruptly, the wide brim of his *gat* striking a small jar high on the shelves behind him. His eyes widen as it twists, slowly, so very slowly. It tips to the edge of the shelf, clinking lightly as it rolls.

I am quicker than I've ever been, throwing myself forward, straining as high as I can on my toes to halt its motion, fingers just managing to brush the cold jar before it rolls over the edge. My heart slams against my ribs and I freeze.

Did the men outside hear?

They are still talking, their voices a low continuous hum from the kitchen. Officer Lee is still as a carving, his head tilted awkwardly to one side, not daring to move in case his wide *gat* strikes something else. We wait with our eyes locked, unable to breathe.

Did they hear? No one comes.

Ever so slowly I push the little jar upright, slide it back carefully from the ledge so it will not fall again. I hesitate before reaching for the ties beneath Lee Yoon's chin. I am slow and careful as I untie the knots that hold his *gat* in place, my raw fingers brushing against his throat, against the stubble of his beard and the warmth of his skin. His eyes on mine as I pull apart the black ribbon and slowly reach to take the *gat* from his head, careful not to let the wide brim touch anything else. I drop it silently to the floor. Lee Yoon straightens now, watching me in the darkness as I lean past him to peer between the cracks in the wall to the kitchen.

The men are still there but they walk toward the open doorway now, taking the flickering light with them as they file out into the night.

Everything is black. I inch myself away from Officer Lee's body and begin to climb silently, awkwardly, over the pots toward the entrance. The kitchen is empty now, quiet and dark. It takes Officer Lee a few more moments before he climbs out after me. But when he does, he follows silently to the open doorway and through to the yard outside, holding his *gat* in his hand.

The chill mountain air almost knocks the breath from my lungs. I wrap my arms around my body and shiver, turning my back to Lee Yoon who still stands in the doorway.

"We are leaving tomorrow," he says quietly. "Be ready at first light."

I stand unmoving, staring at the rising black mountains beyond the courtyard wall. His footsteps crunch closer, the slight drag of his limp, and then he takes my arm, propelling me away across the yard.

I am startled. "Where are we going?"

"You're going to your room. And you'll stay there with the other maidservants until I come for you in the morning." He stops. "Don't go outside alone, don't go *anywhere* alone."

"And you?"

His mouth tightens. "I'm going to speak with Minister Choi."

"What?" But we are moving again, rounding the corner of the building. The door to my room is closed and it is dark within. I wrench myself away and hiss, "Minister Choi will *kill* you!"

"He won't." Officer Lee's voice is confident. "I'm going to tell him I believe the lies he's spun and now I'm going back to the capital to tell those same lies to my father."

"You can't go. It is dangerous, Lee Yoon. Do you really think he will believe that? Do you expect he'll just send us on our way?"

"I believe that is exactly what he wants. Someone else implicated. If he thinks I will point my finger at someone else I know he'll be happy to send us back."

I shake my head, trying to think of another way to dissuade him. "Then what of the letter?"

"I will admit straight out I received it. And that I suspect the people who sent it are that same family Minister Choi has already indicated as the betrayers. It should allow us enough time."

I am desperate, the road red with my brother's blood filling my mind. "He won't believe you."

"He will." Officer Lee bites his lip, expression turning soft. "This is the only way we'll make it back to the capital alive. I have to try."

I grasp his sleeve. "Don't do this. Let's just go. Now."

Officer Lee shakes his head. "They will follow. And they will kill us. You know this is our only chance." He has already made up his mind and no matter what I say it is clear I cannot change it. He attempts a smile, though it does not reach his eyes. "Go inside, brat."

"Then you promise me." I reach for the front of his robes, staring up at him fiercely. "You promise you will be careful. Don't get hurt, Lee Yoon. Promise me."

There is a moment of silence until Officer Lee lets out his breath, something strange within his eyes. He steps back and waits, and I realise he will stay until I have gone inside my room.

Glancing at him once more, willing him to be safe, I slip inside, leaving my straw sandals on the step.

As soon as the door is shut, I hear him leaving, his boots scraping across the yard as he slowly walks away. I am afraid of what he must do.

21

The Last Stretch of a Journey

Nothing happens overnight, nor the next morning.
No one comes to find me.

At dawn I step outside to see Officer Lee already waiting, standing tall in the courtyard, ready with horses and supplies to take me back to Hanyang. He smiles, small and strained, and some of the thick tension inside my belly unwinds. I begin to believe that Minister Choi truly does not yet know he has been marked as the betrayer, nor that his days are numbered.

Lee Yoon has brought guards from the local magistrate to accompany us back to Hanyang. Without being asked, I walk over to one of the older men wearing the uniform and request to ride with him. There is no cart to carry me on the return journey, our destination must be reached much more urgently than a slow rambling cart could allow, so I must sit with one of the men.

I will not ride with Officer Lee.

The journey is exhausting and uncomfortable. My body aches from the excruciating hours spent on horseback, a method of travel I am not at all grown used to. I spend most of my time swaying in agony behind the older guard I ride with. Often my attention is drawn to Officer Lee at the head of the procession. But I do not talk to him, not when we break for midday, nor when we stop to camp for the night. He stares at me questioningly but I continue to turn away whenever he comes near, always at that moment needing to do something else or be somewhere other than where he is. Officer Lee can say nothing, letting me go with a wounded look shining in his black eyes.

Each day we travel, I feel the distance between us grow, stretching until it is a cavern that cannot be breached. Which is exactly as it should be.

As Hanyang draws closer, the freedom I have experienced out here in the mountains slowly slips between my fingers, any happiness I discovered during these long strange days creeping bit by bit from my body.

For this is the last stretch of my journey. The very last thing I will ever do in my life that will be out of the ordinary.

Soon I will be back in Hanyang, returned to the Pavilion where I will live out the rest of my youth day by day.

And soon Officer Lee will ride away through the busy streets of Hanyang and be gone.

I DREAD the sight of the city gates, yet they loom before our party, all of us dusty and dishevelled from our time on the road. Within the city the roads teem with locals and travellers. Officer Lee is immediately approached by two commoner men. Together they speak in quiet voices, often glancing back at me. Kim Jae-gil must have sent them to collect me, to return me to my rightful place in the Pavilion so the deception of my absence is complete.

Officer Lee glances at me, his mouth tight and angry, until finally he tugs his horse around toward the rest of the party.

Already it is time to go.

Taking a deep breath I slide from the guard's horse onto the dusty road, leaving my escort to join the rest of the magistrate's men. They mill beside the main city gates, laughing amongst themselves as they take in the bustling city sights. Officer Lee and I remain alone, the two commoner men hovering further behind, waiting impatiently for me to join them.

When Lee Yoon slides from his horse, I am blinded by the sun shining directly behind him. I cannot see his face, yet he hands me something, fingers lingering on mine.

A pouch. Money.

"What is this for?" My voice sounds strange to my ears, like the whole world is humming, thick and heavy.

"It is the only thing I can do for you," Lee Yoon answers quietly. "You have done the job of an undercover officer so I want you to have the same reward a real officer would receive."

I do not look at him, just stare at the heavy pouch in my hands.

"Seorin *ssi*." Lee Yoon hesitates. "I still do not know anything about you. I don't know where you live, I do not know why..."

I blink. "I don't want your money." I push the pouch back into his hands. "I don't need anything from you."

He is wounded. "This is not ... charity. It isn't pity. It was not meant like that. Surely you must understand me..." He still smiles despite his faltering words. Not a real smile though. There is darkness there, unhappiness, and something else. I'm drowning in that look, my breath catching in my throat.

I cannot have Lee Yoon look at me like that.

I know what I am.

A *gisaeng*. For the rest of my life that is all I am.

"Kim Jae-gil is already paying me." My words are harsh, sharp. Yet they are the truth. "I have everything I want already, Officer Lee. Take it back. I do not need anything from you."

Lee Yoon recoils as though I have struck him, yet it doesn't matter because it has all ended anyway. It is over and done.

Cut it clean away. Sharp and fast.

Or it will linger.

I walk toward the two men who wait for me.

Without turning back I follow them into the crowded streets.

22

A Boiling River, A Calm Surface

The water's surface is calm and still like a mirror, barely a ripple. Yet I know beneath that smooth reflection a current rages. Deep water. So deep the bottom of the river is nothing but darkness, a void. The trees whisper and sway in the chill breeze. Branches hang over cold water, their trailing leaves breaking the surface as the river swells and fades away, the current boiling beneath a deceptively calm surface like a secret.

"Jang Seorin."

I swing to face the owner of the voice, slapping tears from my eyes. "*Nauri* … I … What brings you here?"

I bow low to Kim Jae-gil, startled by his presence. It has been days since my return to the Pavilion, and yet here he is. I return his open smile with a strained one.

"Are you well, Seorin *ssi?*"

For the longest time I cannot answer. "Of … of course I am fine, *Nauri*. And you, are you well? Is it my sister? Do you have news of her?"

He shakes his head apologetically. "Not yet."

I try to smile again, yet a swell of disappointment

clutches my heart. Blinking, I clear my throat. "Have you spoken to Officer Lee since our return?"

"I have. He met with us the same night you arrived back into Hanyang. He informed us about Minister Choi. A pity."

"Then ... no one suspected him at all?"

Jae-gil pushes loose hair from his brow. "I did not, no." He sighs. "You and Lee Yoon have protected our entire movement through your actions in Damjang. I wish I had not needed to ask something so dangerous of you, though." He inclines his head to me, almost bowing. "Thank you for your bravery."

Flustered, I stumble over my words. "There is nothing to thank me for. We have an arrangement and you will repay me with something precious." I smooth my wide skirts to hide my discomfort. I am dressed like myself again, like a *gisaeng*, with hair pulled tight and plaits wound around my head, powder and rouge carefully in place.

"*Nauri*," I ask carefully. "What will be done about Minister Choi?"

"We are still deciding. The leaders will find a way to use him. They find a way to use everyone. For the moment though, we will leave him be."

I am flushed with confusion. "How can you ... he knows of Officer Lee's involvement in this conspiracy. What if he relays what he knows to the king?"

Kim Jae-gil's eyes widen marginally and he looks at me strangely. "Minister Choi knows *many* of the families involved in our organisation, and we have no reason to think he has been telling Minister Park all of it. Not yet anyway. It seems he is withholding information to ensure he remains useful to them. He is no fool after all."

Gathering my emotions, I calm my face. A *gisaeng's*

mask, like the surface of a river. "How can you be so sure he has not already given you away?"

Kim Jae-gil shifts, moving closer through the long wavering grass, yellow and dry from the chill air. When he speaks it is in hushed tones, as if imparting a secret. "The reason I followed you to Damjang was because we received information that the prime minister is trying to expose Lee Yoon's father as a traitor." He pauses. "The mere fact that the prime minister has not just arrested the whole Lee family immediately tells me he has no evidence. It shows that Minister Choi has not yet revealed our names to the king, for Minister Choi's testimony alone would be proof enough to execute every last one of us. And yet we still stand."

I bite my lip. "How will you ensure Minister Choi remains quiet?"

"He will die. Very soon."

I look down at my hands and then back out over the river. "I see. It will all be handled soon."

"Of course it will." Kim Jae-gil flashes a wide smile, confident and certain of himself and his position. "You needn't worry. Your part in this is done. You do not need to think of it anymore. We will soon depose the king and all his madness will disappear with him. Things will become better." Kim Jae-gil walks onto the riverbank to stand at my side, the water swirling past our feet.

"And … my sister?"

"Of course we will find her. Soon. As I promised."

I want so very badly to believe him.

Kim Jae-gil smiles, breathing deep. "It is very peaceful here. These days I do not have time for reflection in places like this, though before the rebellion I enjoyed it very much. Do you walk beside the river often?" He has closed his eyes, drinking in the wind and the sounds of the water.

"Yes. Sometimes."

For a moment it rests on the tip of my tongue, the terrible thing that has happened, the sorrow blooming in my heart, yet in the end I do not speak. I hang my head instead. "It seems different now though than it used to. It feels colder."

Kim Jae-gil smiles. "It is only because winter has almost come."

I nod but still I cannot stop staring at the water. He leans across and lightly touches my shoulder. Startled, I turn back to him.

"Seorin *ssi* … are you certain there is nothing wrong?"

"I am, yes. I'm sorry," I pause. "It is being back at the Pavilion again. I was gone for so long I almost thought … I only need to settle in again." I stumble across my words.

Kim Jae-gil leans closer, morning light reaching through the branches to dance dappled patterns across his broad shoulders.

"Perhaps when all this is done, things could be different for you," he says quietly. "Perhaps you need not continue living here, apart from your sister. With a new king, perhaps you may be released, exonerated from the crimes they say your family has committed."

His words cast spells, I feel them settling across my skin.

Forcing myself to break away, I move until I'm facing the river again, peering into its depths. "I must go back inside. I shouldn't be away so long. They will wonder where I am." Unconsciously I touch the dark jade rose pin within my hair, running my fingers softly across the cold hard surface.

"I understand." Kim Jae-gil steps back, almost wistful. "I do not know when I'll next be able to visit. Things will begin changing soon. But I *will* come back, with news of your sister. I will."

I nod because I want to believe. Yet already doubt has crept inside my heart.

How is Kim Jae-gil different from my brother and father?

All his plans could fail.

And who will save my sister then? There will be no one left.

"*Nauri*," I whisper. "Then I will choose to trust your word. I will wait for your return."

My words clearly please him, an easy smile dancing across his features.

Bowing low without another word, I quickly step away along the woods' path toward the Pavilion. I do not look back.

INSIDE THE PAVILION it is quiet.

None of the girls are laughing or talking, and behind closed doors muffled sobs sound from the rooms I pass. I glide down the hallway in silence and enter the banquet hall to find the headmistress and her bodyguard with the vicious eyes standing by the open window, waiting for me. She doesn't turn around though he does, staring with dark cold eyes. A chill creeps inside my heart. He frightens me.

"What you did to Chungjo is unacceptable," she says.

I lower my head in submission. "I understand, Headmistress. It will not happen again."

"I know why you did it, Seorin, but that is not the way things are done here. You should know that by now. You should have brought your concerns to me."

"Yes, Headmistress."

"You know it was not Chungjo's fault."

I clench my fists tightly but nod in agreement as I am expected to.

"Wol-hyeong was unable to adjust to this place." The older woman turns to face me finally, her elegant beauty not dimmed by age. "She refused to accept her changed circumstances. You and I both know better than that, Seorin. As does Chungjo."

She raises her brows at me and then softly sighs. "I will not force you to apologise to Chungjo for I expect you will refuse me. However, you are to keep away from her from now on, at least until her face is healed and she is able to work again."

"Yes, Headmistress." My voice is less submissive than I mean it to be, and the headmistress clearly catches my tone. Her eyes narrow.

"You are no fool, Seorin, which is why I am so surprised at you. Surely you can see that Chungjo will succeed me one day? What will you do then? She will not keep you around when that time comes."

I glance at my feet. I do not care what happens. I know how Chungjo treated Wol-hyeong. I know her cruel japes and manipulations ground Wol-hyeong down. I should have protected her. I am sick with guilt that I left her alone.

I left her in this place and went to Damjang to save my sister, and what has come of it?

Nothing.

Anger boils beneath my skin.

Chungjo deserved it.

I do not care what the headmistress says. And I do not care if Chungjo's nose heals crooked. I hope it does. She destroyed a young girl and shows no regret at all. I hate her. I will *always* hate her.

Yet my face is calm and empty of emotion. I bow my

head low to the headmistress and tell her I understand my place. It will never happen again. I stare at her bodyguard with my chin raised, as if he doesn't scare me.

I have become such an expert liar.

There is one last thing I must do before I melt back into my old life, before I give up on the spark ignited during my time away from the Pavilion.

Before my lies become my reality.

In the early morning I escape the enclosure, dressed one last time as the brave carefree commoner Jang Seorin. I wander through the market streets as stalls open in the blue light of dawn. Merchants shiver from the mid-autumn cold as they lay out their wares and call to each other.

Crossing the main square I tell myself I am just walking, even as my feet take me to a large stone complex with high impenetrable walls. The police bureau. I do not know what I will do there and argue with myself that I should leave. Yet there is a part of me that must finish this, expel the dreams that have been building inside.

He arrives on his horse, riding slowly down the street with head held high and back straight as an arrow, blue uniform perfectly in place. I stand watching from across the street, hidden beneath the shade of a sprawling oak tree. As he dismounts, a guard stumbles sleepily to take his horse and they speak together in low voices before Lee Yoon limps inside the station complex.

When I am sure he is gone I venture closer to the guard who still struggles to control the horse.

"Excuse me. Please, can you give this to Officer Lee? I saw him arrive."

The man peers down at the small wrapped package, blinking. "*Agassi*, shall I go fetch him? You can give it to him yourself."

I wave my hands in protest. "No! No, please just give him this, I wouldn't want to bother him."

"And who shall I say it is from?" He yawns, softly patting the horse's neck, which now stands quietly beside him.

"Jang Seorin."

I bow and thank the man for his help, retreating across the street to stand once again behind the wide rough trunk of the oak tree, my heart beating fast.

I do not know what I am doing.

Minutes pass and I am about to leave, except Officer Lee comes tearing outside onto the street. Ducking behind the wide tree I remain out of sight, spying as he glances wildly around at all the people walking by, searching their faces. In his hands is my small package, still unopened, clutched between fingers gone white and bloodless.

He doesn't find what he is searching for.

Standing still at the bureau gateway, Lee Yoon seems locked in place, eyes blankly fixed on the road ahead. Finally, his attention turns to the small cloth package in his hands. Slowly he unwraps it.

A jade rose pin. Carved in dark green.

It will mean nothing to him.

Such a small thing, not expensive or special, but it meant something to Wol-hyeong and something to me when I gave it to her, that vivid feeling of family that erupted inside when she smiled in pleasure at this small gift.

I have nothing else of meaning to give him.

Officer Lee stands alone in the street, staring at the pin in his hand. Finally, he rubs his jaw and slowly turns to limp back inside.

I cry as I walk back to the Pavilion. This is the last time I will wear commoner clothes and it is the last time I will ever seek out Lee Yoon. I know what my destiny is, I know everything the future has in store for me. I accept it and am ready.

If my sister is alive then I will live too.

It will be enough, even if she and I cannot be together. Half my promise to my mother fulfilled, the best I can do.

Wol-hyeong is dead. I am told she went walking by herself along the woods' path and did not return. The next day her body was found downstream, tangled in reeds and floating face down in the water.

Drowned.

She left no note behind, so the girls around me continue to gossip. Was it a man from her past, loath to share her with others? Or did her father murder her from shame of what he'd done, selling her here for money?

I know the truth.

The small jade pin was on my table.

It was left there for me when I returned, especially placed so I would notice it, the jade rose cold and hard. Waiting for me.

I tried to help Wol-hyeong, yet I did not do enough. I failed her.

I will not fail my sister.

TIME PASSES AND NOTHING CHANGES.

Chungjo's nose heals crooked and she glares at me spitefully whenever I am unfortunate enough to cross her path. The headmistress negotiates with the minister of defence over me. She tells me he is a patient man and a busy one, but one day when he is ready he will want me and he will come. Jan-sil is the same as always, cheerful and smiling, a ray of sunshine in a dreary world. And I sit every day for hours in silence on the patio, staring at the gardens and practising my *gayageum*.

Months creep by and Kim Jae-gil does not return.

I hear no news and receive no visitors. My life is within the Pavilion's walls.

That is all there is.

23

At the End of Winter

O utside the world begins to change. Yet inside the Pavilion it is as if time has frozen still.

Bare branches reach into clear blue skies and an icy wind flows from the snow-covered mountains into the Pavilion gardens, leaving clouds of white mist clinging to my breath. We go about our daily business in the same way we always have. And during the long bitter winter we are told everyday by the headmistress to be glad of the roof over our heads and the food in our bellies, luxuries not everyone can afford. I keep my eyes down and do nothing that might displease the headmistress, working hard at practising my instrument and avoiding Chungjo.

I never walk the woods' path anymore. I never go to the river.

The winter has been long and hard, and lately we hear rumours filter through from the city outside. Stories of starving commoners and a sickness that creeps through the poorest areas of the capital. Peasants from the countryside amass beyond the city gates, trying to find relief and food within the city limits. Yet as more desperate people arrive, the streets beyond our enclosure become ever more dangerous. Everyone can feel it, an undercurrent of tension simmers within the city, threatening to boil over and erupt.

It seems the city's influential *yangban* families fare just as badly as the poor. Within the halls of the Pavilion we hear dark tidings in the conversations of our noble patrons too, tales of a king so desperate to eradicate untrustworthy nobles from within his court, that no family is safe.

Minister Choi dies in the early weeks of winter.

A peaceful death in his bed is the official word but there are whispers of murder beneath everyone's breath. Not even one month later, we hear the king has declared the deceased minister a traitor to the crown and his remaining family is cast down, the children stripped of their titles and sent into exile.

Kim Jae-gil told me his people would move fast to destroy their betrayer and it seems he was true to his word, for I am sure it is the rebels who poisoned Minister Choi. It is a quiet death, too quiet for the king to be responsible.

Soon it is as if the Choi's never existed, their estates gifted to the rich and loyal Park family for their essential role in bringing out the truth, the Choi's household staff and servants disbanded or resold. I hear that the noble son, Choi Chan Young is executed and his sister, Choi Se-ryeong, is sent far away into exile. My heart aches but I say nothing.

I hear from patrons at the Pavilion that other noble families follow in the same way, marked as traitors and executed as such. I do not recognise their names so can never be sure if they really were conspirators or just victims of a mad king's paranoia.

One name though, I do recognise.

The former nobleman Kim Jae-gil is marked as a

traitor to the king and a leader of a conspiracy against him. A warrant is issued for his arrest. Yet when the military raid his lavish sprawling home he is nowhere to be found.

I hear rumours he has fled north out of Joseon. I do not believe it. I think of the passion for change that blazes within Kim Jae-gil's eyes and imagine I know exactly where he is, huddled in his snowy camp within the mountains.

Plotting his next move.

IT IS on a day like any other that I first begin to hear whispers of the king closing in on the conspirators.

Despite the weather, we sit in an open pavilion overlooking the sparse lily pond of the garden, unlit lanterns hanging from the brightly painted wooden beams above. The lamps move erratically in the cool crisp wind. The sky remains clear and the snowy mountain summits are just visible behind the *gisaeng* house, a sight which has been often shrouded in thick mist and cloud.

I am playing *gayageum* for three young men from the military. They are not as highly ranked as court officials but are still the sons of middling noble families and so must be respected nonetheless. They sit with three of our girls who pour clear liquid drinks, smiling in silence as the men speak openly about the state of the world. My fingers dance across the *gayageum* strings, listening with interest to their lips loosened by liquor.

"It is a complete waste of time," one man mutters, his hair slipping from beneath his black *manggeon* as an alcoholic blush colours his cheeks.

"What else can we do? If they want to start from the beginning, then let them."

"It is not a waste of time!" the third man fires up. "How else is the king going to find the traitors?" He lowers his voice. "I heard their organisation extends right through all official offices in court. Besides, it's been months now and none of the investigators are any closer to finding the people behind it. They have spies within our ranks who sabotage the evidence!"

"But reopening closed cases? It is too much. None of us have time for that."

The second man shrugs and downs another cup, smiling at the young *gisaeng* who gave it to him. "I don't know. It might help to reinvestigate. The superiors might find something they missed the first time. And then we can get this whole thing over with. Until the conspirators are captured we will have no peace."

The other two men agree with that at least, all raising their cups before their conversation turns to less interesting matters.

I am filled with unease that the rebellion has become such common knowledge within the city, something to be discussed casually with friends over drinks. It must mean the king is livid at his inability to find and destroy the people involved. Surely, he is fearful of becoming a laughingstock in the streets. And if he is as mad as I am told, he will not stand for it, even if he must tear the whole of Hanyang apart to accomplish his goal.

I shudder, suddenly thinking of my brother and his terrible humiliating death, only in my mind now it is Officer Lee's face I see, it is him dragged through the streets, his blood spilled across the dirt.

My fingers miss a note and my music falters.

"My apologies," I say, as the three military men stare at me. "I will begin again."

WHEN THE CHANGE COMES, it is so sudden I am left with no time to react. Men dressed in police bureau uniform pour into the Pavilion in the late afternoon, just as the yellow sun slants over the rooftops and shadows lengthen across the yard.

Girls scream as clothing and bedrolls are thrown into the crowded hallways. We are rounded up and pushed through the Pavilion to the banquet hall. Uniformed guards are everywhere, shouting at stragglers to quicken their pace and soon we are all pressed together in the hall, some of the girls flushed with fury and others in tears. The headmistress strides into the room flanked by her body-guard, her face white and bloodless. "What is the meaning of this?"

Police guards step forward as if to hold her back, but one older officer waves his hand and they stand still again. This new officer is short with small hard eyes and a beard of coarse black hair. He turns to face us where we have gathered huddled together at the back of the hall.

"I only want to question the *gisaeng*. All the other serving women may leave," he announces. It is clear from his tone he expects to be obeyed.

The servants turn toward the headmistress and she nods stiffly. One by one they slip from the room, relieved to be as far from the policemen as possible. Those of us still left watch the officer expectantly, waiting for his next move. He strides back and forth, peering intently at our faces but remaining silent.

Finally, the headmistress clears her throat. "*Nauri,*

please can you explain what we have done to deserve such treatment? Your men have destroyed our rooms and manhandled my girls. What is the meaning of this?"

The officer doesn't turn, ignoring the headmistress, a move so disrespectful that Jan-sil gasps. I press my fingers tight against my friend's wrist in case she does anything foolish, for I am well aware of how lowly we are to government officials like this man. No matter how respected she is within these walls, the headmistress is still only a retired *gisaeng*. She is nothing.

"Last year there was a police raid on this *gisaeng* house." The officer's sudden booming voice effectively halts all whispering from the girls. "Tell me, who was not working here at that time?"

Slowly two of the newer girls lift their arms nervously and with a flick of the officer's wrist they are both escorted from the banquet hall. As I watch them leave, I press my hand against my chest to try and calm myself, my fingers gripping the soft gauze of my *jeogori*.

I remember the police raid last year.

I have not forgotten who they searched for.

The officer continues to speak loudly, commanding attention. "Last year a man was followed into this compound. He was a traitor and a conspirator against the king. Yet when he entered this establishment he somehow managed to escape, even though he was badly wounded. And even though this *gisaeng* house was filled with guards."

He stops speaking, his mouth pulled tight. "Explain to me how that could have happened?"

No one says a word. Girls shuffle their feet nervously, the sound of silk skirts loud in the deep silence.

"I believe that man had help." He pauses again. "There are two guards who swear they saw a man with a *gisaeng* that night, alone in a dark room. Though when

179

checking through the statements made by serving staff, there were only two large parties here that evening and both were accounted for in the search."

"What are you saying?" The headmistress's voice is sharp.

The officer finally deigns to look at her, thin lips stretched tight in undisguised disgust. "I am saying that whoever that woman was, whoever helped that traitor escape, I am going to find her." He turns back to us. "I am saying she is among you."

The headmistress gasps. "*Nauri*, surely you cannot believe this? What evidence do you have? This happened so long ago, surely—"

"Shut that woman up!" The officer explodes, waving his hand at the headmistress. Immediately one of the guards steps forward and backhands her face, the older woman falling heavily to the floor. When she next raises her head, her lips are painted red with blood.

I am shoved backwards in a press of bodies as the girls at the front of our group cower, some already sobbing. The headmistress's bodyguard surges forward, hands dragging at his lacquered sword, metal sliding against wood. Immediately all the police guards follow suit, until the headmistress breaks the tension by lifting one hand. She shakes her head slightly at her bodyguard, forcing him to back down, though his chest heaves and his vicious eyes flash with fury.

"I want you all to think very carefully about that night and tell me the truth." The older police officer begins to pace back and forth, my heart beating in time with his steps.

"I know she is among you. I will not leave until you give her up. Does anyone have anything to say?"

I am startled to see Jan-sil slowly raise her hand. I shake my head but she forges on anyway, ignoring me.

"*Nauri*. There was another girl here at that time. But she ... she died. Perhaps she was the one you are looking for?"

The officer nods at her and guards push into our small huddle and drag Jan-sil to the front as she screams in fright. "*Nauri*..." Shock is written across her features. Across the room the headmistress's bodyguard bristles, hands returning to his sword.

"Who was this girl you speak of?" The officer is not moved by the *gisaeng's* fear.

"Just ... just a new girl. She was ... she was new last year."

"And now she is dead?"

Jan-sil nods, stiff with terror. "Yes, *Nauri*. She ... she drowned herself before the winter."

A long silence draws out before the officer finally clears his throat. "Do you think you can fool me by blaming a dead *gisaeng*?" His voice is cold and brittle, but the fury within is palpable, filling the entire room as if he has shouted.

Jan-sil throws herself to her knees before him, head bowed pitifully low and tears streaming down her face. "No, *Nauri*, of course not! I would never! Please!"

"Perhaps you were pushing blame onto others because the one who helped the traitor was you?"

Jan-sil begins to cry harder and I cannot bear it any longer. Across the room the headmistress's bodyguard has drawn his sword though she attempts to call him back, a swell of police guards slowly circling him.

"*Nauri*!" I step forward. "Jan-sil was in the banquet hall for a celebration that night. There were many of us here. It could not have been her."

Silence descends and I hang my head, knowing full well I have now drawn attention to myself. It will be my turn for interrogation now.

Sure enough, the officer strides closer. He is shorter even than me, yet fear still trickles down my spine, my hands clasping my silk skirts to stop them visibly shaking. This small man has the weight of Joseon's entire military behind him, the weight of our king. He is to be feared.

"You were also in the Banquet hall that night, *gisaeng*?"

"I was … I … yes, *Nauri*."

"And how is it you remember so clearly when the others seem to have so much trouble recalling?"

"*Nauri*, I remember because guards interrupted us in the hall." I stay as still as I can and do not raise my head, eyes to the floor.

"And you did not leave the room at all yourself?"

I pretend to think for a moment and then answer firmly. "No, *Nauri*. I do not believe so."

"Liar!" Chungjo pushes her way out from behind two other girls and sneers at me. "You're lying. I saw you leave!"

The officer is silent, all his attention now on Chungjo and myself.

"Her *gayageum* string broke." Chungjo's spite is evident in the words she spits, in the smile that curves her lips. "I remember because the music stopped. And then she left the room!"

"And how long was she gone?"

Chungjo lifts her head triumphantly. "Long enough, *Nauri*." She smiles at me and hatred shines within her big black eyes.

"She is correct, *Nauri*. I remember now." I am calm, standing collected and still. "I replaced my string and then returned to the hall. It was many months ago, my memory has betrayed me." I bow low in apology. "Please forgive this mistake."

The officer smiles coldly. "You contradict yourself, *gisaeng*."

He turns to the other girls, voice booming once more. "Who else was witness to this *gisaeng* leaving the hall? How long was she gone?"

Not one girl answers him, all staring at their feet. Until Chungjo steps forward once more to point at me.

"It was *her*, *Nauri*. I am sure of it! There was blood on her clothes when she returned to the banquet hall. And last year she disappeared for a whole day along the woods' path!" Chungjo laughs derisively. "She told us she was lost! She's a liar and I know she's involved in it. Jang Seorin is the traitor!"

The officer motions to his guards and two of them converge on me.

Just like that.

Backing away, I can no longer hide my fear. "*Nauri*, no! It was simply a broken string! The blood was from my finger. Chungjo hates me, she wants me gone! Please *Nauri*, you must believe me!"

He does not.

I am hauled from the others, shouting and struggling until my belly is struck so hard I fold over and nearly hit the ground. The world spins violently and another sharp blow slams my face, the taste of blood filling my mouth. The world burns black for an instant and when I refocus my face is close to the floor. I sag uselessly between the guards, all breath gone from my body. The ground begins to move, my feet scraping. I cannot believe it has happened like this, I cannot believe it. The long slow winter, the emptiness and the boredom, ruptured so abruptly in this burst of pain and blood. It is too fast.

I am not ready for it.

I catch glimpses of the headmistress's pale bloodstained face, her hand on her bodyguard's chest to hold him still. Jan-sil's tear-streaked cheeks. Then the banquet hall is gone, brilliant sunshine in the garden, feet crunching across the gravel pathways.

Outside on the street people gape and whisper as one of the policemen ties my arms against my body with thick coarse rope, my fingers turning numb and head pounding. I spit blood, wet across my lips and chin, gaze rolling to the sky. It is so very difficult to focus. Black mixing with the bright blue, fringing the edges of my vision.

They walk me forward, holding me upright whenever I stumble, the guards' iron grip keeping my body from the stony road. Lifted, I am slung over a horse, head down, blood rushing. Sharp memories flood my mind. This has happened before. Dragged through my hometown in shame. My mother beside me and my sister, too small to understand. The black in my vision swells closer and I squeeze my eyes shut, wet trickling across my skin. Tears? Or blood mixed with sweat. I do not know, yet I am blinded all the same.

By the time I am pulled from the horse my feet are numb, my hair dishevelled and tugging sharply on my scalp. Up stone steps and through a looming gateway, familiar. My mind runs too thick to place it, still blinking from the mess the guards have made of my face, the ache of my jaw where I was struck. The courtyard beyond the gate is teeming with people, voices shouting and my feet scraping over gravel. The bottom of my once elegant *chima* skirt is now stained thick with dirt. Finally, I gain my footing and glance up; a vast compound, official buildings and uniformed policemen everywhere.

He stands ahead in the middle of the yard, black eyes

on me, mouth open as if he might call my name. Yet it dies on his lips.

Both guards keep walking when my legs stop moving, hauling and dragging. One of them swears though I barely hear his words. When I twist around Officer Lee still stares, face a blank shocked mask, black eyes wide. Then I am pulled inside the darkness of a building and do not see him anymore.

24

Misery

Than cell is cold.

A single chair of thick uneven wood is placed upon damp mouldy hay. They shove me toward it and tie my body tight with thick red rope. This is when the fear should set in. I know what happens within these walls. Interrogation and torture, unbearable pain to elicit a confession, effective whether the prisoner is guilty or not.

Except I am not afraid. Not yet.

Instead my mind is filled with his dark eyes. Soon he will know the truth of me, he will know I am a liar. My body shudders uncontrollably.

The other officer, the older one with the hard expression who took me from the Pavilion, leaves me alone with two guards, men I do not know and have not seen before. They must have been at the Pavilion too, for they talk among themselves as they secure me to the chair, laughing about the chaos they caused and the way their cold-eyed officer treated our headmistress. Their vile words snap me from my stupor and hate burns inside me. It sears through the numbness until I am alive again, my heart slamming against my chest as the terror swells.

I am alone with them for a long time before I hear other footsteps coming closer through the prison. No matter what these men do or threaten I still have not yet spoken. I will not. I understand my situation and am no fool. If I confess the truth my life is done, forfeit. Yet I also know these men are only lowly guards and the real interrogation has not yet begun.

The last rays of dim sunlight filter through high windows, just slits near the cell's roof. Dirty hay lies strewn across the cold hard ground, damp with filth and mould. Through the gloom beyond the cell I see a tall police officer approach with uneven gait. It is only after he has bent to climb through the small open doorway that I realise it is Officer Lee, wearing his blue uniform. I cannot bear to face him and turn my head quickly down to the filthy floor, looking anywhere else except at him.

Officer Lee's voice is low and hard. Unrecognisable. "Get out." He is standing right in front of me but all I do is stare at his feet. Blue robes and scuffed black boots. The guards don't move and suddenly he explodes. "Get out! Get out *now*!"

Startled, they scurry through the small opening and away through the prison gloom, disappearing beyond the other empty holding cells. Lee Yoon and I are left alone and still I cannot meet his gaze. I stretch my fingers behind my back, test the tight thick rope that binds my hands, thinking hard about the pain of my broken lip and face. I do not look up.

"I spoke to the guards." Lee Yoon's voice is trembling, hoarse.

I say nothing.

"You are a *gisaeng*. You lied to me."

I let out my breath in a rush. I had not realised I was holding it.

"You do not deny it?"

"No." My mouth hurts where the guards hit me. "I am what you see."

"And Kim Jae-gil? He knows what you are? He knows the truth?"

I nod again and Officer Lee sucks in a sharp breath. "Then you both lied to me." His voice is strangled and thick. "Why did Kim Jae-gil send you to Damjang?"

I do not know what to say, daring to search his face. I don't know why he asks me that.

"Tell me!" His fury blooms hot in the tiny cell, reaching into everything. He steps back, almost a stagger and I see even after all this time he still heavily favours his left leg.

"I did lie." I finally whisper the words. "I am a *gisaeng*. But you already know why I was sent to Damjang."

"Tell me again."

My eyes meet his in disbelief. "I was ordered to help you find the spy, to help you find Minister Choi!"

His turns his back on me. "I don't believe you."

A wall of tears claws my throat. My voice rises. "You don't believe me? Lee Yoon! Why do you not believe me? It is the truth. "

"Kim Jae-gil sent you to spy on me."

I am taken aback. "He never … how can…"

"He said he would not hesitate to inform on me if I went too far." Lee Yoon's voice drops dangerously low. "He told me he will protect the organisation at any cost."

Slowly I begin to understand his words. "Then you … you told him you were having doubts?"

Officer Lee's jaw tightens. "I did. Long before you and I left for Damjang. I told him. You often asked me questions while we were away, did you not? There was so much about me you wished to know."

Silence, growing heavier by the moment. And then images, the two of us beside the river, me asking why he was involved in the organisation. That moment in Damjang when I pressed him to tell me his worries. I shake my head, thick with dread. "Yoon, surely you cannot believe that I…"

"Do not call me that!"

I flinch.

"You are a *gisaeng*, are you not?"

I swallow, my throat dry. "I am, yes … *Nauri*."

The dirty hay rustles at his feet. "Tell me how you became involved with Kim Jae-gil, *gisaeng*."

"I did not spy on you."

"*Tell* me!"

I breathe deeply, steadying my voice. "He came wounded to the Pavilion one night. I helped hide him."

"Why?"

"I … I do not know. I just did." I peer down at my feet, at my ruined slippers. "I have a sister. Kim Jae-gil said he would find her for me. That is why I agreed to go to Damjang."

"And has he found her for you?"

"Not yet…"

"*Gisaeng*, you have been played for a fool." His voice is different now, softer.

I stare at him. "What do you mean?"

There is pity in Officer Lee's black eyes, infinitely more terrifying than the fury from before. "Kim Jae-gil may seem like a great leader, *gisaeng*, but he has no real authority. He cannot make promises to you. He answers to other men first."

"I do not ... I do not understand. You're saying he will not find my sister?"

"I am sure he will try," Lee Yoon tells me flatly. "Yet the leaders of our organisation give nothing away for free. I doubt they'll have finished with you yet. You'll have debts to pay first before they ever let you see your sister."

"No, that cannot be." I can't breathe, choking on the thick air of the musty cell, the dirty hay and the damp walls. "No ... Kim Jae-gil *told* me ... and I already fulfilled my end of the arrangement in Damjang, I did exactly what I was told."

"To watch me and report back?"

"No!" Frustration rages through my body like fire. "You're not listening! I did not spy for him. Yet believe me, Yoon, I *would* have if he'd asked it of me. In return for my sister's life, I would have done anything!" My voice breaks and I twist feverishly at my bindings, rope scraping at the flesh on my wrists. Furious tears slide down my cheeks until finally I give up my useless bid for freedom and collapse exhausted against my chair.

Lee Yoon has moved to the far cell wall, his forehead pressed against hard stone and hands across his face. I watch him carefully, still breathing heavily from my struggle. He does not move and silence fills the cell, cold and empty like we are strangers.

Finally, I take a deep shaking breath. "Will you leave me here?"

Lee Yoon stands straight. "No. I will get you out." His body is stiff, veins rising like cords against his throat and hands clenched bloodless at his sides. "It will take time. Can you endure it?"

I lift my chin high. "I've endured much worse."

Officer Lee stares. "Have you?"

I falter at his tone, yet his expression shifts once more,

turning blank and cold. "Do not change your story for anything, *gisaeng*. You've helped no one, done nothing wrong. Give me the rest of the night, I'll be back before they come to question you in the morning."

Then he ducks from the cell, striding away along the prison corridor without once turning back. He is gone and I am alone.

They do not wait until morning.

AS SOON AS night falls the officer who arrested me returns with two other guards. The ropes come off and for a single moment I can clench and unclench my hands to bring the blood into my numb fingers. I fight weakly as I'm hauled to my feet. My hands are tied once more, this time to a beam on the roof. My feet barely reach the dirty floor, toes scraping hay. The rough rope tears my skin until blood trickles from my wrists. The officer shouts question after question, demanding I confess. I clench my teeth and say nothing.

The beatings begin when the officer grows tired of my silence. The guards take a stick and though at first I make no noise at all, soon I must scream out. My cries echo within the tiny cell. I tell the men over and over that all I did was replace my *gayageum* string before returning to the banquet hall. It is all I say, no matter what they do or what they threaten.

Later when I have lost all grasp of time, the officer clutches my tear-streaked face between calloused fingers and leans in close. His breath is hot against my cheek, hissing unspeakable horror into my ear, the things he will do to my body if I do not confess. I listen, eyes rolling to the roof which hangs heavy with shadow, until his hand strikes my jaw and I taste fresh blood, seeping from cracked lips.

"Answer me, *gisaeng*! Confess your crimes."

I spit blood but say nothing.

I have seen everything before. There is nothing he can do that will make me change my words.

Afterwards there are no more questions, only the thump of the stick swinging against my body. Bruises flower across my skin and my mouth opens wide with biting screams. On and on until I am gone into darkness.

I OPEN my eyes to candlelight.

Someone is untying me. Lowered to the damp cold floor, my body limp like a child's cloth doll. Hands linger on my face, warm against my cold skin. The world is blurred in shadow.

My name.

I think I hear my name. Someone gently brushes damp hair from my cheek and then the warmth is gone away.

Everything is dark and disjointed. Dim light flickers across dirty hay, across my bloody hands. I try to bend my fingers but they will not move.

Breathing heavily with the effort, I manage to turn my head. Blurry outlines of men, someone shouting. I cannot see their faces and the world turns dark.

MOONLIGHT. The sharp smell of blood.

Straw jabs my skin and a window far above seeps pale blue light.

I wonder if I am dead.

This is a different cell, somewhere else. I attempt to roll but my hands are tied and my feet will not move. The moonlight is so bright it hurts my head, a pounding so strong it reaches deep within my spine until every bone in my body screams for relief. I would do anything to stem this agony. Yet it is all there is.

LATER I WAKE to a figure crouched in the dirt outside the wooden bars, his head in his hands.

"Yoon." I breathe his name and his head jerks up, black eyes burning like stars in the darkness. He moves his mouth but my head hums too hard to understand. Too much noise. My lids grow heavy.

I do not fight as I descend into darkness and lose myself to the black nothingness. It is safe. The pain is gone.

WHEN I FINALLY TRULY WAKE, I lie on a soft bedroll at the Pavilion. The headmistress and Jan-sil both hover nearby and speak in hushed voices. I can barely move, my body heavy with pain, blinking back tears. A sharp breeze blows from between open patio doors, bringing the scent of bare winter gardens. The headmistress sees me stirring and glides over to kneel by my side.

"You are safe now, Seorin," she says without emotion. "Rest."

I lift my hands. My wrists have been wrapped where the rope tore at my skin, my body cleansed of prison filth and dressed in fresh white sleeping clothes.

"Headmistress … how is it I am … free?" My voice rasps.

Jan-sil crouches by my side and presses a wet cloth to my forehead, her face drawn and white. "They brought you back unconscious in a cart yesterday morning, *Unni*. A police officer told us there'd been a mistake and they know now it wasn't you. He said he was sorry. But you wouldn't wake up." Her eyes are red-rimmed from tears.

The headmistress leans close. "The officer said another witness came forward after hearing you were taken in. Some peasant from one of the houses near the woods' path. It seems he saw the fugitive leave the Pavilion through the back gate long before the guards ever arrived to search the complex. But no one had ever asked him."

Jan-sil's face crumples. "I think they are so cruel, they should..."

The headmistress stands abruptly, cutting off Jan-sil's words. She addresses us both sharply. "No matter what we do we are only lowly *gisaeng*. Do not expect justice in this world, Jang Seorin. Simply be grateful you have lived to see another dawn." Her eyes are hard. "Rest and recover. Then forget this ever happened."

She sweeps from the room and Jan-sil climbs up to close the door, her voice low and trembling. "How can she say that? How can she be so calm?"

I close my eyes. "What else can she do? We are what we are. There is no use pretending anything different."

Jan-sil begins to cry. "I know, *Unni*. But it isn't fair." She takes my hand and softly massages life back into my stiff fingers. I try to concentrate on her touch, but I cannot.

"The man who brought me back," I whisper. "What did he look like?"

Jan-sil wipes her tears, sniffling like a small child. "He was very tall." She bites her lips as she tries to remember. "He was handsome with a straight nose and clean-shaven face. There was something wrong with his leg, I think. He limped when he walked. He looked like a noble, yet he was upset, so perhaps he wasn't. I don't know." She shrugs. "That is all I remember. When I saw how hurt you were, I couldn't think of anything else."

I lift my hand to cover my face, a sob escaping. My body shakes and Jan-sil leans close to wrap me in her arms.

"Please don't cry. Everything will be all right. I promise it will. Please don't cry."

But I cannot stop.

25

A Reunion, Bitter

I clutch the note in my hands and walk swiftly along the woods' path toward the river. I have not been here in months and new growth emerges on the bare winter branches overhead. Weeks have passed since I was released from the prison cell and my bruises have slowly faded, yet the thick tension within my heart remains.

One of the serving girls handed me the letter at breakfast. It says nothing except the meeting time and place. I wonder if it could be him, though our last conversation echoes through my head and I tell myself it won't be. I lied to Lee Yoon and he no longer trusts in me. There will be no further reason for us to meet.

I come to the place where the path touches the riverbank and a man is there, standing with his back to me. Beside him a restless horse is waiting.

"*Nauri*?" My voice is tinged with disappointment for already I can see it is not Lee Yoon. This man wears his hair loose, a tie holding it at the back of his head. I am taken aback by how changed he is, face thin, body worn.

"Thank you for coming, Seorin *ssi*." No easy smiles

touch Kim Jae-gil's face today. "I had my people watch the Pavilion for days but you never come outside."

He does not step closer, standing stiffly instead across the clearing. I remember the last time we were here, how we stood close together beside the riverbank, speaking of possibilities and of creating the world anew.

I have not thought of it in months.

"I don't go further than the garden," I reply. "The streets are dangerous these days."

"That is true. Hanyang is changing, and..." He pauses. "You were recovering." He looks at me and waits, but I do not know what to say.

Only when the silence grows too heavy does he break it. "I am so sorry I did not come sooner, Seorin *ssi*." I notice he has black bruising blossoming across his cheekbone, dark against his pale skin. "I heard you were arrested because of me, yet word didn't reach my ears until you were already released." Still he comes no closer. "It is no excuse, yet things lately have been ... difficult."

I nod, reaching for the right words to cover the awkwardness growing between us. "You have had much to do in the past months, *Nauri*. I hear the rumours of changes within the capital. You are making your move."

"Yes. We are making our move." His voice is small and he peers only at the ground.

Lee Yoon's words echo in my mind, growing louder and louder. I do not want to believe he is right. Heart pounding against my ribs, I ask, "Do you have news of my sister?"

Kim Jae-gil says nothing and I begin to wonder if he has heard my question at all.

"*Nauri?*"

"I need you to come with me."

"Now?" I shake my head. "I cannot ... There are

already *gisaeng* who wish to see me fall within the Pavilion. I cannot let anyone notice me disappear again. It is dangerous for me."

Still he will not look at me, hands holding tight to the reigns of his restless horse. "Forgive me, Seorin *ssi*. I must bring you now. There is no choice."

I blink. "What do you mean?"

"Please."

I am startled. He is begging me. Why? This strong bold man is now a stranger filled with guilt.

"*Nauri*, has something happened?" My blood runs cold. "Has something happened to my sister?"

"No. This is something else. But you must come with me."

I am so afraid that Lee Yoon will be right, that Kim Jae-gil can do nothing to help despite his promises. The question coils on my tongue but I am too frightened to ask. Yet if I turn back now, if I cut my ties with him, I will never know, never discover what became of her. After going through so much, can I truly back down now?

I cannot.

Taking a deep breath, I nod. "I will come with you if that is what you need from me."

Relief floods Kim Jae-gil's face. "Thank you."

Immediately without pause he swings into his saddle and motions for my hand. I hesitate only a moment before complying. Soon I am seated behind as he pushes the horse into the mountains. We are in a desperate hurry it seems.

We ride in silence a long time before I hear Kim Jae-gil's voice again, quiet in the empty forest. "Did they hurt you when they questioned you in prison?"

I hesitate before choosing my words carefully. "Not badly. I was there only one night."

Kim Jae-gil laughs, the sound filled with bitterness. "You lie to protect me. Lee Yoon told me what they did to you." He lifts a hand to touch the bruises that swell across his cheekbone.

I am silent behind him on the horse, only one hand clutching the back of his robe to keep from falling. Lee Yoon has been speaking of me. I am flushed with confusion, still wounded by his suspicion, yet also wishing Kim Jae-gil would tell me more. He does not.

"I wanted to be the one to save you," he says instead. "Yet my hands are tied in ways I cannot explain to you. My priorities cannot be what I want them to be." He pauses. "Do you remember what I said the last time we met? Do you remember?"

Standing beside the river, spun dreams of gold, a future for my sister.

A promise.

"It can still be real," he says without waiting for my answer. "But I have made oaths that must be kept. My role in what is coming is more important to the good of this country than my own heart is. I cannot be the man I want to be. Some things are more important."

I remain silent, unable to concentrate on his words, on what he is trying to tell me in such a convoluted way. I want to ask about Officer Lee, how he is, *where* he is, yet part of me shies away from knowing. He will not wish to see me.

The mountain camp is much as it was when I last visited, though melting snow has churned the ground to muddy sludge. Kim Jae-gil helps me from the horse and I glimpse something strange flit across his face, a nervous twitch in the way he holds his mouth that I do not understand. I am filled with a deep sense of unease.

Night has truly fallen by the time he leads me through

the buildings toward the largest tent. Light pours from the open doorway and the voices of men sound inside. I glance at Kim Jae-gil but he will not meet my gaze. Instead he guides me inside, pointing to an empty chair placed along-side a vast table. The men seated there all turn as one as I step nervously toward them, their eyes following me across the room.

A man at the head of the table clears his throat and I glance over to see a *yangban* lord I cannot recognise. He is dressed in richly embroidered robes, not old and yet no longer young. A hard frown twists his face. He inspects me up and down as blood pounds inside my ears.

"Is this the *gisaeng*?"

Kim Jae-gil bows to the man and nods affirmation before taking a seat at the other end of the table, far away from me. I lock eyes with the man to his right and my heart stops beating.

Officer Lee sits there with his face empty.

Immediately I drop my gaze.

"I am told you are a *gisaeng* from the Pavilion. Is that correct?" The lord's voice is booming loud and commanding of respect. The other men at the table clearly take their cue from him, a true leader of the movement. Fear uncurls within my belly, yet I am so distracted by Lee Yoon's presence that my mind moves in circles.

"Oh ho! You were asked a question!" I startle as the other man yells at me, quickly bowing my head to the great lord who still awaits my reply.

"Yes, *Nauri*. I am from the Pavilion."

The man nods his approval. "Good. The minister of defence has taken great interest in you of late, I hear."

I do not look at Officer Lee, I cannot bear him to hear such a thing.

My cheeks burn with shame yet I know I must answer. "*Nauri*, I have ... also heard so from the headmistress."

The men around the table begin talking all at once and I am left frozen in the middle, my head bowed so low all I see are my hands folded within my lap. The great lord must make a gesture, for suddenly there is silence once more.

"*Gisaeng*, your sister has been located."

I stop breathing, sharply meeting his eyes. "My sister, *Nauri*?"

"She is being moved to a safe place where she will not be harmed."

My fingers clench within my lap. "Can ... can I see her?"

"There is something we need you to do first." The lord stands and walks around the table toward me. "If you wish to see her you will do this task for us and do it well. Do you understand?"

I cannot help but glance at Lee Yoon.

He was right.

Kim Jae-gil beside him is still focused on his hands. I force my attention back to the lord, vying for time. "*Nauri* ... is ... is my sister well?"

The man waves his hand dismissively and I understand he has no interest in me or my sister beyond this. We are nothing but a means to an end. I glance back again at Kim Jae-gil, hoping to get my answer from him, but he still purposely looks elsewhere.

"Minister Park is a powerful enemy of ours." The lord's face is grim. "He has thrown his clan's full weight behind my uncle. Yet I believe we can change that using you. He cannot suspect you have ties with us and so already he trusts you."

I stare at him as he returns to his seat at the head of the table.

Minister Park? This lord's uncle?

I do not understand what is being said. I try to think of a reply, anything, for they all watch me expectantly.

"How could a lowly *gisaeng* such as myself make a difference, my lord?"

The man nods his approval and I know I have said the right thing.

"There will be a banquet at the minister of defence's household. It is to celebrate his son's engagement with the daughter of the prime minister. Many courtiers will be present, including many of us you see here at this table. It will be suggested to Minister Park that he provides entertainment from the Pavilion for this event, and I am sure he will particularly invite you on this occasion. We understand that despite his interest he has still not yet personally visited you?"

I clench my fingers so tight they turn white.

Minister Park is the minister of defence, how could I not have known this? I have met the man many times at vast banquets, poured him drinks, known his title but not his family name. And never cared to find out.

But surely the only man Minister Park has thrown his support behind is the king himself. Does that mean this great lord in front of me is the king's nephew?

Dread floods my chest. I am being tasked by the nephew of the king. He is trying to use me to usurp his uncle's throne. I close my eyes as the full weight hits me. Finally, I understand the words Kim Jae-gil spoke as we travelled here. He has chosen the good of his cause over me. He is guilty because he will not protect me from this even after he promised I had no further part to play.

Sweat beads my forehead. The nephew of the king is a

powerful man ... can I refuse him this and walk away alive? Could I protect my sister if I did?

The lord has still been speaking yet I have lost myself in panic and missed his words, until suddenly I am drawn back into the conversation.

"...and when you are alone with him after the banquet, do what is necessary and afterwards take the drug. We will do the rest."

I look up at him. "What?"

"Oh ho!" yells that other *yangban* lord, the one who is small and red. "Such disrespect! Remember whom you speak with if you don't want to be flogged, ignorant slave!"

A cup smashes into tiny fragments across the table, contents spilling onto the floor. Everyone turns to the source of the disturbance.

Officer Lee's chair crashes backwards onto the ground as he stands. Turning without a word he leaves the tent, smashing his fist into the canvas door. The tent flap swings violently long after he has gone.

After a few moments of utter silence one older man hisses, "Fool!" He stands and bows respectfully to the nephew of the king. "Forgive my hot-headed son, my lord. He is foolish and young and does not understand what is at stake. I will talk with him."

"Indeed you must. Yet right now you are needed here." The nephew of the king is impatient, waving his hand. "Sit."

I stare at Lee Yoon's father as he complies.

Officer Lee does not return.

Clearly unconcerned by the interruption, the king's nephew turns to me. "*Gisaeng*. Once Minister Park's defences are lowered and he cannot hurriedly leave the room, that is when you must take the drug." He leans forward and pushes a small vial of clear liquid across the table toward me.

"*Nauri* ... what is this drug?" I pick up the vial with shaking hands. "What will it do to me?"

"It will give you the appearance of death. Slow your heartbeat and pulse until Minister Park truly believes you are dead."

My eyes widen. "Why would I do that?"

The other red lord interrupts again. "We do not need to explain our plans to a lowly slave! Be content with what we've told you and do your job. If you do not there's no telling what will happen to your sister. Do you understand my words?"

I hate this man with every fibre of my being, nearly as much as I hate Kim Jae-gil for bringing me here. Nearly as much as I hate myself for trusting any of them. I peer at my hands and grit my teeth, silent.

Kim Jae-gil clears his throat softly. "It is only natural for the *gisaeng* to ask, Lord Im." He still will not look at me as he explains. "We plan to force Minister Park to side with us. We do not want him dead. Please understand we are not using you as an instrument for murder."

I stare at my hands. "Yet you *are* using me."

Lord Im's face flushes dark but the king's nephew raises his hand to cut the man off. "This is all we are asking of you, *gisaeng*," he says. "Take the vial and after you have entertained the minister make sure to drink every drop before you sleep. That is all."

I do not speak for a long time. "What will happen to Minister Park?"

Officer Lee's father answers. "We will convince him to reconsider his support of the king."

"And me. What will happen to me?"

The lords all glance at one another and then the king's

nephew finally speaks. "As far as everyone at the banquet knows, you will be dead. But later, after an inquest is mounted into your death you will wake up here in this camp, alive and well."

"I won't go back to the Pavilion?"

"No. For this plan to succeed they must also believe you are dead."

"What will happen afterwards, when I wake up?"

"You will be reunited with your sister, far from the capital. You will never return here again."

Reunited? Hope beats once more in my heart, though when Lord Im rises to his feet and scowls at me I am reminded I cannot trust these men. I have already been a fool once.

"Enough questions! We don't have time for this. You'll do what we ask or you won't see your sister again. That is all you need to know."

They are lying about locating my sister.

I am certain of it.

They will use me and discard me. Perhaps the drug is truly a poison that will kill me? But no, even now I am still certain Kim Jae-gil would not go that far. He won't protect me, but surely he would not knowingly hurt me. Yet it is not enough, anger flares within my chest.

I clench my hands as Lord Im walks to the king's nephew and whispers in his ear, eventually bowing low as he leaves the tent. Officer Lee's father does the same and one by one they all trail outside. Soon I am left sitting alone at the table with only Kim Jae-gil and the little vial of liquid.

I stare at him. I feel bold, braver now the other men are gone. "*Nauri*, if I drink this and it makes me appear dead, tell me what will happen afterwards."

He drops his head into his hands. "Seorin *ssi*, forgive me. I wanted to protect you from this but I could not."

I repeat myself in a low shaking voice. "*Tell me* what will happen."

He slumps. "We have secured the invitation of a senior investigative officer, one of our own men, at the banquet. Once the alarm has been raised regarding your … death, he will be called in to investigate. He will threaten to expose Lord Park as a murderer. He will use your apparent death to blackmail the minister into signing an agreement. Once we have the minister's seal, he can no longer move against us for fear we show it to the king."

I gape at him. "Why would Minister Park ever sign such a thing?"

"He will be forced to. It has happened before, one of his *gisaeng* dying. There was no proof at the time but the rumours persisted anyway. He cannot afford for it to happen again. Either he admits to murder and is ruined or he signs the paper and in return our officer clears the evidence."

"The evidence?"

Kim Jae-gil hangs his head. "You." He pauses and then adds quickly, "You must understand, we cannot succeed without Minister Park. We do not have enough men, enough support. Yet with the minister of defence on our side we can openly challenge the king! We can move against him!" He stops speaking abruptly, perhaps realising now how little I care. "Forgive me, Seorin *ssi*."

I stand, collecting the vial and hiding it deep within my robes. "I do not need your pity. Take me back home." I walk outside without waiting to hear his reply, leaving him to wallow in his guilt.

Beyond the tent, the air is cold and sharp, stars above stretching across the entire night sky. I keep walking fast toward the outskirts of the tiny village, heading in the direction of the mountain track, only because I cannot stay still. The dark trees spread across the road as I come to the last building, a storage shed with thick solid walls. I stop and lean against it, my palms spread flat on the cool hardened mud. I take deep breaths, slowing my heartbeat.

"*Gisaeng.*"

The voice startles me, yet I turn slowly for I know who it belongs to.

"*Nauri,*" I say formally, bowing low.

"Did you agree to it?" Officer Lee walks forward, close enough that I must force myself not to back away. "Did you tell them you would do it?" His black eyes are dark with anger.

I snap back at him, "That was not a situation where I was given a choice! I did not hear *you* standing up to the nephew of a king!"

He laughs and I don't like the harsh sound of it, ringing into the darkness. "In the marketplace you wouldn't offer a simple apology to a *yangban* if you didn't think he deserved it! You were ready to be flogged rather than back down. Yet now you hang your head and agree to anything they say!"

"This is different," I hiss furiously. "And you know it. This time I cannot think only of myself!"

Officer Lee steps closer and again I try to move away, except now my back is against the wall of the storage shed and I have nowhere else to go.

"You will do this then? You would ... you ... with the minister?" His voice chokes off and I am so mortified at his careless words that without thinking I reach to slap him. He stops my hand long before it nears his face. We stand frozen, his fingers firm around my wrist.

My voice shakes with hurt. "They have my *sister*. Lee

Yoon, you are just like the rest of them, you do not even stop to think of her. You don't *listen* to me. You pretend to be moral yet you use a little girl so shamelessly!" My voice rises as I attempt to wrench my arm from his grip. Yet he holds me still, his fingers like a vice. I stop struggling and hiss, "I do not care about any of you. I do not care about your foolish rebellion. You think you are trying to save commoners? You are *lying* to each other! None of you care for anything but yourselves!" I am so angry I want to hit him. I think I try. "Should I be ashamed of what I am? Should I be humiliated by you because of what I must do?"

I jerk away but still he won't let go. I hardly know what I'm doing anymore, furious tears clawing at my throat. Officer Lee is close, I do not know how it has happened, he leans against me, black eyes filled with darkness.

"Do not do it then," he breathes. "I can find a different way, I will help you..."

I shake my head. "That man is the king's nephew. Do you truly believe my sister will live if I refuse him?"

"I do not want you to do it, brat." He is so close now I feel his breath on my cheek, his hand curled against my back. Silence draws out between us. His eyes flick to my mouth as he leans closer, close enough that for a moment I think he will...

Abruptly he pulls back, stepping away onto the track, face falling into shadow.

Heavy embarrassment prickles across my skin, flushing my face hot as my breath turns sharp and fast. I hang my head, unable to look at him. I was mistaken. I was a fool to think…

There is only the sound of the mountain wind, rushing through the valley. I smooth my skirts, my hair, reaching up to touch my warm face.

"I do not care what you want, Officer Lee. I will save my sister. I do not care about the rest of it." I take a deep breath. "I do not care."

I walk away into the trees without a backward glance and Officer Lee lets me go, standing alone on the road in the darkness. I do not wait for Kim Jae-gil either. They can send someone else to take me back, I am done with the both of them.

26

A Quiet Place, in Darkness

The Pavilion banquet hall is decorated with coloured lanterns, flickering lights glowing in the darkness. Everywhere embroidered cushions are spread across the floor. *Yangban* men and beautiful girls swathed in bright silks dance, swaying drunkenly to the music my fingers pluck from the *gayageum* strings.

One of the older men trips on his own robes and nearly crashes into me, the smell of alcohol on his breath powerful. Chungjo comes to steady the man, purposely swishing her skirts in my face, hoping I make a foolish mistake in my playing. I glare at her, bitterness invading my heart. Although her nose has healed slightly crooked it has not at all slowed her down. She is still considered the most highly desired *gisaeng* in the Pavilion. I suspect she always will be.

I am busy watching her when Jan-sil collapses beside me in a flurry of blue silk. She whispers breathlessly in my ear. "Did you hear? The minister of defence is organising a banquet at his estate!" She giggles. "He has invited us to go of course, and you will play there for us!" She grasps my arm. "I've never been to a rich minister's house before."

"Go away, *Unni*," I say without looking up. "You'll make me miss a note and then no one will invite me anywhere."

She laughs and stands to rejoin the long low table, with its bright delicacies, ceramic cups, and small porcelain bottles of alcohol. Decadence beyond measure. The men sitting nearby speak loudly and I absently listen as my practised fingers move across the strings of my instrument. One man is a court official judging from his uniform and I suspect the other to be a lowly military officer, though I do not recognise his ranking.

"A terrible business." The official is clearly drunk, his words louder than they should be. "I could not believe it at first."

"How did it happen, *Yeonggam?*" The military officer looks curious. "Was it believed to be natural?"

The older man nods. "That is the official word, but I do not believe it. Lately noblemen have been dropping like flies. Dark days these are and men like us with something to lose should watch our necks."

"Yes, *Yeonggam*. Wise words."

"Indeed." The official lowers his voice, though maybe not quite as much as he thinks he has, considering the copious amounts of alcohol consumed. "The palace is in an uproar. The king is losing his grip on the courtiers and I am sure more families join the conspirators every day. Especially after what happened this morning."

"*Yeonggam*, was Lord Lee one of them? Was he truly involved with the conspirators?"

"Oh ho, fool! Watch your tongue!" The old official peers around to see if anyone has heard but does not even glance at me. Neither man feels the need to curb their tongues before me. Which is their mistake.

"Lord Lee had great influence," the official finally says. "Yet he was not a part of the king's inner council. He had no real power. If he was one of the conspirators he kept it very quiet indeed."

The younger military officer nods, touching his face as if deep in thought. He has been careful with his questions, but it is clear he relishes the gossip and hangs on every word. He pushes his luck with his next question, which is impertinent, yet the official is drunk enough that he doesn't notice or doesn't care.

"*Yeonggam*, how exactly did Lord Lee die? I heard he was ... murdered."

"Rumours! Filthy rumours!" The old official lifts his cup for one of the other girls to fill and then downs it in one gulp. "His son found him in his room mid-morning. Nothing to indicate a murder of course, all perfectly natural. At least that is what everyone wants us to believe."

I concentrate once more on my *gayageum* strings, banishing their conversation from my mind as the two men begin speaking in hushed voices about the refugees that swamp the city. Another nobleman's death. The news these days is always dark. And soon it will be darker still if the king's nephew succeeds in winning Minister Park's loyalty, a prize that comes with an extensive private army. I do not doubt that with more men at his disposal, the king's nephew will not hesitate to strike his uncle. War will erupt on the city streets.

Abruptly the banquet hall grows hushed, enough that I glance from my playing to the open doorway. A servant ushers in a new patron, a tall man whose head is bowed low. He is dressed in dark *hanbok* robes and a wide-brimmed black *gat*.

My fingers stumble and the music falters, though no one seems to notice.

Lee Yoon.

He looks unfocused and pale, his expression strained. He glances around the room until his eyes rest on me. There is no further movement.

"Officer Lee!" The old drunk official staggers to his feet, breaking the thick atmosphere. "We were just speaking about your ... uh ... we were talking..." The official's slurred voice breaks off and there is silence in the room. He swings his arms in a flurry of robes and wine to gesture hopefully that Officer Lee should join them at the table.

"Come, come Officer Lee, drink with us and forget your sorrows ... You!" The official points to Chungjo. "Go bring Officer Lee here and pour him some wine!"

"No!" I do not even realise I am standing until everyone is staring at me. My precious *gayageum* clatters loudly to the wooden floor, forgotten in my haste.

I walk quickly to Officer Lee's side with my head lowered, refusing to acknowledge the other girls. I do not care what they think. Drawing Lee Yoon to sit at the low table beside the blustering official, I pour him a small cup. Our fingers brush as I hand him the clear liquor. He downs it in one shot, dark eyes on me. I pour him another, dread spreading throughout my body.

What was the name of the latest nobleman to die?

Was it not Lord Lee, who was found by his son?

A deep ache stirs in my chest. It had not occurred to me, there are so very many Lee families in the city of Hanyang and yet ... I study Lee Yoon's face. He is impassive, saying nothing and simply ignoring the chatter around him.

Finally the drunk official gives up on his attempts to

draw the younger officer into conversation. The room grows loud once more, buoyed by whispers and gossip, hands drawn to cover faces as patrons peer at Lee Yoon from across the table. I draw closer to his side, leaning into his shoulder as I pass him another drink. I press my mouth to his ear for privacy and whisper, "Is what they say true? Was it … your father?"

He does not turn, gaze locked on the still full cup gripped tight between bloodless fingers. His hands shake.

Then it is true. Lee Yoon's father is dead.

Reaching for his face I gently pull him to my level, moving his chin until his mouth rests beside my ear, hidden from the others in the room by my wound hair and lowered head. It does not matter that he says nothing, I smile slowly and nod anyway. Taking his hands I carefully draw him to his feet, aware the room watches us with interest. I am not sure he understands what I am trying to do, but I cannot leave Lee Yoon here in this room like some specimen to be stared at. Wrapping one of his heavy arms across my shoulders I smile up at him and begin to draw him away. I do not look back.

Perhaps Chungjo will run to tattle to the headmistress that I am not where I'm meant to be. More likely though she will be grateful she sits beside the most powerful lord within the banquet hall while I attend the grief-stricken and limping son of a potential traitor. I cannot seem to care what she thinks.

Lee Yoon says nothing as the banquet hall doors close behind us and I guide him gently along the corridor. Flickering lanterns dance across the floor and all I can think is that Lee Yoon's father is dead. The drunk official said that Lord Lee's son was the one who found the body. I wrap my arm around Officer Lee's waist as we pass two giggling girls who follow behind a well-dressed merchant. Keeping my head low, I ignore them as I carefully walk Lee Yoon deeper into the compound, through the entertaining rooms toward the darker wing of the sprawling house. It is quieter here, emptier, and with one last glance around I slide open the doors to a small room and pull him inside, closing them behind us.

It is dark now, almost too dark to see. Officer Lee stands motionless in the tiny space, his back to me and body stiff. Dim laughter echoes through the Pavilion walls, though within the room the only sound is my breath.

Slowly I walk around him, moving until I am standing in front.

"Yoon *ssi*..."

I break off. His eyes are closed. I do not know why he has chosen to come to the Pavilion instead of sharing his grief with his sisters and mother. I do not know what he wants. Tentatively I reach my fingers to lightly touch his chest, curling my hand around the folds in his *hanbok*, too afraid to touch him properly.

A sob erupts from his body, a hand pressed to his face as he attempts to suppress it. And fails. Slowly he sinks to the floor.

"Yoon..."

I crouch beside him as he rips the *gat* from his head, almost tearing the ties in a bout of sudden anger. The *gat* slams violently against the wall before resting still on the floor, crumpled and abandoned. Lee Yoon's face is streaked with tears.

I want to touch him, want to press my hands to those tears. "Yoon—"

"You gave me a jade pin." His voice is low and thick. "Carved like a rose."

My hands slowly return to my lap, heart beating fast. "Yoon ... I ..."

Silence. Black eyes glittering. No movement. Waiting.

I nod, unable to look away. "Yes. I did."

The quiet draws the words from my lips, stumbling and uncertain. "It was not mine, the pin. There was a girl here, a sweet girl, but she did not survive it. When I … when I returned here after Damjang she was already … gone." I take deep breaths, blood beating faster as unhealed wounds open anew. I failed Wol-hyeong so utterly, so very badly.

"Gone?"

His voice startles me back to the room, back to the darkness, to Lee Yoon crouched before me on the floor. I clear my throat.

"Yes. I'd … I gave the pin to her because she reminded me of my sister. Yet she gave it back."

Lee Yoon's steady gaze does not change. "Why did you give it to me, Seorin?"

"It doesn't matter."

"It does."

I falter. "I wanted..." I do not know how to explain. "It was all over."

For a moment he looks almost angry, his breath expelled all at once. "What does that mean?"

"It was over … and I wanted you to remember me."

Silence.

Something flickers across his face.

"Are you all right?" I whisper but there is no response. We crouch in the darkness together and I listen as his breathing slows.

After a time, I stand to open the sliding doors to the empty garden. Dim moonlight shines into the tiny room, the air chill as it touches my skin. The silence stretches and I take deep breaths of fresh air, steadying my mind as I linger beside the doors.

"Seorin ... I ..." Lee Yoon watches me, gesturing with his head. "Please come. Sit. Please."

I hesitate only a moment before settling on the floor across from him, a safe distance. Already I have revealed so much of myself in this meeting. He is too vulnerable and I give too much. Carefully I steel myself as Lee Yoon leans close.

"The things I said to you, in the prison and at the camp ... I am truly sorry."

I hesitate, unbalanced once more as hurt re-emerges within my chest. "I did not spy on you, Lee Yoon."

"I know. I believe you."

Such simple words. Yet the curling smile falls from my face at his next ones.

"It was Kim Jae-gil himself who told me that you did. That is why I doubted."

"I don't ... why would he say such a thing?"

Lee Yoon presses his hand to his jaw. "We were ... close once. When we were younger. We grew up side by side, though his status is high above mine. Even now he is so certain he does what is right. He cannot bear to see me stray from this path. Kim Jae-gil lost everything to this movement: his status, his name, his home and wealth. And yet I tell him I am not sure I believe in our goal. He is afraid, and he will do all he can to force the pieces back where they belong." He looks at me pointedly, black eyes shining in the moonlight. "You. And me."

I shake my head. "It is not his place to do so."

Lee Yoon glances at his hands. "Lately he has changed much. I have known him my whole life, yet lately ... sometimes I no longer recognise him."

"I pity him, then."

"Pity?"

"Everything has moved so far beyond his control."

Drawing my knees against my chest, I wrap my arm around them, smoothing my tightly wound hair. "I saw it with my brother. He changed much before he died."

"Your brother?"

I smile at him. "I was not always a *gisaeng*. No one has told you?"

He barely moves, only the slightest shake of his head.

"My father was the former vice premier."

I leave it at that, knowing he will have heard the story.

And I am right.

"*Jang* Seorin. Vice Premier *Jang*." His mouth tightens. "Your whole family—"

"They are gone. Yet my sister is not." I hesitate. "Three years ago they sold us. By now, she would be eight years old. But I do not know where she is."

Lee Yoon flushes, voice thick and eyes to the floor. "Brat, forgive me, I … I did not know …"

I watch him yet am unable to answer, and silence beats between us for long moments until Lee Yoon finally lifts his head. What I see in his face frightens me.

"Jang Seorin *ssi*. The king is no madman. I met him today. He called for me when he heard about my father. He was … upset to hear of his death. He really did not know … he still does not know my father was trying to kill him."

His voice breaks and he takes a deep shaking breath. "I do not know what difference it makes anymore. This king or his nephew, they are all the same. Nothing will change. It is only power and politics." He peers at me through the dim light. "I had thought my father was different. I thought he was better than that."

Heart beating hard, I choose my words carefully. "Perhaps he was."

Officer Lee smiles at me. "Perhaps." He turns to the black night gardens.

"Yoon *ssi*, your father. I am so sorry."

His face darkens. "He was killed. The prime minister did it, I know it."

I flinch. "How can you be so certain?"

"I know he suspected my father, put pressure on him to turn and spy for the king, in the same way that Minister Choi did. Yet my father was no fool, whatever else he was. He knew what would happen if he admitted his involvement."

"You think the prime minister ordered his assassination?"

"I know he did." Lee Yoon's eyes burn. "He visited our house yesterday, but no matter how hard he pushed he got nowhere. He must have grown tired of the game." He glances at me. "Poison."

I take a deep breath to calm myself.

"Your father was a good man." I hope it is true, will it to be true. "He would have wanted you to stay strong, to take care of your family in his place. He would have wanted you to keep your sisters safe."

Officer Lee's expression turns fierce. "No. My father would have wanted me to avenge him."

I glance at his fingers clutching tight to his robes, my heart beating fast. "Yoon *ssi*? Does the prime minister have children?"

Officer Lee's expression is strange, as if suddenly unbalanced. "He does. Two daughters."

"You are lucky then. He has no sons to avenge him. There will only be daughters left to grieve."

"How can … How can you say that to me? Why would you? You make everything more difficult than it needs to be!"

"It is the truth. I am not pleading for his life, I'm simply saying you should think about what it means to kill a man first. You said it yourself. Nothing ever changes, it is only a circle with no end."

"And yet you will risk your life to ensure the minister of defence joins our ranks!"

"To save my sister, yes!"

"I will find another way to get Minister Park on our side. And then I will find your sister myself. You don't need to do this."

"You know I cannot go against these men! I have no expectations of you, Lee Yoon. I will save my sister. That is all."

"That is all?" His voice turns strange and choked, leaving me staring down at the floor, furious at him for expecting so much. No one is deserving of my trust. I have learned that many times over.

The dark within the room thickens, the low hanging moon momentarily clouded within the sky. Shadows deepen and gloom extends, creeping between us.

"Yoon *ssi*," I whisper finally. "Why did you come here?"

It is too dark to see his expression as he answers, "Do you want me to leave?"

I shake my head immediately, the word drawn from my lips before I can even think deeply on it. "No."

It seems as if he will say more at this, his chest heaving and his body leaning closer, but this time I cut him off. My voice is firm. "It is late. You can stay here. But you must rest." I stand to retrieve a bedroll, spreading it carefully across the floor. Outside, clouds in the night sky lift and moonlight seeps in once more.

He does not move.

I gently nudge him. "Lie down. It is late and you should rest. Please, lie down."

I guide him onto the bedroll and he complies, stretching out across the blankets, too big, half his body left on the polished floor. His eyes are open, locked unblinking on the dark night outside. I watch his shoulders rise and fall in rhythmic patterns, echoing his breathing. Finally, he closes his eyes.

For the longest time I think he is asleep. Yet as my fingers reach to touch his face I am startled by his voice. I snatch my hand back as if burned.

"Thank you, brat," he breathes. "For letting me stay here."

I don't answer and so Officer Lee rolls to face me, unhappiness etched in the tight lines of his mouth. Exhaustion clings to the sharp angles of his cheeks, skin bleached of colour.

Finally, I nod, acknowledging his words. My mind is filled with pictures of that morning long ago in the village beside the river, of Lee Yoon waiting for me in the sunshine outside the doctor's house. That very first time he smiled at me, eyes crinkling and dimple digging deep within his cheek.

In the darkness now, his eyes are closed tight again, nightmares burning beneath lids, face only bones and sharp lines. The world draws inwards and Lee Yoon no longer has time to smile.

Long moments pass, and when his breathing has turned rhythmic and slow, I reach to touch his hair, pushing stray strands from his forehead and tracing his eyebrows with my fingertips.

Part of me wishes he would wake but he does not.

In the morning he is gone.

27

The Banquet

The archway leading into Minister Park's courtyard is enormous, elaborate wood carvings reaching high into the dusky sky. As our group shuffles beneath the structure, Jan-sil reaches for my hand. Her voice is uncharacteristically hushed.

"Are you nervous, Seorin? Chungjo told me about the rumours she heard … about the minister. What he did to that girl…"

I shake my head, a frozen smile firmly locked in place. "You know everything Chungjo says is a lie. Don't believe her."

The headmistress is not with us tonight, so our group is accompanied by the minister's own manservants, sent to escort us safely to the grand estate well in advance of the banquet. One of the men carries my *gayageum* in his arms, wrapped in cloth to protect the smooth paulownia wood body. I glance at my instrument. Will this be the very last time my fingers touch those strings? Will I truly wake within the rebel camp and be given a new life beside my sister?

Or is this the night I die?

My heart beats hard against my chest. I believe the clear liquid drug burning inside my robes will not kill me when I drink it, simply because Officer Lee would have told me if the betrayal ran that deep. Even after all that has happened I realise I still trust in him. It is too deeply rooted now to change.

The rest of his organisation though, I have no such faith in.

Our party enters the vast manicured courtyard of Minister Park's household. Servants scurry back and forth across the gravel pathways, busy with preparations for the engagement celebration. Chungjo walks ahead, placed carefully at the head of our colourful procession. Every now and then she glances back to me, yet I am careful to avoid her gaze. If I see the smugness shining there I will be unable to hold myself back. I know what she is thinking; the first time a rich lord has personally requested me instead of her and he turns out to be dangerous, a man surrounded by terrible rumours.

Minister Park has killed a *gisaeng* before.

Everyone knows it, though it has been buried deep, no evidence left at all. Despite that, rumours still hum through the city streets, much harder to extinguish. Chungjo's red lips curl when she catches my eye. She is laughing at me.

My feet falter on the crunching gravel and I must force myself to step forward onto the wide stone stairs leading to the main house. I am unwell, sweat beading across my forehead, blood beating in my throat. No matter how I try to hide my emotions, I am truly frightened. Not of Minister Park hurting me, but of what I must do. With every step, the small vial tucked deep within my dress seems to throb, burning into my skin.

Tonight will be my last night. Or it will be a new beginning.

Either way, my world has come to an end.

Servants with slicked hair usher our group along a dimly lit corridor to an open terrace at the very back of the house. Cool night air fills the open structure and a light wind rustles against my hair. Already the large space is humming with laughter and conversation, men lounging at ease before long low tables, cheeks not yet quite flushed, the night still early.

Dusk descends as the other *gisaeng* settle beside the guests, smiles and laughter ringing into the night. I sit away from the main party, preparing my *gayageum* alone in a corner. The terrace has been built over a small lake and the water below is thick with plants, light from the lanterns dancing across the calm surface.

I halt abruptly from my preparations when I see Officer Lee, sitting at the table drinking, his face a storm. It is a long aching moment before I manage to calm myself enough to continue my task.

I did not know he would be here, and I wish with all my heart he wasn't.

The minister of defence presides at the top of the room, watching as my fingers slide across the strings of the *gayageum*. He speaks with his guests, his grey beard glistening wet with liquor. Beside him I recognise the king's nephew, sitting close by, pretending to be drunk. I am not fooled by his act for it is clear how his cup never needs refilling, no matter how much he seems to drink. That man is like a viper, smiling and drinking but all the while he is biding his time, ready to strike. I do not wish to be bitter, yet at the sight of him bitterness floods my chest all the same.

I wonder if the prime minister is one of the men

around the table. He is a man whose face I do not know, yet I hope he is far away from here, at least for Officer Lee's sake. To sit and drink at the same table as your father's murderer is unimaginable, and I cannot help but glance across at Lee Yoon as I play. His black eyes are lowered to his cup and he does not speak with anyone. I think of being alone with him in that dark room, remember the feeling of my fingers pressing against his skin, pushing back his hair as he slept.

Perhaps this will be the last time I ever see him. After tonight I will leave Hanyang behind and go into hiding with my sister. Or I will die.

The evening wears on and midnight passes. The men at the long table become more boisterous by the hour until finally, *finally* guests begin to disappear home or into an inner chamber with women on their arms. Minister Park drunkenly calls for me and I stop playing, hesitating only a moment before walking stiffly to sit at his side, my heart beating fast.

I do not make light conversation as I have been taught. Instead I remain silent and tense beside him, my skin prickling as he drapes an arm across my shoulders. Minister Park is too drunk to notice my discomfort, his coarse beard scratching my skin as he leans close to speak with me.

Officer Lee's eyes burn from the other side of the room as he sits encircled by junior military officers who laugh and joke drunkenly.

Finally Minister Park grows restless and staggers to his feet, pulling me along with him as he bids farewell to his guests. As he thanks each remaining friend for their presence in his home, it's confirmed that the prime minister is indeed present. In fact, he is one of the guests of honour and I am filled with horror at what Lee Yoon must endure to be in the same room. Minister Park leads me by my wrist down the length of the long terrace and toward the inky darkness of the garden. As we reach the walkway leading to the house, I glance back. I cannot explain what I see in Officer Lee's face but I wish I had never looked.

Minister Park brings us through a labyrinth of halls and walkways, across crunching gravel courtyards and through to the far side of the main house. We enter a large dark room with a private garden, a painted screen decorating the wall behind an open bedroll. I assume that I now stand within the minister's private quarters.

We are alone.

"Light a candle," he slurs, collapsing onto the cushions.

I struggle to comply with shaking hands. The flame flickers to life and shadows dance across the painted mountain scene behind us.

The sudden light illuminates his smiling face. "I have been looking forward to your visit for some time." He gestures for more alcohol. Carefully I pour him a cup, which he empties in one gulp.

Minister Park's gaze is unfocused, almost hungry. "Patience is certainly a virtue. You will be all the sweeter for my wait."

I stay where I am, my body rigid. I cannot move. This is the last time, I vow silently. I will protect my sister but I will never do this again.

"Come now," Minister Park breathes. "What is this? A shy *gisaeng*?"

I do not move as he staggers to my side and reaches to undo the knot on my *jeogori*. He pulls the ribbon slowly and pushes the material from my body, until my shoulders are bare to the night air. I am stiff like wood as he reaches around to tug at the *chima* ties on my back.

I close my eyes.

An ear-splitting crash pierces the silence. I jerk back,

startled, as the doors burst open. Two men come crashing inside, a tangle of violence and flashing metal. Minister Park yells and scuttles back as swords slash against furniture, against the painted screen. A low table is broken into jagged pieces, the candle extinguished and everything plunged into blackness.

"What is the meaning of this?!"

A loud crack, like metal on bone, is followed by a man's scream. And then silence. After a moment a voice I do not recognise says, "My lord, please order the *gisaeng* to light the candle."

"You heard him, *gisaeng*!"

I scramble to find the pieces in the dark. Finally, the candle is lit and I peer through the new light. Shadows dance about the room to reveal a man dressed in the uniform of Minister Park's personal guard. He's the man who spoke. He stands with chest heaving and his sword pressed tight against another's throat.

Against Lee Yoon's throat.

28

To Gamble

Lee Yoon has been forced to kneel, his leg twisted and teeth bloody.

My chest grows tight with fear.

"Officer Lee?" Minister Park seems momentarily struck, yet slowly his entire demeanour shifts. Carefully he lowers himself to his cushions, a calm calculating expression stealing across his face. The glazed look within his eyes clears and suddenly I wonder if he was quite as drunk as he appeared. He turns to his guard. "What is this?"

"Master, I saw this man leaving the banquet. He seemed agitated so I followed behind. He was entering your room when I attacked."

"You were trying to assassinate me?" Minister Park seems almost impressed, a smile curling beneath his beard. "Then you are one of those traitorous conspirators, Officer Lee? How unexpected."

I stare at Lee Yoon's blood-streaked face. They will kill him.

"I couldn't find another way," Officer Lee breathes. He seems sick with shock, gaze locked solely on me. I breathe out his name and the minister's head whips toward me like a snake. Immediately I know what a truly terrible mistake I have made.

"You know this man, *gisaeng?*" The minister's brows lower, though he still appears calm. "You planned my assassination together, it seems. Very well." He turns to his guard with a flick of his wrist. "Kill her. Do it now."

"No!" Officer Lee's eyes are wide. "Stop! Minister Park!" He lowers his head, breathing jagged, fast, yet when he rises his expression has been wiped clean, his face calm and completely in control. He stares coldly at Minister Park. "If you kill her, you will destroy everything you have worked for, Minister. You will regret it."

The minister's face twists into a smile. "You threaten me? As you kneel with a sword against your throat? One gesture from me and you will die, Officer Lee. I am justified to do so. As you well know."

"Yet my words remain true, Lord Park." Officer Lee stares at the older man, his gaze burning. "I came here tonight to save your life."

"Master! This man is a *liar*. He came to kill you," interjects the guard, but Minister Park lifts his hand for silence. Though the guard obeys, the blade of his weapon bites deeper into the flesh of Lee Yoon's throat, blood staining the collar of the officer's robes.

Ignoring the metal cutting his skin, Lee Yoon lifts his chin. "Let both myself and this woman go. You know where my family live, Minister Park. If I am lying you will have the advantage."

"Lying about what exactly, Officer Lee? It seems to me I already have the advantage now."

"Show him the vial," orders Officer Lee.

It takes a moment to realise he means me. Startled, I sharply shake my head, heart hammering. How can that help? It will not. It only digs us deeper into an inescapable pit.

"Please, Seorin. Just show the minister the vial."

This cannot be real, everything falling apart and I see no ending where Officer Lee and I escape with our lives. I glance back at Lee Yoon who nods at me. I hesitate only another moment before fumbling within my robes for the small bottle of liquid. I hold it out with shaking hands.

The minister's mouth twists. He does not reach for the vial. "Poison?" He turns to peer at his overturned cup, lying on its side on the floor with alcohol pooled around it.

"Yes. Poison." Officer Lee's voice is low. "If it weren't for me you would already be dead by that woman's hand. She was sent by the leaders of the rebellion to murder you tonight."

I stiffen, blinking as Minister Park and the guard both squint to where I crouch beside the broken screen, my body cold with fear. I cannot understand what Lee Yoon is doing.

Minister Park turns back to Lee Yoon with narrowed eyes. "Why would you stop her? What is it you want?"

Officer Lee smiles. "Tomorrow night our movement will march on the palace."

Surprise flashes across the minister's face, quickly controlled and hidden. "Tomorrow night…"

"The tide has turned, Lord Park, and tomorrow we will descend upon the palace and raise up a new king."

There is silence. Finally, the minister shakes his head, face only slightly flushed. "Officer Lee, I am certain you are bluffing. The traitors do not yet have the strength for such bold action. There are no court officials loyal to you, only lowly men in offices like your own. I know the men in court, they would never agree to what you propose."

Lee Yoon simply shrugs. "They *have* agreed. It is

already set in motion." He pauses. "You think those men you entertained here tonight all back you? They are *our* men, part of *our* movement. You will discover it for yourself tomorrow night." As he speaks Officer Lee gradually pushes away the sword which now hangs loosely at his throat. Neither the guard nor the minister move to stop him as he slowly climbs to his full height, standing straight and tall.

"The reason I saved your life, Lord Park, is because when the dust settles I need a friend at my side. As you can see, I am but a lowly officer. I've not yet had the chance to prove myself to the man who will soon become king, nor will I be rewarded with a better position after the coup succeeds. Amongst the great leaders of our organisation I am … expendable. Yet I do not plan on remaining so. I do not plan on staying a mere officer."

"You wish me to raise you up within the court." Minister Park shakes his head, almost amused, yet a new clarity lights his eyes.

Lee Yoon nods. "Yes. And I am willing to offer you a deal, an opportunity. Instead of dying, I will help you live, I will help you become our ally. Our leaders will welcome your involvement if you remain loyal and they will welcome your soldiers during the coup."

"And what do you expect in return?"

"In return I expect to be rewarded. A powerful political ally is how important men are created, this I understand well enough. The tide has turned Minister Park, and tomorrow our organisation will descend upon the palace and seize the throne. Whose side will you be on?"

There is a long silence before the minister answers. "If I join hands with you and aid the rebellion, what assurances do I have that I will retain my wealth and position after the new king rises to power?"

"There are no assurances," Officer Lee answers without hesitation. "It is in my interest that you live, that is all I am able to offer you. Yet there is no alternative path for you to take, Lord Park. If you do not accept my offer, tomorrow night you will lose everything. Think of your son and daughter, what kind of life do you wish them to have?"

Minister Park is silent, a sharp smile playing at the edges of his mouth. He watches Officer Lee carefully, never breaking eye contact.

"I am offering you a chance, Minister Park," Lee Yoon says. "A chance to live."

Finally, the older man laughs. "Very well, Officer Lee. And if I do accept your … generous offer, tell me, what would you have me do?"

Officer Lee reaches inside his uniform to produce a letter. "Sign this. I need proof of your loyalty if I am to talk the leaders into sparing you. If you refuse to sign it the movement will destroy you as originally planned, whether I return alive tonight or not."

"And if I do sign it?"

"You will provide us with soldiers for the attack tomorrow, and when we win, you will pledge allegiance via marriage of your son and daughter to the families of our choice. You will remain the minister of defence and retain your wealth and holdings. You will be loyal to the new king." Officer Lee pauses and then glances across at me. "And you will not retaliate against this woman who was only following orders. What do you choose?"

Minister Park laughs loudly. "I did not become the man I am today without understanding my limits, Officer Lee. This will not be the first time I have altered my allegiance to survive a war. Maintaining power is about letting go when one needs to. Your first lesson, I think." He smiles, and there is a new coldness about him that has me shrinking away.

"I will sign your letter if..." Minister Park pauses, "...I am offered the position of prime minister."

Officer Lee blinks in the sudden silence.

Finally he nods his head, curt and fast.

Minister Park's smile widens and immediately he waves for his guard to retrieve ink. Lee Yoon bends to set one of the low tables upright again, placing his letter down upon the surface. Carefully Minister Park uses his official seal to mark the page, adding his thumb print, a simple gesture that will surely turn the tide of the impending war.

Officer Lee stares at the paper in his hand and then turns to face the minister. "We will leave now. A messenger with instructions will be sent to you at first light. Make sure your men are prepared in time."

Minister Park smiles as Lee Yoon pulls me up and covers my shoulders with the discarded *jeogori*, grasping my arm firmly between bloody fingers.

The walk out of the vast estate is terrifying and I hold my breath. Officer Lee's limp has become worse and his face is smeared with blood, his breathing shallow and fast. Yet no one tries to stop us, despite our dishevelled appearance. Servants retrieve a horse and Lee Yoon grasps my arm, heaving me up behind him and then we are galloping away along the deserted road outside.

It is only much later when we are far away, hurtling through the empty streets of late night Hanyang that he glances over his shoulder. No one follows.

Tugging on the horse's reins, Lee Yoon slows us to a walk. My hands grip tight to the back of his robes, fingers twisting in the stained material. I sway suddenly, utterly exhausted, and slowly I lean forward until my face rests against his back, forehead to shoulder blade. I whisper, "Does this mean ... war?"

"Yes."

Roads awash with blood and soldiers in the street. Even a fast and sudden rebellion will mean death for many people, nobles and commoners alike.

Such a strange way to start a new world.

"Yoon *ssi?*"

He does not answer, the quiet streets empty and the black sky stretching high overhead, awash with pinprick starlight and a full moon beaming over us. Moon shadows. I take a deep breath.

"Lee Yoon ... tonight ... what you did, I want to say that I'm…"

"Don't," he interrupts. "It may not work, brat."

I hesitate, my fingers tightening against his robes. "Then ... what will you do?"

"The only choice now is to attack the palace. We cannot give Minister Park time to realise I was lying. If he knows we cannot win without his men he will turn against us within moments."

I close my eyes. "Then you will really attack the king?"

"There's no choice. It has to be now, tomorrow night, we cannot wait any longer. I must see the leaders. I will bring you to my household first ... my sisters, and my mother, you all need to leave the city."

I stiffen. "I won't leave."

The horse slows and I take a deep breath, leaning away from him. "I will stay here until my sister is returned to me. I will not leave the city and flee."

Officer Lee halts the horse abruptly. "I do not care what you say, brat. You're leaving the city. Minister Park knows who you are. He thinks you tried to poison him."

I laugh bitterly. "Though in truth I only tried to poison

myself. Listen to me, I will wait here. I will return to the Pavilion and I will wait. The headmistress there is … she is harsh but I trust her to protect me, for a time at least." I push against his back and slide from the saddle, landing heavily on the roadside.

"Brat, please…"

I peer up at his face and press my finger against my lips. His voice is too loud. The small dishevelled houses that cramp the roadside remain dark but this is not a place to speak of secrets.

Officer Lee's expression remains strained, unspoken words tightening his mouth.

I point behind the streets toward the river. "Lee Yoon, the Pavilion is just through there. I will walk from here and you … must go. You know it's true. You must go."

I attempt a smile though my blood runs cold. Lee Yoon is no longer the warrior he once was, his body still strong yet his leg twisted. I reach to touch his hand, fingers pressing over his.

Officer Lee's black eyes flicker.

"Thank you," I say quietly. There is more as well, hanging in the silence. But I do not say the words.

Instead I step back, my hand radiating warmth where my fingers pressed against his skin. I stare up at him, at the blood on his face, staining his teeth.

"Seorin *ssi*…" Lee Yoon's voice is choked, his black eyes deep and dark. "Don't do anything foolish. Be safe. You must be safe."

I open my mouth to return his words but he is no longer there, driving the horse to move again. Stones crunch beneath the animal's hooves. I step aside to avoid the turning beast, and Lee Yoon slaps the horse on the rump and pushes the animal to a gallop. Soon the night swallows him up.

I walk slowly to the Pavilion, quietly slipping through the entrance beside the river where I know no one will be waiting. It is late, the sky almost turning to day with the first faint lines of cloudy blue seeping into the black above.

Inside the Pavilion it is quiet and I pad like a ghost through the halls toward the headmistress's private quarters. I do not wish for anyone to see me. I am certain she will agree to hide me for a few days without letting the other girls know. I hope she will. She doesn't like trouble brought to the Pavilion. After that … I suppose the course of my life will depend on the outcome of tomorrow night.

As I slide past Chungjo's room, whispers hum in the darkness, even so very late at night. It is an old habit that makes me stop to listen with my ear pressed against her door. Information is life within the Pavilion's walls. There is nothing else to trade with, and secrets often mean the difference between a life lived at the bottom or a life untouched by the games played within this house.

The whispers within her room grow louder.

I did not see Chungjo leave Minister Park's banquet, though she was gone by the time he led me to his rooms late in the night. All evening she sat beside the man I later found out was the prime minister himself, all night she entertained Lee Yoon's father's killer. With his lips loosened by liquor, I wonder what that man said to such a beautiful woman.

I hover beside her door to listen as she whispers her new secrets to her friends. Soon I am struck still, my hands shaking at what I hear.

And then I open her door and stride inside.

Soon I am stumbling to the Pavilion's stables. We have pack horses there, and I saddle one as best I can, ordering the stable boy who appears from his room sleepy and yawning to help me. I do not know how to ride but I listen to the stable boy's increasingly suspicious instructions and do the best I can.

Before long I am out in the early morning dawn, blue haze hanging in the trees beside the woods' path. The forest grows darker the deeper I travel and soon I cannot see the city at all.

29

War

I know almost nothing of horses yet somehow still manage to hold some semblance of control over the animal. I am lost, emerging exhausted onto ridges I don't recognise yet passing patches of trees I am sure I have seen before. I try not to think of Officer Lee, who remains behind somewhere in Hanyang in the wake of approaching war.

Time stretches and the sun dawns bright and warm, travelling high into the sky, and still I am lost. Terror building, I forge onwards anyway. So much time wasted. Tears threaten and I know surely I will be too late. Chungjo's words whisper through my mind. A military raid on a secret camp. A rebellion to be quashed in one fell move. Secrets spilling from a drunk man's loose tongue with no one to listen. Except perhaps a *gisaeng*.

If Chungjo did not fear me before she certainly does now. I will not go back to the Pavilion.

My life there is over and done.

By some intervention of fate I finally stumble across Kim Jae-gil's mountain camp, yet it is unfamiliar for I approach it from behind, far from the main entrance I have used before. The trail here is steep and sandy so I slide off the saddle and lead the horse down the rise.

Pushing sweaty hair from my brow, I freeze at a sudden movement in the forest. Behind me I catch flashes of unnatural colour amongst the trees. Immediately I push harder down the trail, sliding and stumbling over loose forest roots and stones. I glance over my shoulder just as a deafening explosion rocks the ground like an earthquake, dust shimmering in the midday sun. I am thrown onto the dirt with my hands clutched across my head, screaming.

The Pavilion horse whinnies and I force myself to stumble to my feet, lunging desperately for her reins for they no longer rest in my hands. Dropped and forgotten when the earth shook. The horse flings herself back onto the path, rearing up and away, shattering through the undergrowth with her kicking legs narrowly avoiding my head. I call after her, sliding on the loose soil. But she is gone.

Below, shouting rings out, loud and clear through the hanging dust. Answering calls spring from within the mountains above and somewhere else among the trees I hear the Pavilion horse scream again, unearthly and blood curdling. And then there is only sudden silence, her cry cut short.

I am too late.

The soldiers are already here.

My feet slip and slide as I throw myself down the ridge, crashing over roots and branches. I reach flat ground and burst from the forest into thick smoke, a storage shed consumed by raging flames, thick trails of black smoke rising into the sky. Everywhere men are fighting, soldiers from the capital locked in vicious blood-spattered battle with the men of the camp. Someone grasps my arm and pulls me into the shadow of a building, grip tight and painful.

"Seorin! What are you doing here?!"

Kim Jae-gil's face is covered with grit and blood. His eyes dart all around as he drags me further from the fighting. I am so glad to see him.

"They're coming in from the back." I point desperately toward the mountain ridge and Kim Jae-gil swears loudly.

"They will surround us. You have to go back!" He grabs my arm to drag me away just as another anguished scream echoes from behind us.

"I can't go back! It's too late. There are soldiers in the hills."

Kim Jae-gil stops, confusion flashing across his face. "How are you here? Did you not take the drug?" He grasps my arm tighter. "The messenger arrived hours ago, he said Minister Park is now on our side."

"Officer Lee ... he found another way."

Kim Jae-gil's eyes widen. "Where is he?"

"Still in Hanyang. I was going to stay there, but a girl at the Pavilion was speaking of a military raid. I thought to ... warn you."

Kim Jae-gil says nothing, gaze dancing across the carnage as he dodges a group of warriors running in the opposite direction. "You were too late."

"I got lost."

"You should never have come here." Kim Jae-gil stops suddenly. "Did Lee Yoon tell you about our planned attack on the palace?"

I nod, distracted by the thick smoke curling into the sky above, by my heart thudding hard against my chest. My ears hum, the smell of burning wood and butchered flesh filling my throat.

"Seorin ... *Seorin*, look at me!"

Startled, I turn to face him.

"If the king's soldiers are here in the mountains with us, there will be less of them defending the royal family." Kim Jae-gil grins suddenly. Too wide, too savage.

"What ... does that mean?"

"It means we will win."

I blink. "Win?"

Looking around at the screaming men and the smoking buildings it seems they have already lost. The shouts of dying men hang thick in the heavy air.

Kim Jae-gil follows my gaze, and his expression changes. "Come with me."

Grasping my arm painfully, he pulls me into the fray, avoiding a blood-covered horse running wild with fear. Kim Jae-gil is agitated, scanning what is left of his camp. "I can't get you out if they've surrounded us." He turns abruptly. "There will be another way."

"*Nauri*, your men ... You said you will win. If you win then we'll all be safe."

He glances at me, clearly torn with indecision, face darkening. He pushes me into the shade of a remaining village building, finding shelter against the mud brick walls. "Seorin *ssi*... you misunderstand me. The rebellion will succeed in Hanyang. We *will* win this war. Yet that will be because of Minister Park's forces, with him beside us we will take the city."

"What are you trying to say?"

"We are *alone* up here. No one is coming. We were not ready for this attack, our numbers are scattered elsewhere. We have won the war, but ... *Seorin!*"

A soldier lurches around the corner, his weapon held high. Kim Jae-gil launches himself at the attacker and within moments it is over, violent and bloody. Kim Jae-gil pulls me away and I step over the fallen body, peering down at the open eyes and gaping blood-filled mouth. My dress catches on everything we pass, until finally I rip it in frustration, fear eating up my insides. Sending my blood cold.

"I must join the others." Kim Jae-gil's attention is drawn to the billowing smoke ahead. "They're burning the buildings ... I don't know where I can hide you."

I shouldn't have come. The truth is written on Kim Jae-gil's face.

Everyone here is about to die.

"Just … go." I step back, giving him the option to leave. "It was my choice to come here, *Nauri*, and … I will find a place to hide. In the woods. Just go."

"There are *soldiers* in the woods! If they find you they'll kill you or ... worse." Distant screams add gravity to his words. He turns and I see the whites of his eyes.

Suddenly he grabs me, pulling at my clothes, grasping my *jeogori*. Stiffening, I attempt to fight him off. "Stop! What are you doing?"

"Do you have the drug?"

"Stop! Why are you...?"

Kim Jae-gil's fingers close on the little vial still tucked inside my clothes. Ripping off the small lid he grabs my chin to force open my mouth. I struggle hard, kicking and scratching, yet Kim Jae-gil is strong. The burning liquid gushes down my throat. Doubled over I spit onto the ground, choking and coughing. But it is too late. I have swallowed too much.

I gape at him. "What did you do?"

Kim Jae-gil drops to his knees. Immediately my body feels strange, wrong. My limbs turn numb and Kim Jae-gil grasps onto me as I lose all sensation in my arms and legs, sinking.

"Seorin *ssi*," he breathes, bowing his dirt streaked face and closing his eyes. "Forgive me. Please ... forgive me."

My body is heavy like rock. I lie still.

"We will lose up here," he whispers. "But I can save you." He leans close, the scent of blood and sweat mixed with smoke upon his skin. "I made all the wrong choices. I would do it all differently if I could. Forgive me for everything."

My mind slows, his words blurring like the sky, swirling colours and the scent of smoke. I can no longer speak.

Kim Jae-gil lifts my body from the ground, hauling me into his arms. My head strikes his chest, barely able to keep my heavy eyelids open as he carries me. I am placed down beside a copse of trees. It is no real hiding place but now I am nothing but a dead girl. There are other bodies here, three dead men laid out next to me on the brown grass.

Four bodies now.

Kim Jae-gil closes my eyes and my mind wanders, the drug dragging me into darkness.

"I will come back for you."

His voice drifts as if from far away.

"If I can."

WHEN I WAKE I am alone.

I'm choking. I cannot move, cannot feel my limbs. I simply lie there, the suffocation creeping within my throat and deep inside my chest. It is the most excruciating effort to open my eyes.

Blue skies. Endless and clear yet tinged with the glow of sunset.

And silence.

I lie still and listen to the winds and the forest.

It grows dark and cold. And still I cannot move.

I push myself until my fingertips twitch and then begin to work on my toes, trying over and over again until finally I feel the smallest of movements. The effort exhausts me.

I dream and this time when I wake I am able to move my head, catching glimpses of the dim shadows of burnt out buildings, the outlines of bodies littering the grass. I begin to cry. Where is Kim Jae-gil? Please let him have escaped. And Lee Yoon, lost somewhere far away in a city at war.

Eventually I manage to roll over, I do not know how long it takes. Forever. I find the body of a man slashed open waist to chin lying across my legs. His eyes stare at the dark sky just as mine had done, but his are empty, devoid of all life. His uniform is a military one which means he is my enemy, but I feel only pity.

When I stagger to my feet there is death and destruction everywhere. I pick my way across the battlefield, falling often over charred wood and weapons emerging at odd angles from the dark grass.

I fall over people too, but all of them are dead so no longer care if I stand on their hands or flesh. There is no moonlight, the clouds overhead thick and black now, creating a darkness so deep I am turned around again and again until I'm no longer sure which way I walk. My throat burns and I try to remember the last time I drank water. I stagger on numb limbs across the deserted village.

"Kim Jae-gil—"

I try to scream his name but my voice is only a rasping dry whisper. Stumbling over to the remains of a building I slide down to rest, hands brushing cloth and coming back red with wet blood. I recognise the clothes of this dead man, I've seen them before. I stare for a long time and then numbly walk away into the forest. I don't turn back.

My mind plays tricks on me now, my body cold and shivering, feverish. My head is full of images, flashing back and forth across my mind as I stagger onwards. The mountains are cold, the air biting at my skin. Frozen fingers even though sweat trickles down my spine.

I see my father's face. He waits ahead between the trees.

In my dream he is crying. He tells me he misses me. He tells me to save my sister. And then my mother forces me to repeat my promise over and over again.

Find your sister.

Find her and live well.

Together.

And then I wake up. The sun blazes overhead.

Far away someone calls, voices echoing through the reaching branches. I cannot make out the words but I muster everything I have and call back, a weak raw sound.

It is enough.

Finally, men crackle through the undergrowth, a small group like a search party. Their faces are drained and tight, none I recognise. One older *ajeossi* touches my shoulder, pity in his eyes. He helps me to sit and gestures for another younger man to bring water. I gulp it greedily as they speak amongst themselves. "Tell him we found the woman."

Someone runs away into the trees and I close my eyes.

"Stay awake," the *ajeossi* urges me, but I cannot.

30

The Shape of Words on Paper

I wake to sunlight. It pours in from an open patio onto my blankets.

For a strange suspended moment I believe it is the Pavilion, except a woman sits beside me with her head bowed, needlework in her hands. She looks up, startled at my movement.

"Lee Da-in," I breathe her name. Officer Lee's eldest sister. My mind is thick and slow. "Where am I?"

"Lord Im's residence. In Hanyang."

I blink slowly. I do not know who that is.

"He is one of the leaders of the movement." Da-in's voice is hushed. "He was grateful for your help and brought you here to ... reward you."

"I don't understand." I glance around the room, at the fine expensive furnishings. "Where is Officer Lee?"

Da-in lowers her head. "He has left Hanyang."

I stare at her. He's gone. "When will he come back?"

"Soon, I hope. He asked me to stay so you would see a familiar face when you woke. He told me much of what happened, Seorin."

"Why am I here? Why am I not at the Pavili—" I break off, the words frozen on my lips.

Whatever Lee Yoon has told his sister about me, I am sure it will not include my time at the Pavilion. She will not know what I am.

Yet Da-in does not blink. "No one wants you to go back there. Lord Im has offered you his home while you recover. You have been freed."

My clouded mind struggles to make sense of her words. "Freed?"

Da-in nods, yet it is clear she is troubled, her expression at odds with her words. "You are a free woman now."

"Why?" Fear curls in my belly. Nothing comes for free, this I have learnt well enough.

"I believe Lord Im plans to offer you a position here. If you choose to take it." Da-in hesitates. "But things are different now, you do not have to do what they ask if you do not wish it."

"Yoon … where is he?"

It takes a moment to realise I already have that answer. He isn't here. Tears threaten but I force them back.

"I am sorry, Seorin. He had to go away." Da-in bites her lips. "Can I get you something? You should eat. You've been so sick." She stands as if to leave. "My brother won't forgive me if I do not look after you properly. Rest until I return."

"Is he well?"

I try to read Da-in's expression as she carefully adjusts her skirts. "My *orabeoni* has been … troubled. Much has changed over the last few days. And much has been asked of him."

"How long have I been here?"

She hesitates. "You were very sick when my brother

found you. The physician thought you would die. It has been five days."

I struggle to a seated position, head spinning. "*Agassi,* your family are safe?"

Immediately tears spring into Da-in's eyes. "My father, he … passed on, but that was before the battle. The rest of us are safe, yes."

My heart beats hard against my chest. If the Lee family still stands it can only mean the rebellion has succeeded, the coup was successful, that the king …

I stare at her, mouth gaping.

"Da-in, is the king dead?"

Da-in hushes me sharply and then quickly glances toward the door, lowering her voice. "Yes. His nephew has taken his place as the new king. There have been many changes in the palace, whole families raised up by the new king, given wealth and titles. And the ones they replaced are just … gone." She lowers her gaze.

Lying down carefully, I turn to face the garden. Outside there are blossom trees in full bloom, petals breaking loose and floating inside on the breeze. Already spring has returned to the city.

Da-in shuffles closer to kneel at my side, her voice still hushed as if afraid to be overheard. "Seorin *ssi,* forgive me, my brother told me some of what happened. He said you were in the mountains when the army attacked?"

I nod numbly and close my eyes. I still feel the drug inside me, coursing through my blood. The mountain camp. Yes, I was there. But it is like peering through a veil of water and the details escape me, slipping at the edges of my mind.

Da-in takes my hand. Her fingers are warm and strong. "What happened there?"

I shake my head. All I remember is blood and smoke. "I don't … recall. I'm sorry." My head aches.

"Forgive me. I have been so thoughtless." Da-in steps toward the door again. "Try to rest. I'll be back soon with something for you to eat. There is water beside you if you are thirsty."

After she is gone, I drink deeply, and then sit quietly for a long time, images from my journey up the mountainside returning. Jagged pieces of a whole picture slowly come back together. I remember the mountain camp, I remember the dead men strewn across the long grass. And I remember Kim Jae-gil telling me they would lose.

My hands clench on the blanket. Is he dead?

I call out to Da-in but no one comes.

I am too weak to rise from my bed, so am forced to sit waiting. My fingers clutch tight to the blankets and my knuckles slowly turn white and stiff. Kim Jae-gil did not help me when I most needed it, he did not keep his promises. Yet it seems by forcing me to drink that drug, he may have saved my life. No matter what he has done I do not wish him dead.

Footsteps return along the hall. Yet it is not Da-in who walks through the door. Instead it is a man, one arm bound tightly against his body with bandages and the other holding a tray of broth. He slides the door closed behind him and we are alone.

My heart slows. "You are alive, *Nauri*."

Kim Jae-gil sits beside me, smiling lightly. "I am."

I attempt to smile back. "I am glad of it. You look well."

He grimaces at his bandaged arm and gingerly moves his shoulder. "Really? I think I have looked better." He smiles again but tension swirls beneath the smooth surface of his skin. "You've looked better too, Seorin *ssi*. Yet I am glad to see you awake." He pushes the bowl toward me. "Eat. You'll feel stronger afterwards."

I ignore it, struggling to sit. "How did you get out? Did many others survive?"

Kim Jae-gil shakes his head, peering at his hands. "A few men made it out alive ... but not so very many. I was lucky." A shadow passes over his face and he grits his teeth, but then he is smiling again, this time with effort.

"You saved my life," I say.

He turns away. "Yet I endangered it many times before that. I don't deserve your gratitude."

"I will give it to you anyway," I say firmly, before hesitating. "My sister?"

Kim Jae-gil says nothing and that is answer enough, my heart sinking deep within my chest. I blink. Perhaps the leaders of his group never located her at all, perhaps it was simply another lie to lure me. I peer into the garden.

Perhaps she is dead.

It has been so many years.

I do not press Kim Jae-gil. I think part of me cannot bear to know the truth. If he simply used me or if his promises were well intentioned. It is over, whatever there was between us. I am glad Kim Jae-gil lives and that is all.

"*Nauri,*" I say finally. "Do you know where Officer Lee has gone? His sister Da-in says he has left the capital."

Kim Jae-gil nods stiffly. "There is a magistrate in the south who speaks out against the new king. Lee Yoon was sent to relieve him of his position. I do not know how long he'll be gone."

I turn to the garden with my face carefully blank. "I see. What will happen to him once he returns?"

Kim Jae-gil shakes his head. "I do not know. He may be granted a position within the court. If he wants that, I do not know." He hesitates. "Please eat. You will feel stronger."

This time I do as I am told and once I begin I cannot stop. Kim Jae-gil watches as I devour the cooled broth and then clears away the tray. As he works, I lean back on my bedroll. "I was asleep for five days?"

"Yes. Everyone thought you would die. I was so very..." His words trail away and he simply shakes his head with another smile. "Yet here you are."

"Here I am," I repeat slowly.

There is a heaviness in my chest. I am not yet sure I'm ready to celebrate my survival. Not when so many others are dead, not when Lee Yoon's father is dead. His family will be grieving, yet even so Officer Lee has left the capital to work for this new king, already at his beck and call.

"*Nauri*?" I hesitate. "What happened at the palace that day?"

He sighs. "Minister Park sent his men to the leaders just as he promised. Officer Lee told me the rebellion overcame the palace easily, within a few hours it was over."

"He was there? In the palace?"

"Not in the initial attack because of his knee, I think. But yes, he was there." Kim Jae-gil is silent for a moment, watching me. "I am told it was quick. The former king tried to escape but was killed by his nephew in the throne room."

I turn away, feeling sick.

Dusk is falling now, twilight covering the garden with a softness that almost seems unreal. I close my eyes. I am so tired, my body heavy and stiff.

"I am sorry. You need to sleep," says Kim Jae-gil.

He climbs to his feet as if to leave, yet footsteps suddenly ring out from beyond the closed door. I expect to see Da-in but instead the angry lord from the mountain camp walks into the room. I stare at him. This small flushed red man is Lord Im? This is the man who has given me freedom, who has offered his home to me? My stomach churns as Kim Jae-gil bows stiffly.

"My lord," he says. "I heard Seorin had awoken and came to see her. My apologies, I should have alerted you to my presence in your household first. Forgive this oversight, my lord."

Lord Im waves his hand dismissively, turning to me instead. "You slept so long, *gisaeng*, we were unsure you would ever wake." He scratches his beard, running long fingers across his chin. "Officer Lee spoke highly of your efforts to bring Minister Park over to our side. An achievement which was of course essential to our success."

I glance at Kim Jae-gil, startled. More lies. Officer Lee is getting good at them.

Lord Im smiles slowly. "Of course, we wish to extend our gratitude to you for the services provided. It has been the decision of the king after much deliberation to award you freedom and a place here in my household. I have heard of your skills on the *gayageum* and will welcome such a ... talented new addition to my household."

Lord Im turns toward Kim Jae-gil, his expression suddenly cold. "I will leave the *gisaeng* to recover and I suggest you do the same. She is not yours to monopolise, Lord Kim." The older man flicks his head toward the door, but Kim Jae-gil does not leave. Eventually it is Lord Im himself who goes, scowling all the way.

Afterwards there is silence. Finally, I lift my chin. "Did the king give me to him?"

Kim Jae-gil shakes his head vehemently. "No! I don't believe that was ... his intention. The king only wished to send you somewhere safe, I know Lee Yoon asked ... but he…" Kim Jae-gil trails off, seeming uncertain. "I will find a way to get you out of here. I promise."

"And my sister, Lord Kim?" I spit out the words, harsh and sharp, yet I do not care. His promises cannot be relied on.

Kim Jae-gil is wounded, hurt shining within his eyes. "I will do as I promised, Seorin *ssi*. You will see."

I say nothing as he walks toward the door. He stops and turns back. "Da-in sent for the physician. They will be back together soon to check on you. Try to rest." He hesitates, almost leaving, body swaying in indecision. Finally, he expels his breath all at once. "I almost forgot. Lee Yoon gave me this. He asked me to give it to you when you woke. It is a letter."

I say nothing, hands clenching my blankets, holding my breath.

Kim Jae-gil stands still for a moment, staring at the letter he has pulled from within his robes, hesitating. Then he walks over and hands it to me. Things must have changed between him and Lee Yoon again, for Lee Yoon has entrusted this task to him. Perhaps their conflict has been resolved. I hope so.

Kim Jae-gil watches my shaking fingers close around the folded and wax sealed letter, clutching the heavy paper against my chest. He smiles stiffly and after another moment walks slowly out into the hall, shutting the door behind him.

When he is gone the room grows quiet and still, darkness creeping inside from the patio. There is no candle burning and the night slowly swallows the little room, shadows curling from the ceiling. The letter is heavier than it should be, and when I carefully open the seal a flash of green, cold and carved, falls into my waiting palm.

A jade rose pin.

The one I gifted Lee Yoon so long ago.

My heart beats jagged against my chest.

Slowly I unfold the thin letter, opening a large soft page covered in messy black ink scrawl. It is the first time I've seen Officer Lee's handwriting. I lean close in the darkness to carefully study the lines and shapes of his words.

The doctor told me today you will live and the worst has passed.

Brat, I shouldn't have left you on the roadside, I don't know how you'll forgive me for that. I don't know how I'll forgive myself. I wanted to protect you, I want to be waiting beside you when you wake. But the king has ordered me south and I cannot refuse him.

Seorin ssi, I don't always have the words to say what I mean, but I will try.

In the mountains I watched you weaving straw shoes and I listened to your stories and I think I have been living only for you ever since. Even if it's hard for you to understand me, please know that I mean it, that I see you every time I close my eyes. That I go to sleep thinking of you.

Wait for me.

Lee Yoon.

I SIT for a long time when I finish reading, clutching the paper and staring outside into the garden as night falls. The jade pin is fastened into my hair. Despite being here in Lord Im's house, despite not knowing where my sister is, somehow I don't feel so alone.

He is out there somewhere.

And he has asked me to wait.

31

A Lush Garden and a Summer Rainstorm

uneral biers carry the wrapped coffins down the street, layered high with bright carvings. Men march alongside with grim expressions. I wipe sweat from my brow, the sun warm and the pressing bodies even warmer. The crowd watches as the bearers pass by, their cries and wails rise high across the swelling city. The main procession is followed by others who carry flags that flutter weakly in the light breeze.

Although my body is still weak, I must support Da-in as she breaks into tears, affected by the grieving families all round us and by her own loss, her father whom she sacrificed to this brief war. I hold her close, her fingers grasping my *jeogori*.

I cannot cry. Even though my own father also died for this same cause.

For the past four years a deep well of anger has festered within my heart for him and what he did, yet now I cannot help but think of Lee Yoon. He nearly sacrificed his family in the same way at Minister Park's house. For me. Unlike my father and brother, Lee Yoon's gamble paid off, yet he was still so close to losing everything … I shiver despite the heat.

Was Lee Yoon all that different from my brother and father in those deciding moments?

The idea has me reassessing my memories; was there perhaps some detail I could not have known? Perhaps my father truly believed he would forge a better world for his son, perhaps his reasons were good despite his ending.

I cannot know for certain.

As I stand and watch the last of the procession, the tear-streaked faces and the clouding dust, I cannot help but wonder if my father is happy now to see his fellow conspirators succeed.

Or perhaps he no longer cares for such earthly matters.

"Let's go back, Seorin *ssi*." Da-in tugs me from the parade, flanked by two of Lord Im's manservants. I glance over my shoulder into the setting sun as the last of the flag bearers disappear from view, swallowed by the crowds at the edge of the city.

"We received a letter this morning," Da-in says. "From my brother. You are being moved to our home today." She looks at me curiously. "Will you be glad of it?"

I stop walking. "I'm to come home with you?"

She nods. "Yes. I do not know how he has managed it, but my *orabeoni* has secured the king's permission. You will live with us until he returns from the south."

I do not move, my eyes locked on the stony ground at my feet. "Da-in … and then what?"

She frowns. "What do you mean?"

I force my lips into a smile. "Am I to be your servant? A storyteller? What exactly will I do in your home?"

Da-in is shocked. "No. You will be our guest."

I sigh, taking Da-in's arm in mine and beginning to walk again through the clouds of dust. "I cannot be a guest forever," I say. "Your mother would resent me."

"No! She—"

I cut her off with a look. I have met Lee Yoon's mother. I know how she would think of me living in her home as a guest. I clear my throat, a part of my insides tearing at what I am about to do, the part of me that wishes to accept stamped down. "I thank you for your offer, Da-in. And your brother. You are both kind. But I will not go."

"I don't understand … you will stay with Lord Im? He is horrible!"

"That he is. And no. I will not stay." I glance at her. "I have made my own arrangements for the future."

She blinks. "But where could you go?"

"Back to the Pavilion." I smile at the look of horror that runs across her face. Gently I say, "It is my home, Da-in."

"My brother will not understand."

"He doesn't have to. He simply needs to accept it as my decision."

She stops walking and grips my arm so I must stop also. "You will be a *gisaeng* again?"

This time my smile is filled with pride. "No. I am a free woman now. No one can force me to do anything I do not wish to do." I take her other hand in mine. "But I am a skilled *gayageum* player, and I am capable of running that establishment one day. I'm strong enough to keep the other girls in line. The headmistress has agreed I will be her apprentice. She will train me to be ready in the future. There is a place for me there."

"A better place than in my home?"

I hesitate. She doesn't understand. There is no future

for me with Lee Yoon. He will protect me and care for me in his house, but his mother will eventually force him to marry another, a more suitable match. I will live like a ghost in his hallways, haunting him and haunting myself.

I have come too far to endure another lifetime of waiting.

"Tell your brother…" I hesitate. "Just tell him I am sorry, Da-in. I cannot accept his offer."

She shakes her head in disbelief. "And what of Lord Im?"

"He will know by now, I sent people to collect my things."

"I think he must be very angry."

I laugh lightly. "I think he will not care. I've been nothing but trouble for him." We continue walking as I chew my lip. "Da-in … your brother…"

She peers at me. "Yes?"

I shake my head. "No. Nothing. Just … please tell him I hope he will be well."

As we walk through the swirling city dust, I take deep breaths, hiding my hands in the folds of my skirt. I do not want Da-in to see how they shake.

AT FIRST IT is strange to live in the Pavilion as a free woman. I have new rooms and new clothes, hidden away in the back near the headmistress's quarters. I no longer must entertain other than with my music. It is strange. And yet as time passes it grows easier.

Everything is just as I remember it, servants bustle through the halls, and the gardens are green and lush in the summer heat. I am welcomed home by the other girls, by Jan-sil in particular, who unlike some others, seems to hold no grudges at the news of my sudden freedom. I earn my keep with my music and am fed well and given clothes to wear every bit as fine as the headmistress's. And after a while I fall into a routine of sorts, walking in the garden, sitting in my quiet room. Sleeping until my body has fully regained its strength. I spend time with only Jan-sil at first but soon the other girls begin to visit and the old routines slowly fall over me again.

There is no one to ask about my sister.

Lord Im could not or would not help me, and I hear no word from Kim Jae-gil. At night I speak to Jan-sil about it. Of course, she has no answers either, though from her I do learn much about Joseon's new king, and the state of our new world as she passes on the gossip she learns from her patrons.

Many positions within the court are cleared out and the previous prime minister is executed for his role in the murder of Officer Lee's father. Minister Park himself is placed into that coveted position as agreed. It seems the rebellion keep their promises when it suits them.

After many weeks Kim Jae-gil comes to visit me. It is the first I see him after our meeting in Lord Im's household. I am seated in the lush Pavilion gardens and do not notice him approaching until he is already standing at my side.

I stand to bow respectfully. "*Nauri*, what brings you here? Have you news of my sister?"

It takes him a long while to answer. "Not yet, Seorin *ssi*. Are you recovered now?"

My heart sinks, but I force myself to nod. "I am. And yourself?" I look at his arm that was so badly wounded but no signs of lasting injury remain beneath his brightly coloured robes.

"I am well," he answers. "Do you mind if I join you? I will not take much of your time."

An air of sadness hangs about him, yet I do not comment on it, returning to my seat. I nod my consent and he sits beside me, holding his body rigid and tense. His silence creeps inside my chest and my heart beats faster.

"Has something happened?"

Immediately I think of Lee Yoon, away for so long, and my sister, but Kim Jae-gil only shakes his head and tells me nothing is wrong, there is nothing to tell.

"I only wanted to see you."

We sit in silence for a time in the warm garden, listening to the cicadas hum around us. When Kim Jae-gil does speak, they are not words I expect to hear.

"I will be married soon."

I am surprised, but my stomach doesn't lurch as it might once have done when first I met him. "Congratulations *Nauri*. I wish you every happiness."

"Do you?" He seems pained, almost disappointed. "It is Minister Park's daughter. I am to become Minister Park's son-in-law."

This is not unexpected news, for Kim Jae-gil is the perfect candidate for a marriage alliance with the Park family. He is loyal and will ensure they never waver in their support for the new king. "It is a good match," I say carefully. "I hope you will both be very happy."

It seems Kim Jae-gil might say something more, though at that moment Jan-sil comes bursting through the trees and he is cut off. I am guilty at how relieved I feel.

"Lord Kim! I heard you were here. Come inside the house. You know the headmistress will want to greet you." She comes forward and takes his arm, pulling him onto his feet. Turning around he bows low to me, then allows himself to be drawn away.

I receive another visitor after that, a little girl with a message. And when I follow her outside the Pavilion's gates there is a maidservant waiting to escort me to a private room in a restaurant in the marketplace. Da-in waits inside, and though she brings no news of her brother, who is still gone from the city, she brings instead warm smiles and kindness. And a burning curiosity about me and my life that I cannot seem to quench.

I answer her many questions about my past honestly and without holding back, and it is through this regular exchange that we begin to see each other differently. Not just as allies who share a connection to Lee Yoon but as burgeoning friends.

Da-in never asks me directly why Officer Lee asked for me to be brought to their home, nor why I refused him, and I do not tell her about the letter he left me. Yet every night I take it from my robes and stare at it, the paper already crumpled and creased.

I am no longer a slave or *gisaeng*, but even as a free woman, with no family there are many things I cannot do. I am not certain of what will happen when Lee Yoon returns home. I do not know what I should hope for and I begin to wonder if I was a fool for ever reading the letter at all.

As the days pass and no one comes to speak to me of my sister, I grow more bitter. This new world has been bought with fire and blood, yet it is not so very different from the old one. I remain the same, even as a free woman I am still powerless and at the mercy of others. There is nothing I can do for myself.

When I first returned to the Pavilion, the headmistress told me I should now live my life how I want, as a free woman out in the world, but I remember how Chungjo watched our exchange from the shadows, a crooked smile painted upon her lips. As if she was the only one who knew better. When I pass her in the hallways now she raises her chin, though I cannot tell if it is jealousy or pity shining within her eyes.

Either way, it seems we now share the same understanding.

The world around us will never change.

I HEAR from Da-in that the Lee family attends Kim Jae-gil's wedding but I do not go. Lee Yoon's mother is surely glad of my absence, if she has thought of me at all, but Da-in later tells me all about it, painting the ceremony in vivid colour. For the first time she invites me to her home, to visit her younger sister So-hye. I am surprised at her boldness and, despite knowing how her mother will despise me, I attend anyway, something about that place calling me.

Lee Yoon's home.

Perhaps I wish to feel closer to him despite everything. I do not know. The emotions surging in my chest are strange and difficult to define. I enter their grand house and spend time in the lush garden telling stories to So-hye, and I keep one hand pressed against his letter. I keep it always, hidden in the folds of my dress next to my heart.

Later in the dusky afternoon I sit with Da-in on the candlelit terrace, speaking quietly together, until loud shouting and thundering horses draw us into the front courtyard. My steps falter when a servant calls that the young master is home. A humming rises in my ears, my veins singing and my heart beating hard. So-hye and her mother already wait with anticipation at the gate.

Stopping at the top of the stairs, I peer from afar as the

four horses mill around the courtyard entrance, followed closely by a wagon piled high with wrapped goods. My eyes flit over the men on horseback, servants, warriors, until finally my gaze locks onto him. He is already watching me, wearing a small crooked smile.

Slowly I step from the shadows of the house.

Officer Lee's mother runs to his horse, reaching high for her son's hand and bringing it against her face. "My son, you've been gone so long. You look so thin." She sniffles and I wrinkle my nose in distaste, though immediately wish I hadn't for Officer Lee still watches me. His smile only widens though, dimple appearing as he slowly draws his horse around and slides from the saddle to greet his sisters.

There is a little girl sitting behind him.

Lee Yoon reaches to help her down and I stare as her feet hit the stony ground. A skinny girl with messy hair and dirt on her face, her dress thin and worn. Her eyes are enormous pools of light filled with terror. Like a wild deer about to flee.

I can barely breathe as I slowly stagger down the stairs toward them all. Everyone is crowded around Officer Lee, servants arriving to take the restless horses and help unload the wagon. I push past until I am standing right in front of her. She is so fragile I almost don't want to touch her. I stare at her face, at a long thin scar running across her cheek to her forehead and I am reaching out and running my fingers across her skin, tracing the line of it as it travels down her chin.

Her eyes flutter closed at my touch and I reach to grasp her face between my hands, falling to my knees at her feet and drawing her forehead to rest against mine.

"Do you remember me?" I whisper. I hadn't realised I was crying but now my voice is thick with tears, my breathing jagged and raw. "Seo-jin-a," I breathe. "Do you remember me?"

Slowly I feel her nod and I press her thin body against mine, wrap her in my arms as we sink to the ground, sobbing as we clutch each other. My sister doesn't speak but I whisper to her over and over that I will never leave her side again, I will look after her forever and keep her safe. It was the promise I made to our mother and I will not break it.

When I finally lift my head the courtyard is deserted except for Lee Yoon. He sits in the falling darkness on the stone stairs by the house, watching us. Slowly he stands and walks to my side, his shoulder pressing against mine as he crouches to peer at Seo-jin sleeping in my arms.

Exhaustion is plain on her dusty face, her cheeks streaked with tears. I cannot stop staring at her as Lee Yoon reaches across to gently lift her from my arms.

I stand too, walking beside him without a word as we cross the courtyard, my fingers itching to touch him. I give in, reaching to press my hand against his elbow, pushing my fingers into the spaces between him and my softly sleeping sister. I feel him hesitate, turn back to me a moment, before he continues walking up the stairs. My hand tightens around his arm as we enter the house, unable to let go.

Inside the halls are dark and I wonder how late it is, the house quiet and cool in the night. We walk silently past the rooms and I am unsure of where I am or where I'm going. I'm only aware of my fingers gripping Lee Yoon's warm skin and the little girl who lies sleeping in his arms. Her chest softly rises and falls.

Officer Lee stops outside a room. Guiding me inside into the darkness, he motions with his head toward a stack of folded bedding and I quickly retrieve the blankets and spread them across the floor. Carefully, he lowers my sister's skinny body onto the soft embroidered bedroll and I sink to my knees beside her, drinking in the sight of her sleeping face. Lee Yoon leaves the room, returning again with water, a bowl of rice, and a flickering candle. He places them beside me and then leans close to gently touch the small jade rose pin within my hair.

I startle but he only smiles, whispering in a low voice, "Your sister will still be here in the morning. Get some sleep."

He is walking out the door by the time I realise he is truly leaving. I raise my hand up in panic to stop him, calling his name so he turns back to me. His eyes shine in the candlelight.

"Yoon…"

My voice shakes and I run out of words. Instead I sit there blinking. I do not know what I can possibly say after what he has done.

Officer Lee smiles, the dimple deepening in his cheek. "Go to sleep, brat."

He slides the doors closed, leaving my sister and I alone. I watch her sleeping face until the candle burns out and I can no longer stay awake.

IN THE HEAVY darkness of predawn, Seo-jin and I slip from our room, padding silently through the dark hallways out into the biting chill of the courtyard. Our feet crunch across the gravel.

Just as we reach the main gates, answering footsteps sound across the yard, tearing closer, uneven and scraping. A hand presses against the heavy wooden gates, holding them closed.

"Where are you going?"

He is dishevelled from sleep, white night clothes loose and morning mist catching at his lips, dark eyes deep and strange.

I can barely meet his eye. "Home," I whisper.

"Home?" He leans close to my cheek, as if he doesn't wish to startle my little sister who stands now pressed against my side, her body shaking. But he is still unable to control his voice, thick and hoarse in the dawning light. "Seorin *ssi*, your home is here."

I stare up at him, startled.

"Did you not get my letter?" He looks winded, his chest heaving, suddenly uncertain and wounded. "Did you not read it?"

My fingers flutter against my will to my chest, pressing against my heart and the paper folded there. "I read it." I nod, my body sways, his words are like threads tangling around my heart, drawing me tighter. Everything I ever wanted. A home for my sister. To stay. To be cared for.

To be loved?

My eyes flick back up to Lee Yoon's, his welling with darkness, glittering now with the rising sun. He looks so uncertain.

And I think again of his future. He is an important man here in Hanyang, he helped usher in the new age, a new king. There are responsibilities placed on his shoulders that he cannot control. I remember again my own nightmares, for I am a woman he can never marry. He will become a court official and I will become a concubine, and eventually, in many years after he has chosen a more suitable wife to bear him many children, I will become a burden. My sister will become a burden.

I will never allow my sister to be a burden. I will keep her safe and loved and cared for. By myself. And there will always be a place for her. I clasp her thin body closer against my side. I will protect her, always. Nothing else will matter.

I lower my head. Whisper the words.

"Our home is elsewhere."

His hand drops from the heavy gates, fingers scraping over rough wood. I don't meet his eyes, cannot look into his face. I cannot bear to see whatever lies there. Instead I usher my sister out of his courtyard into the quiet city beyond, walking together in silence through dusty winding streets back toward the Pavilion.

I stay inside for days, helping my sister bathe, forcing her to eat, to rest. When Jan-sil visits, Seo-jin shies from her in fear and will not speak. I feel as if my heart is breaking.

Every day I tell her she is safe, that I will always be beside her and I take her into the quiet warm garden to sit among the trees. Finally, I hear her voice, the small voice of an innocent child, asking me about the horse she rode on with Officer Lee, asking if we can travel to the stable and visit her. Those words bring hope flooding through my heart. Despite her scars and the horrors she has experienced, my sister still wants to be a child, she still wants to feed animals and look at horses. And soon she is brave enough that Jan-sil is able to join us on our daily visit to the stables. After a while Da-in comes as well, visiting and watching me closely with curiosity in her eyes.

After a week, Officer Lee begins to appear at the Pavilion, always during the day. At first he only follows us at a distance as we visit the packhorses in the stables, until Seo-jin finally seems to remember him from her journey here. After that she is easier with him, especially when he brings his horse to visit her.

I am strangely nervous around Lee Yoon now, no

longer able to meet his eyes, incapable of speaking when he is near. I like to watch them together though, him and Seo-jin, as he patiently talks to her about the horses, my sister's expression loose with amazement and her small hands clutching onto his arm.

Time passes slowly and I hear from Da-in that Lee Yoon is often away from home visiting the palace. She tells me he has turned down a position in the court and is negotiating to move the whole family to the south, away from the capital. I also hear that his mother is furious, as the new position will be a heavy demotion from what she feels he is owed, after the sacrifice of his father to the new king's cause.

But Officer Lee never speaks of it to me. We barely speak at all, always there is my sister between us, or Da-in, sometimes even Jan-sil. But I catch him watching me often, dark eyes impossible to read.

LATE AT NIGHT I sit on my bedroll in the darkness, listening to the rain as it drizzles down outside. The doors to the terrace are flung wide open despite the storm and I watch as the rain washes the world outside clean.

I am alone. Seo-jin has taken to sleeping with Jan-sil lately and I might be jealous if it didn't mean she is slowly learning to trust again, to be happy again. I pull my blankets around my shivering body, rubbing at my brow as the rain falls harder. A knock sounds on my door, a serving girl most likely, and I call her in. Except when my doors clatter open, I am startled to see Lee Yoon standing in the darkness of the hallway.

He boldly steps inside and closes the doors behind him,

limping over and dropping to his knees on the blankets right beside me, wincing as if his leg causes him pain.

I lean away in confusion. "What are you doing here?"

Lee Yoon follows, moving closer like he has every right to be here, like his presence is not strange at all, determination in his eyes.

"I'm here to ask you to come south with me," he says.

"South? I don't…"

He shifts closer, his voice low. "I've taken a position in a small town in the mountains. As a local magistrate. Seorin *ssi*, I'm asking you to come with me."

I blink. "My sister…"

"She will come as well. Both of you, together."

He stares at me, his eyes pools of darkness, his hand hesitant as he reaches slowly to touch my cheek, fingers running carefully across my skin. "No one will know us there. We can be whatever we want to be."

I barely breathe but do not move away. Slowly, he smiles.

"I think you will say yes, brat."

A rumbling clap of thunder resounds throughout the Pavilion, echoing as rain crashes harder, spilling through the open terrace doors. I lower my gaze, breathing hard. "Why?"

His hand is warm as it travels along my jaw. "Because you carry my letter inside your *jeogori*." He grins in the darkness, slow and wide. "That's what Da-in told me."

I falter, no idea how to react to this side of him I've never seen before. "Da-in told you … that?"

He nods, eyes locked on mine. He grins again. "It is true?"

I try to turn away, to deny it, yet Lee Yoon reaches to pull me back, laughing quietly at me. "Ho! It is!" He looks pleased.

"You cannot truly mean it," I whisper. "You cannot truly wish for us to come with your family. Do you know what people will think?"

His smile disappears. "I don't care what people think. I do mean it. I mean it."

Rain pours through the open shutters, drenching the blankets, pooling on the floor. I feel the mist of it settling against my damp skin but Lee Yoon does not move, he watches me and I think he is waiting for me to speak but I do not know what to say.

He leans closer, his dark eyes on mine. "Stay with me."

His mouth is on mine and the touch of him, the taste of him, the warmth, it is all that fills my mind.

"Stay with me. Seorin *ssi*, you love me, I know you do. Stay."

I do not answer, but my hands gripping his shoulders, my fingers reaching into his hair, my tongue and teeth against his, they seem to be enough for Lee Yoon.

When I wake, it is with Lee Yoon's arm flung across my belly, his face pressed close against my hair. The weight of his arm makes it hard to breathe but I do not move and do not wake him. His steady breath tickles my neck and I shift to watch his face as he sleeps.

There is darkness beneath his eyes, yet he seems different now, mouth soft as if he is dreaming good dreams.

I listen to his breathing, steady and even. Reaching over, I touch his skin and run my fingers through his hair. And I let myself imagine this new life, this impossible chance for something different, slowly now becoming real.

If I choose it.

I imagine sitting on an open terrace beside Seo-jin, teaching her to sew like my mother taught me. And I imagine asking Lee Yoon for a *gayageum*, playing it for him at dusk, when the two of us are alone.

Light slides in through cracks in the shuttered screen doors and sends patterns dancing across his bare skin.

Lee Yoon's breathing changes as he wakes.

Want More Korean Historical Fiction?

Thank you for reading *Promise Season*, which is Book One in the Promise Series.

If you enjoyed it, please consider leaving a review, which helps greatly in sharing this work with other readers.

For more historical fiction set in old Korea, sign up to Lee Evie's bookclub for fiction updates, and receive a FREE BOOK written by Lee Evie:

Barely Fields: A Joseon Love Story

www.leeevie.com

PROMISE THIEF

Book Two of the Promise Series

A girl with no future.
A man with no past.
A choice.

During the long dark midwinter, the sky turns black and snow drifts heavy through the stark streets of sprawling Hanyang. Within the stifling walls of the Pavilion, the city's greatest entertainment house, a *gisaeng* slave girl is driven inexorably to the edge of her endurance.

Chungjo is ambitious. Beautiful. Cruel. A slave girl who submits to no-one and destroys all who stands in her way. Yet a mysterious stranger thwarts her plans at every turn, craftier than she could ever have anticipated, a young man who is her match.

Soon a dance begins. Who will discover the truth first? Who will destroy the other?

A dark and romantic historical adventure set in old Korea.

Sign up to Lee Evie's monthly bookclub for all the latest on her historical Korean fiction novels:

www.leeevie.com

PROMISE DREAM

Book Three of the Promise Series

A girl with one secret.
A man with many.
A journey into the wild.

Rain hisses across the rooftops of the Pavilion, Hanyang's greatest entertainment house. Within its stifling walls a lonely *gisaeng* slave girl strives to hold together the scattering pieces of her life and protect a terrifying secret.

When a mysterious lord from the far north unexpectedly buys her as his unwilling concubine, Jan-sil must decide if she has the courage to deceive him, her very survival hanging precariously in the balance. Yet as they journey together through a perilous world of rain and mist, Jan-sil's loyalties begin to waver.

To protect her secret, she turns to a vicious bodyguard who desperately frightens her. And who might also be her one chance at freedom.

A dark and romantic historical adventure set in old Korea.

Sign up to Lee Evie's monthly bookclub for all the latest on her historical Korean fiction novels:

www.leeevie.com

A SONG FOR LONELY WOLVES

Book One of the Joseon Detective Series

A missing woman.

A frozen body.

A damo *slave girl, determined to solve the mystery.*

1590, Korea.

At the foot of a jagged mountain range, an isolated village lies in muddy snow. In the dead of night a young woman vanishes from her bed, rumours of a fearsome ghost with no face echoing in her wake.

Dan Ji arrives into the long winding valley with her own ghosts, determined to prove her worth as an investigator and solve the mystery. She is a *damo*, a tea servant of the police force, tasked with cooking and cleaning for her superiors and sometimes, with performing undercover police work.

With only the officer in charge on her side; a hard young man with a bloody past, Dan Ji must convince the local Magistrate and his provincial policemen to trust her judgement. As mistrust brews, a frozen body is unearthed from the deep snow.

As a *Damo* of Joseon's police force, it is not within Dan Ji's nature to leave a mystery unsolved.

A dark historical mystery set in old Korea.

Sign up to Lee Evie's monthly bookclub for all the latest on her historical Korean fiction novels: ***www.leeevie.com***

About Lee Evie

LEE EVIE is a historical fiction author.

She writes with a focus on Korean history and loves dark adventures with a heavy dose of danger and romance.

When she's not writing, Lee Evie can be found watching drama, which she will do for hours on end. She believes drama watching is the ultimate joy of life. Even when they make her cry.

An avid photography and travel lover, Lee Evie thinks stories are the most precious gift to the universe.

Sign up to Lee Evie's monthly free bookclub for all the latest on her historical Korean fiction novels:

<u>www.leeevie.com</u>

Acknowledgments

Huge thank you to my family and friends who not only support my writing every step of the way, but actively get involved to help. Special thank you for Gus, Rory, Margie, Cathy, S0ssy, Anna, Jane for the new ending, Novelist's Circle, massive gratitude for Sue and Kristy's help, Kirsty, Nicole, Mo Yang. Thank you to my Korean cultural editor, Kim Stoker, for your thoughtful suggestions on language and history, and to my past Korean language teacher and wonderful current friend Lee, for introducing me to everything.

Finally, thank you to the people who create those wonderful dramas, which inspire me to write and give me joy every day.

Made in the USA
Middletown, DE
17 October 2020